For Dad

A Gentleman's Game

As flies to wanton boys, are we to the gods;
They kill us for their sport.

> William Shakespeare
> *King Lear*

Once the game is over, the king and pawn go back in the same box.

> Italian proverb

OUT

BY THE TIME I was thirteen, I was pure.

They came to the driving range without clubs, without any intention of practicing themselves, and they leaned against knotty oak trees, swatting mosquitoes, smiling to each other and shaking their heads. Watching. Some went *mmm mmm* like there was butter on their lips, and some stood with church faces, quiet and grave and stiff with wonder, studying me as I launched ball after ball out of the shadows. A sweep of air pulling my shoulders, the hum of iron tearing soil in my hands, the hollow click of steel smashing into Surlyn that made a white-haired woman *oooh,* made her leather-skinned husband whistle. Someone else might say *nice turn,* or *nice rip there, boy,* but Mr. Logan always said, "Pure, Timmy. Absolutely fucking pure."

Charlie Logan had a face like the ass end of a ham, red and shredded by the bottomless cup of Scotch that grew from the end of his arm. He was lopsided without his Styrofoam tallboy of Johnny Walker Red and a few flakes of ice. The caddies called it a Logan soda. The secret perk of caddying for Charlie was that he was soupy-eyed oblivious to how much he drank, so when he traded his cocktail for a five-iron, the caddy on his bag that day could filch a few healthy mouthfuls while Logan rubbed his eyes, waiting for the golf ball at his feet to stop swaying. "Keep it full," he told his caddies. "My bag. Try the front pocket. Might find something in there." They always did, and Logan never noticed the caddies' faces when they returned his soda, their eyelids pulled taut at the corners, their lips curling back inside their mouths.

"Timmy, that goddamn swing is gonna take you to Augusta," he said, white bits of skin hanging from his sunburned lips. On a sunny afternoon, and sometimes on one that wasn't so sunny, you could find Charlie napping on a bench at the range, cup teetering on his medicine ball of a belly, not a drop spilled on one of those afternoons when he had been drinking since noon in the men's grill, speaking too loudly about his three-putts, paying and collecting on bets, calling everyone he saw his old friend, on one of those afternoons when you didn't have to ask the bartenders for rounds, because at Fox Chase Country Club, you don't ask, and you don't pay.

You just get.

"I've seen swings, hell, I had a swing. Damn, damn decent swing," he said, running his fingers through his scalp, looking at his palm. "Ungrateful bastards." He shook a few loose hairs from his hand, then laughed and spread his legs wide for a solid base. "Put potential in one hand, spit in the other, see which fills up first. Understand?"

"Yes sir."

"Your father must be a proud man," he said, not waiting for me to answer. "If I had a son like you, well," he looked at the empty metal buckets toppled in a mess around me, "you'd be hitting twelve buckets instead of ten."

He chuckled and smiled at his drink. He had two daughters I saw at the club at Christmas and Fourth of July parties, girls whose mother colored her hair to match theirs, three blondes with hair spilled down between their shoulder blades, just touching the tops of their asses. They matched their outfits as well, and the gentlemen went slack-jawed when the trio strolled into a Christmas gala, draped snugly in red velvet, chins up, shoulders back. And there was Charlie Logan, a little bit behind, soda in hand, green blazer and patches of gray chest hair poking out of a golf shirt, his eyes looking like they might slip down below his nose, his wife walking in front of him as if he were some unfortunate brother.

His girls were not golfers. They didn't go through the ranks of the junior clinics with the other members' children. Fox Chase was a club for gentlemen, owned by and open exclusively to three hundred and fifty bond-holding members. The clubhouse was tucked back at the end of a long winding drive, behind trees so thick with needles that people drove past the place every day of their lives, never knowing what was there. The rules of the club allowed wives and daughters to use the driving range and putting green at their leisure, and on Tuesday mornings and Sunday afternoons the course was all theirs. But Charlie called such policies an embarrassment, and no daughter of his was going to tee it up at his club, not on any day.

"The way you turn on that ball, it's just," he said, his words sliding into a wheeze as I took my address, quieting my body, thinking without a thought. And in a moment I was watching a ball roll upward against the air, hanging there on the breeze before falling fast and straight and knocking up against a thin metal sign. Two hundred yards. On a dot.

"That's pure, Timmy," Charlie Logan said. "Absolutely fucking pure."

There was something in my bones to turn like that. A golf ball at my feet, a pause in my shoulders, and a silent, effortless click.

I was tall but not big, a quiet sort of large. My limbs were lanky and elastic, and that mattered. Physicality mattered. There were all the intangible ways of being good at golf. The real players were coated with a dust of something that the others couldn't have—talent, luck, confidence, charm even— it was that gift in being gifted, and golfers chased it in circles, in seven-thousand-yard laps of short grass to discover that some people could do, and some people could want. And while being graced with talent was good, being tall was simple. Physics mattered. Longer limbs meant a longer arc, which meant more speed at the club head. That meant more momentum at im- pact, and it all meant more violence tearing through two ounces of golf ball.

I grew tall without growing awkward, and by thirteen I could look most of the men at my club in the face. Including my fa- ther. When you are small, the idea of being taller than your fa- ther is strange and implausible and a little unfair. You expect it to be a real moment when your head rises above his, fireworks and a page in a scrapbook, a line penciled and starred on the edge of the kitchen doorway, 5'10"—age 13. But one day I was look- ing my father level in the eyes, and on another day his eyes were somehow lower than mine, and it was like everything else in life that just goes ahead and happens.

I could beat balls at that range for hours with no sense of time, just ball after ball after piles of balls. But when the shots were

all scattered out among the weeds, there were times when a burning would start up in that space where my spine is wide above my
hips, where the bone would feel too thin and too hot. My back
would bunch up into lumps of bone and muscle, purple and black,
and my shoulder blades would pop as I lay in bed, telling myself
I was falling asleep. There were times when my fingers ached to
where I couldn't hold a pencil, when I would wait until morning
for my hands to go fluid again to fill in the answers on my school
assignments. Calluses the size of nickels covered both my palms.
They didn't hurt, but there were times when my father would
catch me staring down at my hands, and he would make a sound
with his nose and tighten his eyebrows and tell me calluses were
natural, and he would remind me then that no, they didn't hurt,
no matter how large or hard or orange in color.

When he came to see me at the driving range, he did not hover
over his son like the other fathers. He didn't stand behind me
with his arms crossed. He didn't lift his fingers to his lips and
watch the pieces of my golf swing, studying me as if I were something to be deciphered. The other fathers stood close, reminding their boys of their bad habits, shaking a finger at the same
mistakes, but my father would only stop for a second to tell me
to stay in the shade because that Irish skin of mine was fertile
soil for melanomas. If he saw that the back of my neck was getting pink, he would shake his head slowly, as if it took all his
strength to do so, and tell me that only a real jerk would stand
out here in the sun with skin like mine. Then he would turn
and walk off toward the clubhouse, his shoulders hunched, his
hands tucked deep into his pockets.

He never turned to see me watching the way he walked. He
never caught me looking for that touch of fear in the way his
feet never dragged. Sometimes he came back down the path

with a blue tube of sunblock and sometimes he didn't, but what stays with me is an image of my father that's stuck between silence and unrest, and I watch, waiting for that image to change—his wool cardigan sweater hanging from his shoulders, thin and yellow, his back curled over an iron blade he said they would never make again, his eyes moving from ball to hole, hole to ball, ball to hole, the concentration pumping in his temples, his scalp lined with effort. It's the preparation I remember, never the contact that came after.

"This is where I find my strokes," he would say as I watched him at the practice green, choking down on that eight-iron and bumping a ball across the grass carpet, making it check for just a second, then release and roll and curl to the lip of the cup, where ball after ball would die, hanging on the edge, the odd one turning over into the hole and rattling around the bottom. "I have to find them somewhere. I can't go hauling off like you young gorillas," he said. "They don't ask how. They ask how many."

On an afternoon in late July, I was beating my driver, launching shots over the fence at the end of the driving range. I gripped the club and wrung sweat from my fingers, ball after ball jumping off the screws. I watched them move out into the orange light. They would be gone for just a second when I would hear the sound of branches rattling from the other side of the fence.

"You're gonna kill someone doing that," my father said.

He had been standing behind me for I didn't know how long.

"There's no one back there. There's no one else here," I said, quickly teeing up another ball, coiling my shoulders, cranking another one out of the park. There was the sound of leaves rustling, and then a hard ding from one of the tractors hidden in the brush that grew beyond the range.

"Hey, Hank Aaron," he said. "You drive for show, putt for dough. There's no pictures on a scorecard."

Speaking in clichés was a safe way for us to converse without talking, and golf was full of them. Banal truisms were passed between golfers like secret handshakes.

I turned to look at my father, the afternoon light settling on his face. There was age all over him, his cheeks raw and marked with tan blotches, his lips thin and liver-colored.

"Jimmy Shaw's dad was up here watching him, and he said I should charge people to watch me swing." I tried to laugh when I said it. "There was a little crowd up here before," I mumbled, looking down at the five striped balls left to be hit.

My father pulled his hands out of his pockets, rough with gray hair and a touch shaky. He folded his arms in front of him, tipped his head to the side.

"You're a lucky kid, Timothy Price," he said.

"I know," I said, and I tore at another red-striped range ball, boring it straight and hard into the center of the fence.

"You do? Do you know why?"

I stopped and looked at him, then looked down at my palms, which were pink and covered with black bits from my worn rubber grips.

"Because your father doesn't push you," he said. "Because you play if you want to. If you don't, I'm not going to be the one who makes you. I won't be one of those fathers, Timmy, standing up here and looking over your shoulder."

"I know."

"Norman Dane's in the grill right now, talking about Myles doing this and Myles doing that. I won't live my life through my sons, Timothy," he said. "Would you want a father like that? A father who never leaves his son alone, pushes him until the kid hates his guts? Is that what a kid wants? Is that what you want?"

He didn't wait for an answer, because of course I didn't. And of course I did.

He turned and walked back toward the path, and I watched my father lower his eyes and take careful steps. Fireflies had begun to light up along the walkway, pale green lights flickering around the clubhouse in the distance, everything around us having slipped into the slow summer darkness.

I stood there waiting for the buzzing to start up in my fingers, wishing for another hour of daylight and a hundred more balls.

MOST DELAWAREANS CAN'T tell you what Delaware means. My fourth-grade teacher told us it was an Indian word for *first state*. Her name was Mrs. Weber, and Mrs. Weber would have preferred I didn't raise my hand and ask her how something could be named "first state" when the states were still colonies. But I did, and I told the class that it wasn't an Indian word, but rather the name of the first Englishman to tread Indian soil, Thomas West, Third Baron De La Warr. She put a star sticker on my desk and told me I could put my head down and rest since I already knew so many things.

I knew about the name of our town as well. New Water. Most of my neighbors don't know, or believe, that my hometown is named for a border point on the underground railroad. New Water, where South water met North water, a small safe stretch along the Delaware River that was almost Philadelphia, almost up to Erie and across. Some say the town was named by Dutch or Swedish explorers, but what most seem to agree on is that today, nobody really cares. It doesn't concern me either, though I know there was a time when it did, when I was a child whose father had raised him on the whats and whens of Delaware history. A part of me I don't hear anymore still reveres Caesar Rodney and Thomas McKean and the poor patroons at Swanendael, because my father believed in knowing the place you came from, that once you knew enough about that one spot in the world, you would never need anywhere else.

My father's name was James Patrick Price, and he was the lone CPA of JPP Accountancy, a very local firm located on the first floor of a converted Victorian in New Water. He had eighty or so clients that he worked too hard for, and he shared the first floor with Alfred D'Angelo, an Italian attorney who advertised his business on a large spotlit sign in the front lawn, SPECIALIZING IN ALL LEGAL SPECIALTIES—SLIP AND FALLS, DIVORCE, WORKMAN'S COMP, MISC ACCIDENTS. On the door, a brass sign the size of a cereal box read JPP ACCOUNTANCY. My father told new clients to look for *Slip and Falls*. He didn't talk much about his fellow tenant, except to complain about the man's heavy black cigars—Italian taffy, my father called them.

My father wore gray and navy blue suits to the office, suits that always had another year in them, no matter how they had started to soften in the shoulders. A tailor tidied up the cuffs each summer when my father would wear short-sleeved button-downs to work, white pilled cotton behind solid burgundy ties. He wasn't tall, or short, and he had gray-black hair that was thin across the top, a few windy threads covering his sun-spotted scalp, a face with more sag than wrinkle. He would walk through the front door at the end of the day with a boxy briefcase and watery eyes, and he would kiss my mother on the forehead before he lifted his lapel to his face and sniffed, scrunching his meaty Irish nose to mutter something about those goddamn cigars.

My mother was smilingly indifferent to most things. My father would spend his entire weekend at the golf club, leaving her at home on the couch. He would return home with bourbon in his eyes and sit on the edge of his chair, replaying his round out loud, and she would nod and smile and pretend to understand what he was telling her about each bad lie and bad read and each damn lip-out. Three, sometimes four nights a week, I would skip the dinner she had cooked for a few extra hours at the range. When I'd come home in the dark with a cold bone-chill in my fingers, I would always find a plate of food in the oven, a salad in the refrigerator made how I liked it, just lettuce cut up small. My mother would sit at the table and keep me company while I ate.

"Tell me all about your day," she would say, and I wouldn't talk about golf though it was the only thing on my mind. I didn't want to remind her of what she had lost to golf, a game that was like my father's mistress, the younger, smarter, better thing that he loved blindly, that shook him out of bed on his days off when the sky was still gray behind the curtains. She was a golf widow, but she never showed contempt for that thing my father and I couldn't do without. The only thing that really troubled my mother was the heat, and she hated the heat more than anything. She was actually afraid of it. In November, she complained about it being muggy. I would bring her iced tea and fresh ice cubes, and in the summer while my father was at work I would make the air-conditioning as cold as she asked, even though he would have thumped me for keeping the thermostat at sixty-eight degrees.

Her hair was a deep, unreal shade of brown, and she had it dyed every third Thursday. Her face was thin, skin with the same white gloss as her china plates, and most days my mother seemed much older than my father, if only because she was so settled into her life, on her green chair in her clean living room in her air-conditioning. Next to her chair on an antique iron stand sat her yellow box of vitamins, filled with a selection she ordered from the saleslady in our neighborhood who sold them out of her station wagon, a woman with a relentless purple-lipped smile stuck to her face. Some of the vitamins in my mother's box were for hair roots, some for teeth, some for pain, and some were plastic with small print on them, the ones that put my mother in a glassy-eyed place where she smiled without looking happy.

I was four years younger than my brother Casey. We grew up in the same house with the same meals, same whispered prayers, same rules, the same smell when you opened the door, nutmeg and Endust. But Casey and I were never the same. His face looked sour and small, too small to hold whatever it was that rippled at the sides of his forehead. He hated things—people, conversations, us—but I think the thing he hated most was the way he was made, as if his veins were not wide enough for the heat in his blood, pushing it all around too fast. He hated the things that made it so he couldn't sit still at the dinner table, couldn't smile when someone told him to, couldn't win or lose without something behind his eyes snapping, his face going flush, a temper flashing through his muscles that seemed to scare him as much as it did us.

Casey had wide shoulders and muscles down the back of his neck. When he flexed, he could squeeze his forearms into baseballs. His hair was a deep red with thick oily curls. He looked nothing like my father or me, and I would have believed he was adopted if my mother didn't tell the story of an uncle Brendan we never met, her older brother who was a redhead just like Casey. Uncle Brendan apparently drank too much and spent nights in jail. She said he was killed in a car accident before my brother and I were born, but she always made a point of saying he died at thirty-three.

My brother didn't have friends. He had a stereo. While we were growing up, a boy would get dropped off at our house from time to time, carrying an album or a magazine, and he would go up to play in Casey's room, sometimes twenty minutes, sometimes a few hours, before we heard yelling and a thump above the kitchen. A short while later, the boy would leave our house beneath his mother's arm, a bloody dishtowel pressed against his nose, perhaps a bag of ice against his eye.

"Hitting? Is that how you make friends?" my mother would start, and Casey would turn and head back up the stairs and put on a record I didn't know he owned.

I was nine years old when the game began for me.

It was a sticky May afternoon, and my father and I were washing his car in the driveway. He drove a black Buick that I could never remember being new, and together we slapped on the Simoniz, rags and blue goop and elbows and towels and shoulders—it was all breathless and red-faced and it made me worry about his heart, rubbing and waxing and rubbing again, as if by working the rags hard enough he might turn the cloudy metal into something else, something he deserved, something I could feel in my hands as I polished away, the car rocking on its tires, my father pushing on his black Buick going gray.

I dropped my rag in a bucket and wiped my grimy blue fingertips on my T-shirt, and without stopping to think why I shouldn't, I asked him about my mother. I asked him why she looked so sleepy some days, why some days she would drag Casey to the grocery store by his ear or push me around the driveway in my Big Wheel, and why other days she would hardly blink. She would sit in the air-conditioning with a glass of iced tea in front of her, stirring it until the ice cubes went to water, her skin rubbery and tired, and when I asked her what was wrong, she wouldn't answer except to flash me a smile. There was something in it all, I knew there was, in the stirring and the air-conditioning and all those ice cubes in August.

My father tucked his chamois into his belt. "Your mother?" he said, as if he had never heard of her. "Why? What's wrong with your mother?"

I kept my eyes to myself. I picked up my rag and kept to the polishing.

"Some people, adults, have better days than others," he said. "Is that what you're asking?"

I shrugged my shoulders and rubbed the blue cream in circles.

"Your mother had a spell after you were born," he continued, voice low like he was talking to himself. "It's common. It's not an uncommon thing." He picked up a new towel, rolling the clean cotton between his fingers. "But it just," he paused, turning back to the car, "it lasted." Whether it was pills or Casey, a son who was a load too much for a couple who didn't have children until later in life—something made it last. Something made it so my mother was the worst kind of quiet. It made her sweat in December.

*　*　*

When we finished with the car, my father walked into the garage, and he came out with two golf clubs. Their silver shafts lay across his open palm. He sprinkled plastic golf balls in a spot in our backyard and laid a metal cookie tin in the grass, fifteen yards away. It was rusted and golden, and it made a deep *ting* sound as ball after ball landed in it.

"This is where the strokes are," he said to no one in particular, focusing his breath on the way his hands held the club, the iron dragging through the splotchy grass and sliding through the ball, gentle, clipping white plastic and spinning it through the air, balls bouncing off the metal, ting, tin, tin, *ting*. I watched and bit my nails, nibbling a blue paste that tasted like poison.

"Junior clinic at Fox Chase starts next week," he said as he walked to the tin, dumping the balls out, tossing the metal dish toward where he had been standing before. He started chipping back across the lawn, his fingers locked into one grip that glided back and forth, club sweeping the grass and the tin clanking.

"Sunday afternoons," he said. "Only takes an hour."

The clinic at Fox Chase Country Club was a free instructional program for members' children and grandchildren, a first taste of golf for young hopefuls that would segue into private lessons that summer with the teaching staff at fifty dollars an hour.

My father wasn't asking me if I wanted to go. He wouldn't ask, afraid to push. He just threw those words into the air, *clinic starts next week, only takes a hour,* hoping I might pick them up and find some use for them.

The spring before, my father had taken Casey to the junior clinic, and I don't know if he ever stopped regretting it. It was a predictable mess, a disaster that ended with Casey blowing into the house like a storm and yelling at the walls about the most awful afternoon of his life, how the kids up there were a bunch of pussies, how he would never pick up a golf club again or wear one of those shirts with the queer collar and the little alligator. *Pussies, pussies, pussies. Pussies dressed in saddle shoes.* Casey chewed on the words as he took the kitchen scissors to his white golf shirt. He cut out the Izod alligator and taped it to the refrigerator, mounting his kill there for the rest of the family to see.

When my father walked into the kitchen and saw the Frigidaire, he didn't take the alligator down. He stared at the small green patch and moved his chin from one side to the other, shaking his head about a boy with wild red hair and cheeks full of an anger that seemed more permanent from year to year.

There was a part of me that needed to go to that clinic and learn their game, not just to please my father, but to do with a smile the thing my brother refused with a fist. *Golf, gooolfff, goff*—it sounded so big, so beyond a child that a nine-year-old couldn't help but want to touch it, shake it up a bit, lift the box and see how heavy it was. But there was a touch of fear there too, fear in not knowing how deep it might go, the dark stairs that were *Fox Chase Country Club,* with its crossed arms and its worn mahogany, its old members with their papery skin, their scent of piss and aftershave. It was a place that made a child understand things like impropriety and probity, a place that first made me feel the burn of embarrassment behind my eyes. Walk here, don't walk there, don't speak now, speak now and speak clearly—and don't dance through a sand trap on a Saturday afternoon, waiting for your father to stroll up the eighteenth fairway, or a man in a large blue blazer will shower you with spit and angry words, and you will taste your first doubt in what you know about things as simple as sand and beaches and games. I cried on a bench until my father finally walked up the last hole, and there he explained to me something called etiquette that, like everything in that place, was hovering just above me, like it might all come down with one wrong move.

Yet there was something of my father there in that tin in the backyard, in a game of sticks and balls that seemed about as complicated as marbles with the pace of a Sunday morning.

"I know how to play golf," I told him as the pendulum continued to swing, ting, *ting*. I held an orange butterfly by its wing that, up close, was wiry and black and ugly.

My father stopped and smiled at me. "*You* know how to play golf?"

"Yup." I grinned to myself and whispered, "Yes I do."

"Uh-huh. We'll see about that," he said. He walked back into the garage and came out with another club, a five-iron he had cut down with a hacksaw for my brother. The sharp end was wrapped in black electrical tape for a thin grip. I might have swung the thing twice. The weight was all wrong, the club head full size but the shaft split halfway, and I could barely swing it around my body without taking a step backward first, then stepping into it like I was swatting a baseball.

"Here's your ball," he said, setting up one of the plastic practice balls on a tee, "and there is the green." He pointed at his Buick sitting in the driveway, clean and shining silver and black.

"Your car?"

"Uh-huh."

"You want me to hit the ball at your car?" I said, unsure if he was waiting to see if I was dumb enough to try.

"Absolutely. There is no doubt in my mind that you can swing until morning, and you cannot hit that ball to that car."

The Buick sat there in front of us, less than twenty yards away, wide and steady, a box of metal and shine, and at my feet, a miniature Wiffle ball I had seen my father send sailing over the house a hundred times, a one-man volley from front yard to back, backyard to front.

"Or maybe you don't know how to play golf," he said, crossing his arms in front of him.

I wrapped my fingers around the grip, squeezing the tape, locking my wrists. I looked up at my father in Sunday khakis worn white at the knees.

Tilting his head, he said in a tired voice, "Come on, Timothy. Let's see it, my guy the little golfer."

I lifted my front foot up, wiggled my hips, dragged the iron weight back behind me so that it all toppled over backward, and suddenly I was flat on my ass.

I popped back up and brushed the grass off the seat of my corduroys.

"Try again," my father said, laughing, "try as many times as you want." He walked over to the car, ran his finger along the hood and listened to the tight clean squeak. Leaning against the car, his body between my ball and my target, he looked at me with impatient eyes and said, "Well?"

I lifted the club up as far as I could, not much higher than my shoulder, and I dropped it down hard into the earth like a hoe, barely nicking the ball. Again, I picked it up and dropped it, and again, until I was not swinging but hacking, chopping at the ground. No metal *ting* but the sound of solid pounding soil, torn grass and an iron edge turning over the dirt. I watched the club head crush the little ball, plastic folding in on itself and sinking into the mess, and me not trying to hit it backward or forward or anywhere but out.

"Goddamnit, Timmy!" My father's hand grabbed the shaft in midair. "Jesus Mary and Joseph, what the hell do you think you're doing?"

I was out of breath when he yanked the club out of my fingers.

"You're chewing up the goddamn lawn!" he said. "Is that how I do it? Is it?"

I looked down at the ground, a ditch and a pile of grass and earth that, after a moment, did not seem very large at all.

"Maybe you aren't ready for the clinic," he said, stomping off to the garage. "You certainly aren't ready for a golf course."

He returned with a bag of grass seed. He sprinkled the yellow seed into the soil, shaking his head, saying things as I walked away about lawns and fairways and sons and respect. He didn't remember that I had baseball practice on Sunday afternoons, same exact time as the clinic, so if I was ready or not didn't matter because I played left field on a team in second place.

The following Christmas, I unwrapped a box and found a collared shirt inside with the Fox Chase Country Club logo embroidered in green on the breast pocket. My father told me to try it on right there, so I slipped it on over my pajamas. It was two sizes too big and the sleeves stretched down below my elbow. My father smiled at me like he hadn't seen me for years.

"You look like you're ready for the tour, Timmy," he said. "You look like a little golfer there." He didn't tell me the clinic was just a few months away, and I didn't tell my father I already knew how to play golf. I didn't remind him that I would still have Little League on Sundays.

My brother threw a ball of wrapping paper that bounced off the side of my head.

"Nice shirt." Casey laughed. "That stupid thing fits you like a nightgown."

He was right. And I wore my gift all morning.

TEN YEARS OLD and I was surrounded by the blank faces of children wanting to be elsewhere, kids flopping around, swinging their arms to beat away the boredom. Some stood still with drool dangling from their lips, staring at the sky and imagining all the other things a bright Sunday afternoon could be. Behind each child loomed a larger frame, a father or grandfather, most of them sporting cocktail smiles with eyes gone milky from the men's grill where they had been sitting since noon, stewing amid roast beef sandwiches and cigars and highball glasses, waiting for their wives to drop off the little ones for the afternoon clinic.

I stood off to the end of the group with no one behind me, my father either out on the golf course or tucked away in the grill, a room where children and women were not allowed, a wood and leather lounge where a fake antique placard read, G.O.L.F. — GENTLEMEN ONLY, LADIES FORBIDDEN.

The head professional's legs were sausages stuffed into a pair of polyester pants and he smelled like onions and mustard. His face seemed larger than his head, round and tan and without a conspicuous chin, and we listened as he introduced himself, Raymond Mann, PGA professional. He rolled up a smile and said something about how he made the cut at *the* Open once, so we better all listen hard and good, which made the fathers chuckle and smile at each other. I stood quiet, feigning interest, ten years old and afraid not to listen, but the younger kids, boys no older than six or seven, twirled in their places and pulled at their fathers' slacks, some whining about *bathrooms* and *mommies,* some looking nervous in a way six-year-olds shouldn't.

Little Amanda Norton had a look on her face like she had turned down the wrong hallway and wound up in a room with urinals. Her blond hair was almost white, pulled back in a ponytail, and she was taller then most of the boys. Behind her stood history, her father, Richard Norton III, the president of Fox Chase Country Club and the grandson of one of the original founders. It was clear from the paintings hanging in the clubhouse that Norton III was the product of Norton I, a tall man with a long face and a thin bony nose that looked ill suited for breathing. The living Norton had the same chalky face, deep-lined cheeks and hair that was jet black, presumably from a dye job because every few months he would come to the club looking like he had used shoe polish for shampoo. He placed a hand on each of his daughter's shoulders, his fingers tapping in a thinking rhythm.

Next to Amanda stood a boy I recognized from a Fourth of July barbecue the year before. His name was Myles Dane, and I remembered the short-game display he put on at the practice green beside the club's patio where the rest of us children were sweating over blackened hot dogs and flicking watermelon seeds to the squirrels. My mother was sitting at our table, listening while a woman with hard white hair slurred something about airfares to Orlando. My father leaned back in his chair, eyes dreamy, like he was not at our table at all. He was watching Myles Dane, a boy with pronounced shoulders and lean, athletic muscles that seemed to pour into the golf ball. The back of his neck was flaky and red, his brown hair faded a summer shade of yellow, and it looked like Myles lived out there in the sun with his pitching wedge, stalking that island of short grass. He chipped three balls in a row into the heart of the cup, and my father watched with a look in his eyes like something had just occurred to him.

Myles's father, Norman Dane, was six-foot-plus with small glasses and thick, stringy arms. He didn't stand behind his son at the clinic, but rather stood over in the shade with Charlie Logan, who was there for no better reason than he was always there. The two were laughing about something that made Charlie bend at the waist and show a mouthful of wet brown teeth. My mother once told me that Mr. Dane *developed* real estate, like that was the best thing one could do to something, to *develop* it. All it meant to me was that Mr. Dane developed himself a silver Ferrari that Myles rode home in, and that it was a very different thing from being a CPA and driving home in a Buick.

We waited anxious as the pro inspected our grips, our hands trying to remember what he had said, how he had done it—left thumb down the shaft, fold the right thumb over, keep the V's in your hands parallel and pointing over the left, no, right shoulder. Raymond Mann checked us one by one, shaking his head at boys who looked up at him, their fingers tangled and timid, folded more for prayers than for a golf club. He walked from child to child, waving his shadow over us and saying, "Now grip's the thing, son. If you don't get that grip down, might as well be swinging a wet noodle. It's all in the grip, only thing between you and that little ball."

Raymond passed me by with a sniff and a comment about a "textbook interlockin' grip," and he went to the boy next to me, Jimmy Shaw, a left-hander who was perfectly mixed up. Everything about V's and knuckles that he had barely been able to remember, all scrapped with a chuckle and a "You got it all upside down, son. Lefties got to do it all opposite, or you'll have to play the course backwards." Jimmy dropped his chubby hands to his sides and made big I-don't-want-to-try-anymore eyes. His father thanked Raymond Mann for the help.

Jimmy came from big people, and to see his father swing a golf club was to disbelieve even as you watched it taking place. The soft folds of his body took turns sucking in and blowing out, rolls pinching and folding, his hips somehow getting out of the way as the golf club spun around three hundred pounds of dentist and smacked a ball the size of a deviled egg. It was part golf swing, part golf wobble.

Jimmy was his father's son. His cheeks looked like he was perpetually holding his breath, and his clothes were too big for him in a way that said his mother didn't expect little Jimmy to be much different, that she knew it was in the genes.

Raymond picked up an eight-iron and hit a few balls out into the range, each one starting low and rising up against a wall of air. The children around me began to bounce in their shoes, impatient for their turn to make those balls in front of them go, but, I could have watched Raymond swing all day. I followed the rhythms in the contact, flash after flash of metal slapping the dirt, all that focus in his face as he watched the balls soar and skip and pull back next to the 150 marker. I watched him in his backswing as an inch of pallid flab slipped out from between his cotton shirt and polyester pants. He looked back at the group of us with a smile that said *that's how the hell you do it,* pushing his shirt back into his pants with a meaty hand.

"Now if I could only putt," Raymond said. "I wouldn't know any of you."

Laughter trickled down the row of fathers behind us.

"Alright, Wilson here is gonna make sure you guys, and girls," Raymond pointed at Amanda, "get all straightened out now. He's a heck of a teacher, and always lookin' for a new protégé. But I want you all to remember, that if you don't remember anything else from today," he said, laying his palm across his chest, "remember that this here game, is a gentlemen's game." He smiled. "And a ladies' game. The way you conduct yourselves, boys and girls, is always more important than how you play."

The fathers nodded their approval. Raymond clapped his hands together like a dealer leaving a card table, and a young man named Wilson with mirrored sunglasses stepped in front of us. His golf shirt was buttoned to the top button, and he had a black goatee that didn't connect at the corners of his mouth. He didn't break a smile as he talked at us about golf and how *hard* it was, how it would take a lifetime to master, how patience was important because the game drove many a good man mad. Again, nods from the fathers. Wilson the assistant pro told us that golf was a game that rewarded work, a game without excuses, a game of you against yourself. He talked about golf as love, golf as everything, golf as addiction and golf as disease. He talked three feet over our heads, speaking to the men behind us, and the only things that our young ears were hearing was that golf was a game for grown-ups, and that games for grown-ups were not really games at all.

The group spread out, lining up along the front of the range with a safe amount of room between us. Wilson explained to us that these clubs weren't toys, and he told us a little story about a boy who wasn't paying attention at this very range when he was knocked in the head with a pitching wedge. His name was Harold, and he was never quite right again, his head a little heavy, his words a little backwards, and the poor kid had to be a Fox Chase caddy for the rest of his life. This made all the members laugh, including Charlie Logan, who had been sleeping standing up against a sycamore tree.

Whatever we might have learned that day, none of it amounted to anything resembling a golf swing. Twenty-seven children had basically been provided with a weapon and just enough space and instruction to be legitimately dangerous. A yellow-haired boy at the far end of the line was throwing balls at a red-haired boy next to him. A skinny boy who needed his nose wiped was holding his club by the wrong end, swinging the rubber handle at the ball and laughing to the boy next to him who had decided to practice baton twirling with his five-iron. A five-year-old was pulling his shorts down around his ankles and peeing on the ball in front of him, which made Amanda Norton shriek with laughter and made an anxious father come scoop the small boy up in his arms, a boy who, unfortunately for the father, was not prepared to stop what he'd started. Next to me, Jimmy Shaw was crying between whiffs, his father standing behind him and whispering, "Okay Jimmy, atta boy, that last one was almost . . . now just nice and easy."

Myles Dane was stationed off at the end of the range, separated back in the corner as if he didn't want to be contaminated. Wilson stood behind him, nodding, mouthing something to Mr. Dane that made the man smile. Myles's every swing was identical, same turn, same tempo, same smart look on his face as he followed the ball out into the range. It was all very gorgeous, very sleek, a performance that, like his father's Italian racer, looked wonderfully expensive. There in front of us was time and lessons and a father who couldn't possibly develop real estate all the time because there needed to be hours for his son. A swing like that was built beneath a shadow.

I thought to myself that there was a boy who didn't get to play baseball, and I wasn't sure why that made me so happy. I didn't know then that baseball was over for me too, that now there was golf, and there would always be golf. Only golf.

I watched Amanda laugh as she topped shot after shot, dribbling balls to a spot a few feet in front of her. She covered her mouth and scrunched up her nose, embarrassed, then hurried to grab another ball and tee it up again. Mr. Norton was shaking his head, saying, "Amanda dear, now remember what the man said, hit *down* on the ball, *down,* now just concentrate a little," but she was smiling and swinging and turning like a ballerina, knocking the ball on every third pass.

"Oh, no dear, your grip is all wrong, honey," her father said as he stepped forward to grab her hands.

But he didn't. The club swung back and, *click,* like stone on concrete, it cracked his forehead solid center, Amanda's best contact of the day. Her father stumbled backward, his fingers holding his forehead as he dropped to one knee.

Amanda shrieked so loud it sounded fake. Fathers scurried around the range, rushing toward the clubhouse, others rushing to pick up Norton III and be the first to brush off the back of his pants. Someone yelled, "Call an ambulance," and someone said, "There's got to be a doctor here. There's got to be a doctor." Charlie Logan stood amid the action, soda in hand, eyes like slits as he called out, "Call an attorney! Ha! Hope she's got herself a good lawyer." The laughter dribbled from his lips.

Jimmy Shaw was no longer crying. He licked an orange Creamsicle and watched two men lift a dazed Mr. Norton up by the armpits, a red line blossoming on his forehead. One of the fathers told Norton that he might want to see a doctor to be safe, but not just then, and the men took turns patting their president on the back, a clumsy congratulations for taking a five-iron in the face. Charlie Logan offered him a sip of his soda, which Norton declined with both hands.

When Wilson and his mirrored glasses came to watch me swing, I did what I thought I was supposed to do. I cranked one good and solid, hundred and a half out into the range. It didn't feel entirely lucky, like I could do it again if I tried. Which I did. And then I did it again, my right hand feeling like it was part of my shoulder, a sweet snap, and the ball moving gently from right to left against the plain blue sky.

"Clinic's for beginners," Wilson said, eying me over the top of his sunglasses. "You can hit balls up here if you want, but we're out here to help the new kids."

"I am a new kid."

"Right."

I saw my reflection stretched across his glasses.

"I've never hit a golf ball before. My dad hits them in the back-yard, but . . ."

"Great, kid," Wilson said, "you just keep swinging."

Something behind the mirrors was bothered by what I had done, as if the way I was striking the ball was irreverent. He left me alone for the rest of the afternoon, but I would catch him glancing at me, peeking from behind the other children, grinning at me with one smarmy side of his mouth. I looked around at that romper room of junior golfers, hardly the sound of iron clicking Surlyn coming from anywhere along the line, and I knew that I was doing it right, that I could and they could not, and I wasn't too young to look at Wilson the assistant pro and think, *fuck that guy.*

Snap after snap after snap and each a little easier, less thought with each pass until I was not thinking at all, things in my body telling me what to do instead of me telling them.

The crunch of iron spikes on concrete came down the path behind the range, and I turned to see my father in his sweater, walking with his head down and reading a scorecard. Behind him was a caddy, a small boy with bones for cheeks who was carrying my father's brown leather bag that looked like it was made from ripped-up saddles. The boy wore one of the bright yellow hats that all the caddies had to wear, and the brim was marked with a dried white line of salt and sweat. The clubs rattled as he dropped the bag off his shoulder, and my father dug a dollar bill out of his pocket and handed it to the boy. The walk to the range was barely a hundred yards, and my father would have preferred to carry his bag himself had that not been entirely unacceptable. It was one of the things about the place that defied reason until it was tucked beneath the word *etiquette,* where it became superior to reason. A golfer would spend hundreds, even thousands of dollars on a bag that smelled like new shoes, gold stitching advertising his name, a little extra to fill it up with titanium and graphite and flashy headcovers that substituted for price tags because everyone in the place knew that the new Nukehead Plus driver cost $399 on sale. And after all that, after matching the towel and stuffing the bag with tees and unspecific knickknacks a friend had brought back from Scotland, a player won't even pick it up. Assemble your prize, and never let it be seen on your shoulder.

The caddy tried to look surprised when my father handed him the money.

"Timmy, come over here," my father said. "Meet Jamie Byrne."

I put out my hand. "Nice to meet you."

The boy stared at his feet like he was thinking of something to do.

"Hello," he said, extending his hand small toward mine. I looked down at it, and I saw that his right thumb was just a bony nub. It was pink at the tip and it didn't extend up to the first knuckle. By the time I could think not to stare, I was already staring, and the caddy pulled his fingers away and stuck them in his pocket. He thanked my father for the tip, and I watched him hustle back toward the clubhouse, two small bumps for shoulders and a pink neck, and I couldn't imagine how he carried a golf bag long enough to break that sweat stained in a circle around his head.

"Is there something wrong with that caddy?" I asked my father. "Did you see," I wrinkled my nose, "his hand?"

"Kid's got no thumbs," he said as if it were something to be admired. "He's a real hard worker, though. So let's have a look and see if you learned anything today."

He leaned on his club, no smile and his eyes waiting, and I imagined for a second that what he was leaning on was a Buick, shining black and silver and blue.

I hurried to place a ball on a good spot of grass, and I thought of every single piece of instruction I had heard that morning about angles and moves and turns. I swung quick, all wind, and I looked out into the sky to see the dead blank sight of nothing.

My throat felt stuffed with tissue, the ball sticking to that tuft of grass like a rotten albino toad.

"Hold on, that was just a practice one," I said, not pausing to gather myself but swinging again, keeping my head down, *down,* so this time I was able to watch the club sweep past the ball, missing it by a good four inches.

"I was whacking them before," I said, "that guy over there saw, the guy with the glasses."

My father chuckled like he was bored and said, "Thank God I'm not paying for this."

I went solid for a second, frozen over the ball. My jaw tightened and I turned back bitter, stretching muscles over bones and snapping them free. No thought, just heat, and there was a push through the ground and a ball slicing through the air with that *whoosh,* not soaring, but barreling outward and away.

I turned to watch my father's yellow sweater disappear behind the oak trees surrounding the practice green, where he would find those strokes, the things that might be hiding there. He didn't see me hit that ball, and I told myself that was fine, so that I might believe that it was. It was fine because even though I could do it, it was still his game and he played it alone. Better to leave me here, better for him to be down at the practice green, chipping from all sides, looking for the center of that circle.

I turned and looked back at the clubhouse, and halfway down the path I saw a yellow hat poking out from behind an oak tree. I quickly went back to hitting balls, showing off, slamming them out into the grass. I would peek back once in a while to see that the caddy was still watching me, and then I would look down to the practice green to see that my father wasn't.

THE AIR WAS April, cool and bright and everything smelling like a fresh towel in your face when you step from the shower. The days began to stretch themselves, and the return of those late afternoons was everything to a golfer. A few more hours, a few more holes. There would be enough light, my father told me, for a quick round after school if we hurried along. Meet at the tee at three o'clock, get out and back in three hours because my mother was making her pot roast. This time she asked us not to come home with excuses.

It was the kind of spring day when things move on a little quicker without trying, the April afternoon when I was eleven years old and I first beat my father.

Three o'clock sharp. We stretched on the tee box, our quiet twosome, and he smiled at the way I was watching the first hole, looking to see where my drive was going to land. Charlie Logan once explained to me that it was the thing separating those who played golf from those who were golf. It distinguished weekend golfers from those who played the game like it was all buttons and switches, those who made the questions fit inside their answers.

"It's the difference between the likes of you, and the likes of this old bag talking to you," Charlie Logan said, swallowing a mouthful from his Styrofoam cup. "When I move on the ball, Christ, I'm just hoping for contact. You," he said, pushing his cup toward me, "you smooth-as-silk sons a bitches, you fellas aren't thinking about hitting the damn thing. You're just thinking about where it's going to end up. You're *seeing* it. There's not one damn smidge of fear in your swing," he said, his eyes staring out at nothing. "Give anything to know what that feels like. Give my left nut. And that's the bigger one." He laughed, the folds in his face lifting into a smile.

On the first tee that afternoon, my father slid the headcover off his wooden driver, its lacquer worn yellow, the face chipped and softened around the edges. "That's not where you're supposed to hit it," he would say when I pointed out the wear and tear around the sweet spot, "and they don't make them like this anymore, Timmy. This is what Ben Hogan used to swing, an old spoon just like this."

In our garage, hanging above my father's neglected tool bench, there was a black-and-white framed photograph of Ben Hogan's one-iron shot at Merion. The picture was cracked and bowed from the yard sale where he'd picked it up. My mother wouldn't let it in the house. It was a view of Ben Hogan's backswing from behind, his stature perfect in a way that cannot be held longer than an instant, that cannot be posed or drawn or sculpted. I agreed with my father when he talked about golf being the one game that allowed for those singular moments, those small visions of pure success, pure purpose, pure unity of effort. Other games blur past, run, score, win, loss. But golf is a flow of pauses, a pace of moment after moment, and sometimes, at some point in that progression from tee to green and green to tee, there is a Ben Hogan at Merion, a club set straight across his shoulders like a carpenter's balance, his cap tipped humbly on his head, a white ball rising toward a gray green deep in the distance.

My father teed up his ball and asked me if I wanted any strokes. I told him I didn't.

"And what are we playing for?" he said.

"I don't know. What do you usually play for?"

"The fellas usually play for drinks. Or money. Or real estate. Do you have any of those?" He smiled.

"I've got some money."

"Not that I don't give you, you don't. What fun would that be for me, taking my own money?"

"We can play for drinks," I said.

"Right. We'll stop off for a round on the way home. And your mother would cook me instead of the pot roast. I'll tell you what, we'll have ourselves a gentleman's bet."

I slipped my hand into a crusty leather glove, the fingers shriveled from rain and sweat. "What's a gentleman's bet?"

He took a slow practice swing and watched an imaginary ball move out into the afternoon light. "It's a friendly bet. A bet for honor."

My father's swing wasn't like the one hanging in the garage. It was chopped in half, his arms and legs disagreeing on what they were trying to do. His driver struck the ball with a heel thud. It knuckled over and dove down into the rough.

"Jesus Mary and Joseph," he muttered through clenched teeth.

I bruised a drive that rolled to the spot the hole suggested, right center of the fairway to get back to a pin tucked left. When I used a pitching wedge to drop my second shot six feet below the hole, my father looked at me like I had changed colors.

"Who showed you how to do *that*?" He pointed at my ball as we marched up to the green.

I shrugged my shoulders and didn't look at him and tried not to cough on the pride swelling in my throat. I rolled the ball into the bottom of the cup, and it went down with the sweet rattle *gulp* that only birdie putts have.

The fifth hole was a tight snaking par five, a tunnel of trees bending right then left. A dry creek bed ran down the left side of the fairway, and the other side of the ditch was marked out of bounds. White stakes were placed back in the woods there, in the shadows and the leaves where no one went to look for lost balls. It was too deep and it was dark in the daytime. It was where Fox Chase ended and somewhere else began.

A soggy black carpet of autumns past, a million leaves and my father's ball was beneath one of them.

"You should probably just drop one," I told him.

"I'll find it. Golf balls don't grow on trees. That was a brand-new ball."

He inched down into the ditch, stepping onto a loose stone and almost breaking his ankle. He kicked over rocks and I walked ahead to my ball. I dropped my bag in the fairway, and to my right I spotted someone standing on another fairway. Through a crowd of blue pines, I saw a boy in jeans and sneakers standing a few paces beyond the tree line. I knew that at dusk, fence-members would hop their way onto the course and play a few free holes at Fox Chase in the last bits of daylight. They were usually guys from the public courses, older men with softball cleats instead of golf shoes, carrying sticky old golf bags from the trade-in sports shop. If a member spotted a fence jumper, he would usually look the other way, happy to allow a Joe Sixpack a couple of holes, ten minutes of night golf for the workingman. But I didn't look the other way, and I stared at the figure until I recognized the boy and remembered his name, Jamie Byrne, the kid with straw-blond hair poking out from under his caddy hat. He was trying to hit a golf ball, and as I watched him I understood how that kid carried bags twice his size, sweating that ring of salt into his cap. He was all try. He didn't stop once, not once to think or reconsider as he whiffed shot after shot. Jamie Byrne just whipped the club around his body like he was throwing back a sledgehammer, the club falling down to the ball and missing again.

He grabbed another club off the ground, swinging and holding on with eight fingers and finally knocking a dribbler along the grass that ran ten yards and sat down in the rough. Another ball came out of his pocket, and Jamie set it up on a tee. He waited over the ball, turning his chin, teeth clamping the tip of his tongue, perhaps thinking of the next shot and trusting it to be perfect.

That pause before the swing begins is a small moment of simple faith. It's one of the reasons we play, for that quiet before contact when it might all go right, when we might believe we were better than ourselves. And as Jamie lifted his club back, then threw his body forward to pull it on through, I watched that moment slip through his fingers, the club getting loose from his hands, banging and twisting across the fairway.

"Jesus Christ! Get the hell out of here!"

I turned to see my father waving his five-iron like a sword. He stomped his foot at the ground and spat as he yelled. "Go, get out of here!" A dozen yards in front of him, a fox stood frozen at the edge of the fairway, a gray squirrel hanging limp in its teeth. The fox was small with sharp ears and dark eyes, burnt-orange fur the color of my brother's hair. It shot its eyes from my father to the woods beyond the creek bed, then to me across the fairway. Two hundred acres of open grass and this animal found itself in a corner.

When I turned to look for Jamie, I saw him running hard for the shade of the tree line where the link fence was lowest. He left his golf balls behind, no bag, running with golf clubs cradled in his arms like a bundle of twigs.

"Go on, get out of here!"

The fox dropped the squirrel from its mouth and sprang across the creek bed. It scratched its way up the bank and disappeared into the woods, twisting through the tree trunks until it was just the sound of fast-beating paws on leaves that were still wet from winter.

"That thing could have had rabies," my father said. "Somebody's going to have to do something about that." His hands were shaking when he reached into his bag, taking out a new ball and dropping it in the fairway.

You would hear the talk about there still being foxes at Fox Chase, but it seemed like such an obvious myth that I had not believed it. I had seen the paintings in the clubhouse, men in red coats leaping fences on white horses, a little red blur trying to escape at the corner of the frame. And now I had seen a fox, and I thought that there must have been something better to chase, something bigger to hunt that they could kill and stand over. It seemed as pointless as chasing a dog around the backyard or a cat around the kitchen. I wondered why they needed all those people in a mob, why they needed all those horses.

On the sixteenth hole, my father stood over a perfect lie in the heart of the fairway with a three-wood in his hands. He made two poetic practice swings, then took one sideways rip at the ball, sending it worm-burning along the turf and into a muddy creek that crossed the fairway. I had never heard the word *fuck* come from my father's mouth before. It sounded accidental, two syl-. lables like he wanted to stop halfway, fu-*uck*. He wrapped his three-wood around his knee, bending the shaft into a boomerang. It didn't bend back. I looked away as he snapped it in two and dumped the pieces into his bag. I slowed and let him walk out ahead of me, watching him kick and curse and crawl his way in. He looked old, which he did sometimes, but with all that ungraceful anger I thought for the first time that my father looked like a fool.

I only let myself think it for a moment.

By the time we finished, the light was just a cold blue shadow between the trees and the night above us. After eighteen holes, there were two scores. Mine was lower by five.

My father looked over the scorecard, adding up the numbers. "Eighty," he said.

"I think it was seventy-nine."

He looked at the scorecard again, his brow tight over a short list of simple numbers that were somehow tough to put together.

He ran his fingers over and down his chin and said, "Right, seventy-nine. Well done."

He tucked the card into his back pocket and said, "You are eleven years old, Timmy. *Eleven.*" It sounded like an accusation. "I have never broken eighty in my entire life."

Eyes lowered against the breeze, my father turned and headed back up to the clubhouse. I watched him pull the scorecard out of his pocket and turn it over in his hands, looking to see if the numbers had changed.

We drove home in a silence that said we had both had enough for one afternoon. My father walked into the kitchen and set the scorecard up on its side on the breakfast table. It took us a minute to notice the smell of electric heat and to see the slippery pink loaf of beef waiting in a black pan on the counter. The kitchen was warm like the oven had been broiling for hours.

My father didn't panic when he saw her in the family room, sleeping sideways in her chair, grape juice dripped down the front of her blouse. Her hair fell over the armrest, and her shoulders, small and crooked, stretched at the corners of her shirt. One knee faced in, one faced out. Her face lay on the edge of the chair, her lips open and pushed against the upholstery. The sound upstairs of my brother's stereo. She slept, drums throbbing against the ceiling.

My father helped her off the couch and up the stairs, holding her by her waist, and she apologized until she cried while he told her not to worry. We had eaten already, he said, a quick bite on the way home.

She stopped crying, and she lifted her head and said, "You promised you wouldn't." He said it didn't matter, we could save her roast for tomorrow.

My father came downstairs and made a pile of peanut butter and jelly sandwiches. We ate dinner across from each other in silence, a scorecard for a centerpiece. My father mashed up the bread in his mouth, eyes studying his sandwich like it was covered in fine print. I tried not to think about the boy on the course and his hands and how they told us grip's the thing. I didn't stare at the roast on the counter, thinking about why we were eating sandwiches again. I didn't wonder if the man across from me wished he had beaten his eleven-year-old son.

My father and I sat there eating our dinner, both of us not thinking the exact same things.

OUR HOUSE WAS a simple house, small the way suburban homes were small before people needed patios and skylights and a third garage. It was dwarfed by the new homes popping up around us in New Water's panicked wave of residential construction. Hundreds of families with minivans instead of station wagons flooded our northern Delaware town, the latest mid-Atlantic suburban alternative to New Jersey. My father bought our home from an original New Water family, before the new developments were plotted and produced, before all the horse farms were sold, before the tree-filled hills that rolled on like sleep with colors you couldn't see the edge of were flattened and combed into neat brown lots. Coughing yellow machines came and readied the land for rolls of new sod. They left their tracks all over.

The latest edition of New Water houses comprised five or six architectural designs shared between eighty homes, each home trying to distinguish itself by way of aggressive landscaping and longer swimming pools and shutters of an unexpected color. Our house was an old custom job, a one-of-a-kind colonial, and I knew my father took pride in that idea—smaller, but better. There was no spiral to our staircases, no wraparound wooden deck, no smart-looking bevels. We had two garages, one for the station wagon and one barely wide enough for the Buick. It took my father three reverses to squeeze it in.

Six rosebushes grew in front of our house, blooming full and wild below the front windows, and picking, pruning, holding those buds in his hands was the only thing I can remember my father really giving his time to around our house. Stuck between homes with vanilla-icing stucco and overmulched flower beds where the tulips didn't take, his rosebushes seemed to bleed color, and it wasn't rare for a passing car to slow for a closer look. My father would inspect each leaf and petal with his fingers, picking off bugs and brushing the wrong colored dirt away from the black soil he poured over the roots and fed with scoops of his special blue powder. On his knees in front of those bushes, or curled over an eight-iron at the practice green, my father could lose himself in a tight-eyed preparation. Preparing for what, I never knew, but I always feared that it might be nothing.

Part of what made those bushes great, my father would say as he chuckled and pulled on his belt, was that they were older than half the houses in New Water. Smaller, but better, and my father believed it.

Casey moved up into the attic when he was twelve years old, and my mother left his room untouched, a sewing machine in one dusty corner, a stack of her *New Yorker* magazines spilling up-ward in the other. The door was kept locked and the air inside had a bitter stink. My father wanted to turn the room into an office, but she said no and no and no, as if she thought Casey might someday put on a smile and come down from the attic and push his bed back into his childhood room at the end of the hall.

When he moved to the attic, my brother staged his act of rebellion as something vicious and adult, something someone his age shouldn't have the hardness to do. I didn't tell Casey that I knew his inspiration was *The Brady Bunch*. We had both watched Greg Brady move into the attic on a half-dozen reruns, but if I had told my brother that his insurgence was as defiant as chocolate chips and linoleum and Sam the butcher, he would have cracked his knuckles on my eardrum.

We were out by the rosebushes when my brother showed me the proper way to throw a football. Casey was very good at football. He just wasn't good at teams. Not an obvious athlete, he ran half bent-over, his arms swinging unnatural and his feet a bit flat. Yet there was something very basic that my brother understood about finding the football and hurting the person who happened to be cradling it, and that made him the least-known star on the high school varsity. They wore Penn State colors, no names on their backs, and the other football parents referred to my brother as *that linebacker*. They didn't know Casey Price. Their children were not his friends. He didn't sleep over at their homes the night before the game, but they all cheered for that linebacker on Saturday when he threw his head into the pile. They barked when he picked up an opposing player and swung him down like a sack of dirt. When he wrapped up a tackle, Casey punched with his biceps, squeezing the breath out of a running back, and the crowd would scream and wonder where his parents were, where was the pin that read *My Son Wears #44.*

My father would be sitting quietly at the top of the bleachers, just a few rows behind, wearing a wool cap when all the other dads were wearing Philadelphia Eagles hats. He would skip golf on Saturday mornings when Casey had a home game, a twisted-up newspaper in his hands, rocking in his seat and mumbling through his teeth at the referees. On those autumn Saturdays before the air went from crisp to frozen, I would join my father in the stands to watch Casey rumble around the turf helmet first. My mother never came along. She thought the sport was an awful idea, and when we came home she didn't want to hear the final score. She just wanted to know that Casey walked off the field at the end.

I would watch Casey stretch before the game beside the other boys, and to me, he threw a shadow over all of them. Some of his teammates were taller, some were thicker, but Casey was bigger in the way you expected smoke to come out of his face mask, in the way he would hardly lift his hands when he was doing his jumping jacks. He was giant in how he wore black socks when everyone else wore white, in how his helmet looked like a windshield after a long drive, smeared with colors and bits of the other team. His pants were always the filthiest, muddy and sagging in the knees, his fingers cold and black and dangerous in the way he never closed them into a fist, roaming the field with claws pried open. And in the way Casey ran, hulking, nose first, as if he could smell the contact coming.

He had run that way since we were small children. A Monday when I was too young for school, I watched from our front window as my brother ran laps around our house in the rain. Casey splashing through the puddles without shoes, sopping brown socks falling off his toes. Lightning grabbed at the trees in the distance as the big drops splashed all over the yard. I watched him run, and I watched my mother go chasing after him, shaking a pair of his galoshes in the air. Few things in our house could bring on a firestorm like Casey's rubber rain shoes. He loathed them with a passion, yet my mother was of the school that nearly all childhood maladies—pneumonia, mumps, meningitis—could be traced to either wet feet or wet hair. So that morning she chased him in her yellow bathrobe, her bare feet slipping around in a pair of my father's galoshes, yelling at my brother to stop, please, until she wasn't yelling anymore, and she was standing in the rain in the middle of our yard. She dropped Casey's rain shoes in the grass and looked at me watching her from inside, and I stood there wondering how a person could cry that much, her face, her hair, her clothes all dripping wet.

It took Casey half the afternoon to help me figure a way to launch a spiral across the front lawn. The old football was slippery gray and bloated like a basketball, too round for my fingers to grip. On one side of the ball, my father's name was written in a child's deliberate cursive—*Jimmy Price,* faded into the leather. I laughed when I read the name, turning the ball over in my hands.

"I think this is the original football," Casey said as he grabbed up my pass out of the dirt. "It was Dad's when he played in high school."

I imagined my father striding toward the end zone in loafers and khakis and a yellow cardigan. Football players didn't turn into shortish golfers with sunken cheeks and pointy shoulders. But Casey told me my father was pretty tough on the field, an All-County tackle back when tackles could be five-foot nine. Casey once told me about going down to games at U of D with my father to watch his Blue Hens, back when I was still a toddler. They would drink hot chocolate and freeze their asses on the metal bleachers, and my father would tell stories of the glory days of Delaware football, watching Chuck Hall and Tom Dimuzio and Gardy Kahoe, and every game he would explain to my brother why Delaware Blue Hens wore the same helmets as Michigan Wolverines. What Casey didn't tell me, what he didn't need to explain, was that this was all before my father became a member at Fox Chase and fall Saturdays became a time for golf.

Casey flipped me the football.

"Hit me, I'm going deep."

He bounced on his toes, then darted across the lawn. I leaned down low and jumped off the ground to toss the ball as far as I could, no spiral, the football flailing sideways in the air. Casey looked back over his shoulder, stretching his arms and his fingers and his whole body, and the ball slid into his hands, no smack, just the smooth purchase of worn leather in his palms.

And then the screaming. More like a growl, really, Casey shouting between his teeth, the muscles taut in his legs and arms. He was motionless in the middle of the rosebushes. Thorns in his arms and his cheek, the sharp branches grabbing his clothes and pushing little red dots into his skin.

I ran to try and help, but when I pulled Casey out by his free hand he groaned loud in my ear, a long green thorn squeezing into his thigh. The front door banged open behind me.

"Goddamnit, Casey!"

My father grabbed my brother by the shoulders and lifted him out of the roses, and this time Casey didn't make a sound as the branches dragged lines across his legs and arms.

My father quickly got down on his knees, his hands fumbling to push the roots back down into the soil. He picked at the bush, returning each branch and petal to its proper spot. He stood and brushed off one hand against the other, big dramatic slaps. "Somebody better tell me what the hell happened here." He didn't look at me for a second.

Casey stared at me for a moment, his hand pressed against the cut in his leg, his chest moving up and down as if he'd run a hundred yards to get under that football. He didn't look me in the eyes, instead he stared at a spot between my shoulders, swallowing deep breaths. My brother shook his head, and he turned and walked away.

"Hey, get back here. Don't turn your back on me, mister!"

Casey walked down the driveway and out onto our street. There was nowhere for him to walk to, not in New Water. We didn't have a corner or a playground or any place you could find by foot that wasn't just like here. I didn't know where my brother was going. Ours was a neighborhood of neighbors, all the white houses put there for the people to pass by.

THE RULES GOVERNING PLAY at Fox Chase decreed that junior golfers couldn't play before noon when the tee was reserved for bondholding members. Some faceless caretaker of those rules made an exception for a handful of us, for the nascent talents they would let out of the stable in the morning. A dance around the paddock, we would shoot our low numbers and the members would marvel at the amazing things that could happen at their golf club.

On one of those mornings, my father and I matched up in a foursome with two men I had never met. Both were tan with tall bright smiles and they wore pressed slacks and starched cotton shirts for Saturday golf. There were effortless members at Fox Chase, men like these who wore privilege around like a handkerchief tucked smartly in their breast pocket. My father was not one of them. He had to work at belonging, and even a sixth-grader knew that meant he never would.

One of our playing partners' names was Peter Staeger. I asked my father if that was the Staeger of Staeger Savings and Loan, and he nodded, unimpressed, piloting our golf cart in figure eights through the pine trees as we searched for another one of his brand-new Titleists.

On the eighteenth green, I lined up a ten-foot putt for a seventy-five. When the ball looked inside the cup then spun off the lip, I started to laugh.

"He's not perfect," said Mr. Staeger. "I was starting to wonder if you'd ever miss one."

Two birdies and three double bogeys for a plus four, seventy-six. We finished and said *it was a pleasure,* shaking hands, and *let's do it again.* Peter Staeger didn't shake my hand. I was taller than his playing partner, yet he still patted my head and shook up my hair and said, "Way to go, kid."

Staeger shoved a wad of cash into his caddy's hand and turned to my father. "Bring Timmy into the grill room, Jim. I'll buy the boy a sarsaparilla." But my father answered no thanks without looking at me to see how much I wanted to go behind that door, the bronze sign that read GENTLEMEN ONLY PLEASE, the door's heavy dark wood with its moaning gold hinges.

On our way to the parking lot, we walked around the clubhouse instead of through it. My father didn't go inside and take that opportunity to buy a round and brag over old-fashioneds about his son breaking eighty before he was shaving. He didn't gloat when Staeger told him I looked like a walking scholarship to Stanford, and he didn't even smile when Staeger's partner asked him if the milkman was a scratch handicap.

My father had the floor to boast, loud and obnoxious, and I wasn't surprised when he didn't take it. My mother called it one of the glories of being Irish, an inborn conviction that misery was a virtue, joy a sin. But to me that was all bullshit. We weren't Irish, we were suburbanites. My father's stone face had nothing to do with where my grandparents came from. It had to do with guts.

After I put my clubs in the trunk of the Buick, my father pulled the scorecard out of his back pocket and flipped it to me. "That's really something, Timmy," he said. "If you're old enough to do that, I think you're old enough to go out and earn a few dollars."

The following saturday, my father dropped me off at 6 A.M. at the end of the long winding driveway up to Fox Chase Country Club. I was wearing a clean white T-shirt like he had told me to, one of our old white towels wrapped nervous around my fingers.

My father said good luck. He explained that gentlemen take their game seriously, and one thing that won't be tolerated is a caddy who doesn't take it just as seriously.

"It's a good summer job. And it will make you a better player, Timothy," he said as I stepped out of the car. "There's a lot to learn up here. Pay attention to these guys."

I nodded.

"And stay out of everybody's line," he said as the station wagon pulled away through a cloud of its own smoke.

As I walked up the driveway in the early morning light, carrying a towel instead of my golf clubs, it was as if I was seeing the place for the first time. The white clubhouse in front of me was a grave sort of building, a tall oak doorway shut beneath dark windows, columns supporting a roof of slate shingles. There was one peak to the building, a muted steeple above the doorway, and rooms stretched out from the entrance like shoulders and arms. I stood there thinking how the place looked asleep, a large snoring whitebeard I should tiptoe past.

A wooden flagpole rose out of the grass in front of the house, red, white and blue nylon snapping tired in the morning.

I turned and saw a long black Mercedes pull into the driveway. The entrance to Fox Chase was set back a half mile from the road, and not even the neighbors were sure what was hidden back in the woods, the clubhouse with stiff columns and starched corners, miles of green stretched over what some called *the hidden gem* of the golfing world, a club where men waited ten years for the chance to mortgage their homes to pay the initiation fee, and did it with a smile.

The cricket sound of sprinklers clipping water was everywhere. The Mercedes rolled past me with a yawn, and a man with shock-white hair sat small in the driver's seat. I wondered about that man and how he, perhaps many years before, first found his way back here, to this spot in front of this house where a flagpole stuck out of the ground like the mast of a buried ship. Who told him about this place, how did people know about it? It was hidden and quiet and admission was tough. At the end of the driveway, there wasn't a sign.

I walked around to the back of the clubhouse where golf carts were buzzing, tires swerving on edge, a busy mess sliding into row after row of white carts. Caddies jogged from cart to cart, tying bags to the back, tightening straps, hustling from the clubhouse and back down to a small metal hangar. Raymond Mann stood at the center of it with sleep crusted under his eyes, barking orders that everyone seemed too busy to hear as the carts zipped from the hangar like bees from a nest. I could taste the work in the air, bitter and early, chilly morning sweat.

A few members in pleated slacks and V-neck sweaters stood off to the side of the commotion, sipping cups of coffee, steam rising up around their smiling faces. They looked like they were trying hard not to be serious, away from work and out of the house on a Saturday morning. These crack-of-dawn golfers, I would later learn, tended to be either retired curmudgeons with no patience for playing behind anyone, or young men with young children and young wives who were red-eyed from a week with the kids, who at some point along the line might have said *it's the golf or me.* These husbands always took a cart and were first in line at the tee, tearing around the course and quietly settling their bets and, God willing, making it home by noon, the hero with a sack of McDonald's. They didn't take caddies, and they never talked about golf and their wives in the same sentence.

"Caddy, hey, caddy," called a round man sitting by himself in a sagging cart. He was lighting a cigarette that looked like a toothpick between his fat fingers.

"Hey, do me a favor, kid, clean this stuff out," he said, pointing to some hairy orange peels jammed into a compartment in the front of his cart. I hesitated for a second, unsure who he might be talking to, but before I knew it I was standing there with a handful of orange rinds, still lost but doing my job—I was confident in that. Someone had told me to do something and I did it. No questions asked, no need for a thank-you, no matter that the peels felt like spiders in my hands.

"You loopin'?" a voice came from behind me. I turned and saw a man holding a clipboard. He had a waxy white face with skin like a cutting board, all nicked and pockmarked. He was wearing a wrinkled golf shirt with the Fox Chase logo on the chest. "Where the hell's your hat?" he said.

"I've never been up here to caddy before . . ." I started.

"Well we've got enough kids for the season, sorry 'bout that. But thanks for stopping by," he said, turning away before his sentence was finished.

"My father's a member here, he said to come up here to caddy. He's Mr. Price," I said. I had a vague notion that at that moment and in that place, it was the only thing to say.

"You Mr. Price's kid?" He turned and eyed me, suspicious. "You're the kid Wilson won't shut up about."

I couldn't remember who Wilson was at first, and once I did, recalling my reflection stretched across his sunglasses, I felt a self-conscious sort of thrill in the idea that he knew my name without me knowing his. It was a simple thing, but fascinating, and a little frightening. Perhaps he thought I was special, maybe, or pure, *fucking pure,* maybe lucky, or maybe he couldn't shut up about how my game was bogus, a show for the members, an expensive-looking swing on a spoiled little shit.

"Lewis Holmes, caddy master," he said without shaking my hand. "I'm in charge of the loops. I put the caddies out, so if you want to be a caddy, I'm the fucking man. And I don't care who your daddy is. If you want a loop, Lewis Holmes is your daddy."

Caddy master—it sounded like someone with a whip and a chaw, someone who failed at everything else he'd tried. But that morning, I was sweating at 6 a.m. and I was lost where I was standing, and it was all intimidating enough.

"You're big enough for doubles," he said. "We'll put you out with someone who knows what the shit they're doing. You know your way around the course?"

"Yes."

"You never caddied before?"

"No."

"Shit, then pay attention to what the other guys do, and stay out of these people's way," he said, pointing to the men with the coffee. Lewis Holmes handed me a yellow cap with the FC logo on the front, CADDY #36 embroidered on the side. I put it on, the starched brim sticking up cheaply on my forehead, and Lewis nodded. "If you want to be a member's kid, be a member's kid. If you want to be a caddy, be a caddy," he said, wiping his nose with his finger, then tapping the brim of my cap with it.

Raymond Mann leaned his pork chop of a chin out the pro shop window.

"Lewis, get your ass back in here and tie it to this counter," he said. "Phone's ringing and I'm in here doing your damn job."

"Caddy hole's over there," Lewis said, pointing to a set of stone steps that led beneath the clubhouse.

I heard voices coming from the stairs, then a little laughter, then words jumping on top of each other, *fuck* over *pussy* over *pieceashit,* getting hotter, inching upward to the top of the stairs. A roar, and then nothing. The hush seemed to squeeze my toes as I stood on that first step. I waited for the voices to roll back into a hum before I made my way down. I tried not to go too slowly.

The walls were cement and the sound was stone, and as I looked around the dark room, I couldn't tell exactly where it ended. The ceiling stretched back over row after row of wooden racks, each row packed tight with golf bags. There was a lightbulb above an industrial sink where warm water was running, bubbling up green and soapy. There were shadows and corners I could not make out. And around the sink, in between the racks, on benches, on buckets, curled up on towels on the floor, there were men. Boys and blank stares, wrinkled eyes, four-day stubble, thick biker beards, cheeks pale and swollen and pink. There were faces everywhere.

I sidestepped to the edge of the room and leaned up against a
bare space of wall, trying not to make a ripple in the routine as
men took deep drags on cigarettes, pulling the fire down to their
fingertips. Boys my age, some smaller than me, arm wrestled
and told jokes and whipped each other with their towels. Bring
a towel, my father told me, every caddy needs a towel for wiping clubs and spotting balls. A tall boy with a ponytail and thin
eyes wound up his towel tight as rope and snapped it, cracking
it on the cheek of a smaller boy across the room. The faces all
laughed until there bubbled a spot of blood, when they grabbed
the tall boy by the neck and hands and legs, and they held him
down while the smaller boy softened his face with punches.
They did not let him up until an older voice said *enough, knock
it off fuckos,* and I sank back against the wall, scared and amazed
and clenching my fists, no idea what I might do with them, and
I watched everyone go back to doing nothing, more jokes and
more waiting while the boy with the ponytail licked blood from
his teeth. After five minutes, the two boys were arm wrestling
and laughing and snapping towels at each other's head. I re-
moved my hat and felt the stitching, Caddy #36, and I looked at
the numbers around me on hats that were worn brown with
sweat, scorched pale in the sun, and mine ripe and yellow as fruit.

A man wearing a blue windbreaker ate a cinnamon bun with
a plastic fork. The man next to him held the butt of a white-
filtered cigarette in his palm. The skin on his face looked like it
had died days before, and he told the man in the windbreaker
that he was *a son of a whore* for eating that in front of everyone,
all gooey with syrup, the white sticky smell of it. The faces were
hungry. I watched the man smile and chew with his mouth full
of sugar, and I could feel the room wanting it, as if there were

something about the place that made you feel not quite full. Maybe it was the smell—rotten vegetables—or the shape or the sound or the name of it, *the hole,* or maybe it was the way all the colors in the room were brown.

Maybe it was the waiting.

Hours went by.

I stood, then slouched, then slid my back down the wall and let my ass go numb on the concrete. Faces changed with the minutes. Bags came in and bags went out on caddies' shoulders, and sometimes there was movement and purpose all over the place, and sometimes there was just waiting. I stayed out of the way, the way I was told.

Lewis Holmes came down into the caddy hole with a small sideways smile. He was cocky with a sunken chest, and it was obvious that he took pleasure in bossing around men twice his age.

"Jamie, grab Norton's bag and get up there." Lewis tapped his pen against his clipboard to show he was thinking. "Take Price with you. Give him Parker and Mollit."

Jamie Byrne stepped out from a group of boys in a corner. His feet shuffled to the center of the room, hands tucked in his pockets, and he asked in a voice more polite than I expected to hear in that room, "Price? You mean *Mister* Price?"

"No." Lewis scanned the room until his eyes fell on mine. I took a half step away from the wall, then paused.

"Well for fuck's sake, waiting for an invitation, Long Ball?" he said.

"No, I'm not."

"Ladies and gentlemen, we have a bona fide member's son in our midst," Lewis said. "He says he wants to be a looper, so let's everybody give him a nice round of applause."

Lewis Holmes clapped to himself. A man with green finger-nails spat on the floor and said, "Whoopty-fuckin-do. I ain't been out in three days."

"Plenty of loops to go around today, fellas," said Lewis. "He's got Parker and Mollit. Anyone else want that shit loop?"

Nobody lifted their head to answer him. "Didn't think so," Lewis said.

Jamie looked me up and down, acting as if he'd never seen me before. "I'm out with a first-timer?" he said.

"You'll be fine. Just make sure he doesn't go running off building castles in the sand traps." Lewis dropped two bags in front of me. "Stay up with your players. And pay attention to Jamie."

I put one on each shoulder and walked up the steps with the feeling that this was all some terrible prank.

Jamie Byrne was the kind of kid who, the first time you saw him, everything looked the wrong size—blue eyes too large for his face, bony ankles swimming around in his sneakers, strands of hair hanging over his eyes like cobwebs. But you would only think that the first time you saw him. Before our loop, he gave me a mild rookie shakedown on the first tee.

"Okay, so here's the important stuff. If you mess up the simple stuff, it's really bad. The most important is to stay up with your golfers. And never say anything unless they say something to you, and be quiet, I mean *really really* quiet when they go to hit the ball. Rake the sand traps after they hit out of them, and make sure you rake over all the footprints, especially yours. And stay off the greens. I'll take the pin. You don't know about lines and stuff yet. A line's the imaginary line between the ball and the . . ."

"I *know* what a *line* is," I interrupted. "I play golf here. My father's a member." It sounded awful, but at the time it sounded safe. The faster I could get that out, I thought, the better my chance of not getting my nose bent sideways.

I was dumb as a fucking eleven-year-old.

"Yeah? Well mine's not, so good for fucking you," Jamie said, lifting the bag to his shoulder, teetering a step, then hustling up to Mr. Norton while I trudged behind. The round was quiet for Jamie and me after that. I stayed off the greens. I stayed out of their lines.

I used my legs to lift the weight of the bags. At first, they were a numb steady load balanced across my shoulders. After five holes, gravity dug in, and I was hauling two anchors chained to my shoulder blades. There was no balance. Clubs rattling, the sweaty leather straps slipping down my arms and dumping the bags to the turf. And when they didn't slip, the bag straps were piano wire burrowing into my shoulders. I stumbled and walked and wondered if my forehead might actually split at the center, and I didn't even try to smile at Mr. Mollit, a shrunken actuary who made jokes out of telling me what I was doing wrong, trying to mask his frustration because he played gin with my father. He didn't do a very good job.

"We'll make a caddy out of you yet," he called back over his shoulder. "You'll learn. Now you should always walk behind your golfer, but never too far behind. And never, now never hand a golfer a club with the headcover *on*. It's hard to hit the ball like that," he said, faking a smile. "But you'll learn."

And I would. I would learn that what he was doing was not trying to help me, but setting me up to be stiffed. Poor pay for a poor job, that was only fair. More than a few members railed at their caddies for the entire round, regardless of the quality of the work, in order to create the illusion of a shoddy job and save themselves from having to pay for good service. These men were not worth one splash of a caddy's sweat. They didn't join a private club because they believed they deserved it—these members joined for an empty first tee and no weekend greens fees. They were small men who feared nothing more than not having a pile of money to die atop of, men with no understanding that service work at a country club, a workplace of fifty employees and 350 garrulous owners, is made tolerable only by dollar bills moving from palm to palm. These members played the least, complained the most, and because they did not flex dollar muscle around the club, they blew hot words on the cold ears of those who would smile and do nothing. These men found white scratches dug into the driver's-side door of their Sunday playthings, and if that brought on more complaining, the white lines would reappear, longer and deeper, until the gentlemen either closed their mouths and opened their wallets, or surrendered and had their wives chauffeur them to and from the club. It had been three years since Mr. W. Mollit last parked his car in the lot at Fox Chase, three years since the caddies decided to turn his front quarter panel into a key-cutting station. He had learned, just as he promised me I would learn. He would make a caddy out of me yet.

And I would learn that the caddies who lasted were the ones who convinced the members they cared deeply, never letting on that there was nothing less significant in the world than which way a putt broke, or if they thought the shot was a seven-iron, maybe a six. A private club like Fox Chase could never be small enough, because to the individual member there was only one member, his needs so pressing, his round of golf so paramount—he would never accept that his caddy didn't find him as interesting as he did. To survive in the golf business, you had to listen with closed ears. Ignore the members and lose your job. Pay them attention and lose your mind.

It was leather-palms work, big-shoulder work. They were good people, the caddies at Fox Chase, doing good work, the members all agreed. But a caddy's work was good only in the way that nobody else would do it. It wouldn't be long before I knew that there were two kinds of people in the world—people who carry things, and people who own the things they carry.

Mr. Parker, THE other half of my first loop, said little and made few motions he didn't need to. He plodded forward with his head down, mumbling profanities under his mustache after each bad shot. And there were many. These men were not players, they were might-as-well golfers who teed off around 10 A.M., no rush home, men with such intense boredom in their eyes that they could have been doing anything or nothing at all—they just happened to be playing golf. They did not love it, but it kept them moving forward, kept them chasing a white ball, kept a boy like me chasing them.

We were a threesome, and Jamie carried singles for a man I recognized from the clinic, the club president, Mr. Norton. He was Jamie's steady loop, and in all the time I knew Jamie, he never told me how much Norton paid him, and that was very uncommon among caddies. A looper always tells how much his golfer paid. It was part of the caddies' loose sense of etiquette— like golf etiquette, but with *fucks* and *pussies* and punching allowed. Every caddy knew how much every member's bag was worth. We had to, because there was nothing more maddening than slaving for five hours and getting stuck by a stiff you didn't suspect. It made you bend putters and piss in golf bags. It made you draw lines with your keys.

But Jamie never told what Norton paid. It was definitely a good bit of cash, enough to make it his steady. Some golfers don't play in the rain, some don't play without a cocktail. Richard Norton didn't play without Jamie Byrne on his bag. Byrne takes Norton, no snapping fingers, no tapping of his clipboard, no bullshit from Lewis because Jamie was the looper he knew he couldn't bump. Norton never tired of taking the same caddy. It was the game's highest virtue: consistency, consistency, consistency.

"Did you know that your father played his first round of golf at Fox Chase with myself and Mr. Parker here?" Mollit said as we walked down the fairway, smiling at his feet as he spoke. "God, I'll never forget it. Do you remember that, Donald?"

Mr. Parker didn't look up from where he was kicking at the tall grass off the fairway, searching for a ball I should have been helping him find.

"It was the first Saturday morning after he got his bond. I spotted him out in the parking lot, sitting on the bumper of his car and changing his shoes out there in the open." Mollit chuckled. "I had to show him on into the locker room."

"Caddy, did you see where my ball went?" Parker asked, hands planted on his hips.

"No, I'm sorry, I didn't."

"And then I remember waiting for him at the first tee, and here comes Jim with his clubs tied to one of those squeaky pull-cart contraptions they use at the municipal courses. Mr. Parker asked him if he was playing golf or driving a rickshaw. Ha! We all had a laugh about that. But we got your father straightened away soon enough. I still give him a little ribbing once in a while. Good man, your father. Tell him I let you use a pull-cart today," he laughed. "He'll get a kick out of that."

"Goddamnit, where the hell is that ball? It was just off the fairway."

I walked over into the rough and found Parker's MaxFli sitting deep in the wiry grass. I stepped on the ball and mashed it down good into the turf, and I found that much funnier than the pull-cart my father hadn't taken out of the garage in years.

I could not remember the last five holes, not even as I was walking them. There were steps and hills and no breeze and a burning at the top of my spine. It felt like my temples had opened up and someone was pouring in the pain. I spent the last hour struggling to lift my knees and promising myself I would never do this again. I would paint houses. I would mow lawns. I would wax the car until my palms went purple, but I would never, ever put myself through another day of caddying.

When I put the bags down for the final time, leaning them against the rail at the clubhouse, Mr. Mollit handed me a five and a ten and said, "Keep at it, kiddo, tell your father I said hello," and Mr. Parker handed me a twenty-dollar bill and said, "Would have been more. Could have been more."

I watched as Richard Norton slipped Jamie a tight wad of cash and gave him a nod that said they weren't one-dollar bills.

On my way out to the driveway where my father would pick me up, I passed the pro shop window and saw Lewis Holmes moving inside, following me along the glass toward the door until it swung open. "Hey! Where do you think you're going?"

"I'm going home. We finished."

Lewis Holmes made it very clear that I wasn't going anywhere, not until I took my bags back down to the hole and
scrubbed every speck of dirt from Parker's and Mollit's clubs.

Downstairs, most of the crowd had cleared out, newspapers
and cigarette butts and a cool quiet left behind, and Jamie
was there leaning against the sink, pouring green soap over Mr.
Norton's irons. I watched his fingers grip a steel brush, scratching the brown off the club faces. I stared at his hands and the
two pink nubs working perfectly, covered in water and suds and
wiping a white shine across the steel edges.

"How'd the member's boy do today? Make some money?
Gonna go show your daddy?" Jamie said without looking up.

Upstairs, my father was a friend and a client and a man who
drank highballs on Thursday evenings, but down here, he was
a number, a bag and a slot, #221. My father was a brown leather
sack with faded headcovers and a torn strap that was worth
eighteen dollars of your effort. Say Price in this room, and a
caddy would go to a space on a rack and pick up a bag. He
wouldn't run.

"I didn't mean to sound like a jerk out there," I said. "I just
didn't want you to think I was an idiot or something."

"Don't worry. I do."

"I'm not like a snob or anything."

"Right. Hey," he said, looking up at the wall in front of the
sink, "you know what a line is? Wow, I bet you do."

"Yeah, I do. And I also know I suck at caddying."

He laughed, then thought about it and laughed again. "I'm
surprised they even let members' kids do this. You might sprain
a pinky or get a sunburn or something."

"Well I'm not like those other kids, like that Myles Dane kid
or anything."

Jamie smiled.

"You ever see that Ferrari? Geez," he said, wiping the clubs dry with his towel, "that is an automobile."

"Yeah, it's awesome. Fast."

"They probably don't even know how fast. Man, if that was mine," he said, speaking more to the clubs in his hands than to me, "I'd race that thing like you wouldn't believe. I'd take it to Germany, on the autobahn, or I'd drive it all the way out to Montana. They don't even have speed limits there."

"How can they not have speed limits?"

"It's true. My dad used to live out there, doing forestry and stuff. He had to kill these bugs that were eating all the bark off the trees. He'd drive his truck into the mountains in the morning and back out at night, and he said there were no signs or cops or speed limits anywhere. That would be the place to take a Ferrari. Not even one sign, not nowhere."

Jamie took his time dropping each club into the bag's proper slot.

"Did you ever see Norton's Bentley?"

"No," I said, "what kind of car is that?"

"It's sort of like a Rolls," he said, rolling his neck around his shoulders. "It's awesome. I'm surprised you don't know about Bentleys. Every member I've seen has a pretty decent set of wheels."

"My dad drives a Buick, an old one. I'm not a rich kid."

"Uh-huh. Well my dad drives a paper truck," Jamie said. "It's not very fast."

A thin man with white hair in his ears was reclining in the corner. "Members' kids come in here all the time," he coughed, "not none of them usually come back." His face was sweaty with a thin scar trailing along his jawbone. "You gonna be back, rich boy? Or are your shoulders hurtin' too bad? Go get a job down at the pool, go and play grab-ass all summer." The man laughed and hacked up something chocolate-colored onto the cement.

"Your shoulders break in," Jamie said. "It gets easier. The first loop of the year is always the worst. It burns. Burns like hell, doesn't it?"

"Burns like crazy," I said.

"That's my last name, Byrne."

"I know. We met before, but you might not remember. My name's Timmy."

Jamie unchained his bike from a pipe in the corner. "I know who you are," he said.

I followed a few steps behind as he pushed his bike up the stairs. He walked it around the pro shop and out to the parking lot.

"See you around. Maybe," he said.

"I'm coming back," I said, but Jamie didn't look back to respond. He turned his hat around on his head and climbed atop a bike made for someone twice his size. I watched him push and stand on the pedals until the wheels began to turn.

JAMIE BYRNE WAS right. My shoulders didn't get stronger, but they did break in, and it did get easier, and I kept coming back like I told him I would. We were out on the course a few weeks later, caddying together on the first Tuesday of summer vacation. Jamie carried for Norton with me on what he told me was a B-loop, an upgrade from the stiffs Lewis started me with.

"Someone must have said you didn't suck," Jamie said, pointing to my bags. "Bastian pays twenty, maybe twenty-five, but Walton might be good for thirty."

He was—fifty-five more dollars, and I had no concept of what this money was. I envisioned things like boats and televisions, a swimming pool with a slide, Lladro for my mother's collection, Disney World and go-carts and sports cars with sliding red curves. My father snuffed out those dreams with a four-percent college fund that was not open to discussion. When I asked him if I could use my caddy money for new clubs to replace my mismatched hand-me-down set, he told me, "It's the arrow, not the Indian."

While we were washing clubs after our loop, Jamie asked me why I would want to play golf. I could tell he meant it as a dig, and that I shouldn't mention spotting him out there, hacking and whiffing and running scared for the fence that April.

"It's all old people," he said. "It's not kids, it's all old guys and old ladies, all wrinkly and old. You don't run. You don't jump or slide or sweat even."

"I sweat."

"But it's not even a real *sport* really," he said, scrunching up his face.

"It's sort of a sport. And it's not all old people."

"Seems like it."

"I don't know why I play, I just do," I told him. "The weird thing is, I'm actually pretty . . ." I stopped myself. "I'm not that bad at it, so I keep playing."

"I hear you're real good."

"Where did you hear that?" I said, looking around to see if the other caddies were listening.

"I hear it. I don't know where. From someone. Everyone's blabbering about something around here."

"But who was talking about me? I'm not bad, but I mean, I'm not great at all."

"You don't have to freak about it. I don't care if you're a *golfer*. I might be a golfer someday. I might be a member here too, and I might even let you carry my bag. First you have to get better at caddying though."

"I thought you said golf was just a bunch of wrinkly people."

"It is, but I'm talking about when I'm a wrinkly old person. I'll just pull up here in my Rolls-Royce. You could even park it for me."

"Thanks. Maybe I'll give you a couple lessons, half price," I said, snapping my wet towel at the back of his leg.

"Screw that. It'll be me teaching you, Mr. Pro Golfer guy," Jamie said.

He lifted Norton's bag up over his head, grunting as he pushed it back into its slot on the rack, #113. "I don't know. It just doesn't look like all that much fun to me," he said. "Is it really any fun?"

I thought about it, if it was any *fun,* and it seems to me now that maybe that is when you begin to grow up, when you separate fun and laughter, when the things you enjoy are things you work at, things that keep you awake with doubt and wonder and worry. Things you do alone.

"It is fun. It's not really a sport, I guess. It's a game," I told him. "It's a big game on a big field with lots of rules. It's a gentlemen's game."

"Right, gentlemen," he said as he polished Mr. Norton's driver with a purple towel. "A real bunch of gentlemen."

I kept coming back to caddy at Fox Chase, through the weekends and the summers from that summer on, until there was nothing Jamie Byrne and I didn't talk about.

Jamie Byrne kept coming back until he stopped.

THE NEW CLUBS came in a long box covered in clear tape on an ordinary day in July. My father dragged the box into the kitchen and told me, "This is it, kiddo. Next set of clubs, you're paying for them."

His fingers tore the tape away in loud strips, and he rolled the fresh black grips in his hands, rubbing the caramel wooden club heads. "You should be able to do something with these," he said. "Now this, *this,*" he said, shaking the three-wood in his hand like an old man using his cane to complain, "this is commitment, Timothy. This is what one gets when one commits, when one *works.*"

A Friday morning and the heat stung in my nose when I walked out the back door, an orange summer haze draped over our yard. Commitment meant signing up for a golf lesson with Raymond Mann, not because it would make my game any sharper, but because my father wanted to be sure that his investment was met with some accountable discipline. It was like going to the doctor for feeling well, but I signed up for an early lesson, early enough so that I might finish and still catch my first A-loop—Dr. Brown was playing with a guest. "Guaranteed sixty bucks," Lewis told me, "if you don't go fucking it up."

My new arrows slung over my shoulder, I stopped my bike halfway down our driveway when I heard my brother's voice chasing my father out the door.

"It's important, Dad," Casey said, his feet following my father's shadow down the front walk. "The station wagon's crapped out again. The store closes at six and I have everybody's money. I'm the one that's supposed to get the tickets."

Casey made a habit of eating dinner in the attic. When we ran out of dishes, my mother knew where to find them, around his bed, beneath trails of hungry ants. But the previous two evenings, my brother broke with routine and ate London broil, then sloppy joes with the family, too excited about Bruce Springsteen coming to the Spectrum to dine up there alone. He owned the conversation, telling us about collecting money from half the football team, guys who didn't even like Bruce Springsteen until Casey started playing his tapes in the weight room. The concert had sold out in thirty-seven minutes, but a friend at a local record shop had a block of floor tickets he was willing to sell if Casey could pay in cash by the end of the day.

In his short-sleeved shirt and tie, my father climbed into the Buick, Casey standing by the window and waiting for an answer.

My father rolled down the window. "I told you I would take you. I'll be home at five-thirty. Will that be enough time?"

"Yeah," Casey said. "Five-thirty."

"Don't you have a lesson, Timmy?" my father called to me as he backed down the driveway.

"Yeah, I'm going," I said.

"Aw, isn't that cute, the little faggot has a golf lesson."

I pedaled to the end of the driveway where I was safe. "Springsteen sucks," I said, and Casey sent me off with a firm middle finger.

The walk up to the driving range with Raymond was surprisingly polite. I expected a boisterous beginning to my lesson, but Raymond quietly stepped up to the practice tee, dropping a bag of balls in the grass and running his hand over his round olive face. He was a club pro, and club pros gave lessons and organized foursomes and yelled at their staff when they were too slow, when they were lulled into the pace of the place. His job was all orders and action, so that morning it was strange to see him so sluggish with thought. But I would hear about it later, down in the hole, about a member who didn't like the way his clubs were being cleaned and decided to write a letter to the Fox Chase Board, complaining that Raymond was too comfortable, lazy and set in his ways, that they needed new blood running their pro shop. So Raymond was nodding hello to all the members as we passed, treading gently because club pros got one-year contracts, no matter if they had three kids and a mortgage.

"Are you ready, Timmy?" He smiled. He took me through grip, stance, swing. Check, check, check. He gave me a gadget club that would bend in half if you swung it out of plane. I didn't. He lined up clubs on the ground, propped balls beneath my feet, drew a V on my right hand with a marker. I swung with a weighted club. I swung with a broomstick. I checked out with a clean bill of health.

"I feel like I should give your father his money back," Raymond said, hiking up his pants until they hung from one of the rolls in his belly. He lifted my new five-iron out of my bag, fluffed up a ball on a tuft of grass. "You said you haven't been taking lessons with anybody else?"

"No. Just the lesson I had at your clinic."

Raymond filled his chest with air. "It's like I tell all my students—if your fundamentals are right at the start, you can't make a bad golf swing."

He swept the five-iron back, his weight sliding into a slot behind the ball, but instead of clicking off the club face, the ball dribbled across the range, kicking up other stray balls as it rolled.

"Chee-rist," he said, teeing up another ball. "Well there's someone I know who might be able to help you, a guy by the name of Foster Pearse. He used to caddy here when I was still an assistant. D'you ever hear of him?" he asked me.

"No."

"Well, if your father's interested I'll make a phone call. Foster might be able to help you out," he said. "There isn't much else I can show you up here. I don't teach what you were just doing. I teach hackers how to break ninety."

Raymond swung again and sniped a toe-hook, a sharp *clank* vibrating at the end of the shaft. He turned the club upside down, eyeing it for a moment before he wiped the mishits off the club face with his thumb.

"Those are nice sticks," he said, and he gently dropped the five-iron across my bag.

*　　*　　*

LEWIS SHOOK THE two golf bags in front of me as he whined, "These guys tipped me extra for a good looper today. Is that gonna be you?"

"Yes."

"We'll see about that. If you blow this one, you're roaded. And I'll road a member's kid, don't think I won't."

Caddies didn't get hired, so they didn't get fired, but they did get roaded—pushed out to the road, not to return until whatever they did was forgotten.

Sixty-five dollars later (minus five to Lewis for his generosity), I was riding my bike out through the parking lot, my calves and shoulders aching with the pleasant soreness of effort. I stopped pedaling when I saw it there, parked stubborn on the cement, the Buick still bright from the coat of wax I had given it three days before. I looked at my watch: 5:45.

When I walked through the front door, I saw Casey sitting in the living room with my mother. She wore yellow polyester and she was busy painting her fingernails the color of fingernails. I watched Casey teeter on the edge of the sofa, staring out the front window, anger washing over his face. It was like watching two cars on an icy road, slowly sliding toward each other—there was nothing you could do but watch and wait and know that there was going to be pain. Casey wouldn't ride his bike to the record store. He would wait for my father. He would give him time to break his promise, good and final.

Waiting was one of the things Casey was not good at at all.

"What time is it?" he asked my mother, his eyes watching nothing come down our street. When she didn't answer, pretending she hadn't heard the question, Casey slammed both feet on the floor, rumbling the metal ducts in the walls. He stood and blew past me, his hair twined and wild from pulling at it all afternoon. He headed out the front door, slamming it shut behind him like a fist.

The sun was touching the tops of the houses in the late afternoon, and my mother and I watched at the window as Casey came out of the garage. He carried the pitching wedge my father used to practice with, and he walked over to the rosebushes lining the front of our house. Solid clumps of green and thorn and fat dying blooms. My father had tended to them before breakfast that morning, watering the roots, feeding them his special blue powder, picking beetles from their leaves with his fingers. And it was later that afternoon when his son tore them into garnish. Branch ripped from branch and buds burst into petals, my brother swatting the flowers like baseballs. The pitching wedge sliced the rosebushes to pieces, and Casey grunted with each blow, his arms and shoulders fighting to get back into the damage. He hacked away all the leaves and colors, no more pruning to be done to bushes that were now wiry brown fingers reaching up out of the soil.

My mother and I watched in silence, afraid to speak or look at each other. Hundreds of petals lay stuck in the grass, some turning over in the breeze, tumbling across our neighbor's lawn. When Casey finished, he stood there staring at the bare stumps, panting hard with lines of water running down his face, a hot wetness touching his lips.

My father pulled down the driveway that evening after the golf was played and the stores were closed, and he did not do anything but stare at the branches. He did not ask what happened, and the way he wasn't surprised—the way he took it without a word—was the saddest part of all. He walked to the garage and carried out a large trash can, and he filled it with what he said distinguished our home in a neighborhood where all the houses looked the same.

When spring came the next year and some of the branches started to sprout—a few green spots clustered on the broken ends—my father did not bother to prune them. He let those that could grow, grow until they died out. He did not water them. He did not feed them his special blue powder.

MY FATHER PILOTED the Mercury station wagon past acres of farm-land, the earth turned up in long, straight rows, a few shabby horses nibbling grass off a tight sloping pasture. The drive was forty minutes to a town that was hardly a town, a space that was both Pennsylvania and Delaware, a spot deep in the heart of mushroom country. I watched the farmhouses perched above their fields, set well back from the road and miles from their neighbors. They were beautiful old homes with Dutch doors and wooden chairs on the lawn, some of the homes bright with a new coat of paint, their exteriors heavy from years and inches of enamel. Yet as we passed I could not help but wonder where the people in those houses ordered their pizza from. Could they get delivery? Could they get cable? I wondered if they ever went to the movies, or how far they had to drive to get to the mall.

When I went to roll down the window, my father said, "Mush-rooms. You don't want to do that," and the air from the acres hit me, a faceful of sweet-smelling shit.

"They say he's the best. Best teacher in the area is what Raymond Mann told me," my father said as he pulled down a bumpy brown road. He drove past a dried-up pond with a dock reaching out into the mud, around the corner of a low and long building with walls that were piles of gray and silver stones. The building had dozens of doors with numbers painted on them, rusty steel doors to what looked like cell after cell. They were mushroom rooms, my father explained, where they blended up earth and manure and water and seed and let the mushrooms bloom in the dark, damp closets.

We drove past a farmhouse with red paint peeling off the walls. Tattered shingles fallen from the roof lay stuck in the lawn. My father slowed the car and glided up to a landing that looked out over a large rolling field, an ocean of yellow grass and yellow dirt, spotted with green, red, white flags sagging tired and sideways. The grass rolled out to the faraway shade, a fairway without edges, touching farms in the distance that were all green and blue. And there on the edge of the landing stood a man, tall and airy and blending into the backdrop, a thin flag with tangled blond hair.

I opened the door and the odor settled in the back of my throat, a brown stink that made me gag. I breathed through my mouth, exaggerating like I was suffocating.

"Knock it off," my father said, lifting my bag from the back of the car, throwing my golf shoes at my feet. "Be polite. Show the man what you can do. And listen to what he has to say."

"But it stinks out here," I said.

"Do you know how much I'm paying for these lessons? Do you want to know?" He had to fight to keep the number from jumping from his lips.

"I want to go back to Fox Chase," I said. "I want to go back to the range. I don't need a teacher."

"Timmy, I told you. I am not going to push you to do this," he said, picking up my bag and dropping it in my hands. "But we came a long way, so get the hell out there and listen to what that man has to say."

The man had wispy yellow hair that curled around his neck in the breeze. He stared out at the open field, arms crossed above a small belly. Foster Pearse was his name, and he lived on an old farm where he gave lessons by special appointment, taking on new talent by referral only. It seemed as if I was the only one who didn't know about Foster Pearse, but it wasn't long before I heard the stories and the way the members at Fox Chase would brag, *my son got a couple lessons with Foster Pearse last week, he's playing the golf of his life.* People said Foster was a three-time Pennsylvania boys' champion. Some said he won the U.S. Amateur when he was nineteen, and some said he lost the tournament when he missed his tee time, but either way, no one was sure what came between seventeen and thirty in that mushroom field for Foster. There was a year at Georgia Tech and an abandoned scholarship, then maybe some time playing on the tour in Japan, a few years on the big island of Hawaii, supposedly, where he played golf with a squad of heiresses, adulteresses, millionaire divorcées. Eighteen holes in the morning, then torches and roast pig and tall sweet drinks. Some said he spent most of the year following Jerry Garcia, from San Francisco to Philadelphia and back again, while others claimed that Foster was just back for a short while, teaching golf for cash, trying to cover the debt he'd piled up while hustling golf matches out West. Or maybe not at all, but those stories thrilled the members down in New Water, the legends wrapped around their golfing bigfoot of the mid-Atlantic country club. No one seemed decided on whether it was romantic or heroic or stupid for Pearse to give up on a game like that, a talent they said used to drip from his fingertips.

This best player to ever come out of the area only came out of his farmhouse to teach a few bright hopefuls—at their great cost and inconvenience, instructing only at his private range, a neglected field and a barrel of crusted yellow balls. His skin was tan, his cheeks and eyes and ears all a smile. There was an easy gold stubble covering his face. His khakis hung low on nonexistent hips, and in leather sandals he was well over six feet. His gait was relaxed as water.

"Mr. Price," he said, extending his hand to my father, smiling as if shaking hands was amusing. "So this is the kid," he said. "Raymond Mann tells me you've got quite a swing on you."

"He's really something. He's a five handicap and he's not even twelve yet. Timmy said he wanted to commit himself, so I thought we should find the right instruction for him," my father said. "I have no idea where he gets it from. He beats me all the time now."

"And how's your game, Mr. Price?"

"Well, let's see," he said, sucking air into his chest. "I'm carrying about a twelve. I was down to a ten last summer, but that was all my short game. I can't hit it like these young gorillas."

"Ahh, yes, the gorillas. Now there's nothing wrong with a twelve handicap, Mr. Price. That'll win you some dinero."

My father nodded a modest maybe not, which was all very immodest since he was a fourteen on his best day. He went and sat on the front of the station wagon and read the paper while Foster led me over to a spot where the ragged farm grass grew tight and soft like a fairway. He toed a few balls out of a shag bag and said, "I think you know what to do with these."

"Should I stretch?" I asked him.

"Do you want to stretch?"

I thought about it for a second. "I think so."

"Well don't hurt your brain thinking about it."

I looked down at the balls, scratched and cut and caked with dirt.

"I guess I should," I said. "I'm a little tight, from the drive and all."

"I'm sure you are," he said. With his front teeth he bit off the corner of a fingernail, then blew the little white slice off his lip. "So stretch away."

I wrapped two clubs around my torso, twisting, bending at the waist and gripping the backs of my ankles, letting my back lengthen and pop. I looked at my bag on the ground, the clubs spilling over one another.

"What should I hit?"

"Timmy," he said, pushing his hands into his pockets and looking me straight in the face, "here's the deal. The one thing I am sure about in this game, the only thing I know about anything really, is that this is not a team sport. I'm watching, buddy. So you show me why you're here."

I looked back to catch my father peeking over the edge of his paper. Ten minutes paid for, and I had yet to swing a club. I reached into my bag and pulled out a seven-iron.

"I hit this a lot," I said. I took a dozen swings, blasted a dozen shots that drew gently from right to left, the balls curling down to a spot somewhere beneath two feet of farm grass. I hit fades that rose high into the air and softly leaned away. I choked down on the club and hit ten more, knockdown shots that clipped the tips of the weeds before ducking into the grass as if hands had reached up and grabbed them.

I stopped and looked at Foster, who I could tell was trying not to smile.

"Are you kidding me?" With the toe of his sandal he flipped a ball up into his hand. "What I want to know first is, what the hell is a kid your age doing hitting the golf ball like that?"

I looked down at the club in my hands as if the seven-iron was the one he should be asking.

"I don't know," I said.

"Exactly. You don't know. You never think about it, do you?"

"Not really."

"Good. Because that's the hardest thing to teach somebody—how not to think about something. And that little beat before you hit the ball, that moment when your head's empty, and there's no time, and there's nothing around you—that, in my opinion, is the only reason anyone should ever play this game. Or any game. For that peace. You know what I mean?"

"Not really."

Foster nodded. "Exactly." He rubbed the back of his hand up and down the scruff on his cheeks as he thought.

"So how long have you been playing, Timmy?" he said without looking at me.

"It's my second year."

"Well you'll probably never know how other people feel when they pick up a golf club. I see them up here all the time. At some point in their life, someone, somewhere convinced them after they shot 125 that this game was bigger than they were," Foster said. "Are you afraid of golf, Timmy?"

"No," I said. "I'm not *afraid* of it."

"Well it isn't like that for everybody. People who love this game, they'll play golf like they're begging the course for mercy. And that is because they have no idea what golf is. Do you think you know what golf is?"

"It's . . . a game," I stammered.

"Sure, it's a game. And it's not a game. But more specifically, golf is a ball," he said, showing me the ball in his hand, "and it's a hole, a hole that's a whopping two and a half times bigger than the ball that fits in it. Just a ball and a hole, but for ninety-nine percent of the people out there, they'll never believe it. They'll never be able to believe it."

Foster sidearmed the ball out into the field, then looked at me with wide eyes to see that it was all sinking in. I almost nodded.

"You don't understand a word I'm telling you," he said.

"No, I think I do."

"Did your father make you come up here?" he said, turning to watch the screen door of the farmhouse bump against the door frame in the breeze.

"Yeah, he did."

"My dad would have made me take lessons with me too." Foster kicked over the bag of balls at my feet. "Well let's make sure he gets his money's worth."

He picked a broken tee out of the grass and set one of the balls on top of it. "I want you to stand on one foot, and I want you to hit that ball."

I started to smile to show I got the joke, if it was one, which it wasn't.

"Go ahead. Stand on one foot. Like you're doing the hokey-pokey."

I stared back at him blank-faced.

"Haven't you ever been to a wedding?" he said, wiggling his right foot in front of him. "One foot in, one foot out. Come on, champ, step up there and hit the damn ball."

I set my club behind the ball and tried to hold it steady as I lifted my left foot. I pulled the club back and flipped it through, tipping over backward on the right side of my ass. Foster picked me up with one hand.

"There you go. There's your introduction to the most important part of the game. Do you know what it is? You tell me what Timmy thinks is the most vital ingredient to the golf swing."

"Grip?" I answered. "That's what Raymond told us, that your grip is most important."

"Not for you. For a duffer, yes. I have guys up here that look so uncomfortable holding the golf club, you'd think they were holding someone else's dick. Pardon my language." He looked over his shoulder to see my father still hidden behind the *Wilmington News Journal*. "I know you don't think about your grip, Timmy. That's what they tell you you should think about. What else is there to the golf swing?"

"Stance? Maybe your alignment, or your take-away . . ."

"No, no, no." Foster shook an open hand at my face, then held it still in the air. "I'm talking about *balance*. Balance, balance, balance. I don't care if you're forty or eighty or not even twelve, the only thing you need out there every day is balance. It's the only true athletic part of the game. You need it in your swing, you need it in your head," he said, rapping a knuckle against his temple. "I'm talking about highs and lows equaling out to nothing, until every hole is the right hole, and every shot is the right shot. Good, bad, mistakes, successes—when I'm done with you, Timmy, maybe I can convince you they don't exist. Do you ever take a bad breath? Do you—a bad freaking breath?"

Happy to finally have a response, I spoke straight at him. "Maybe. It smells out here."

Foster blew out a deep breath and smiled. "You know, I don't even smell it anymore. That's when I know it's time to leave for a while, when the smell doesn't bother me anymore," he said as if he was trying to tell me a secret in a crowded room. "But the point I was trying to make was that swinging that club, for a kid like you, it's like taking in air. It's like taking a leak or eating a sandwich. It's not right or wrong, it's just done. And I'm right about that, because it was the same way for me. It's golf in your gut and your balls and your heart. It has nothing to do with bullshit tips on a driving range, or trying to win tournaments or shoot this score or that score, gotta go out and make this par, that birdie. All of that—is horse shit. All you have to think is balance, until you're not thinking it. That means playing on that even keel, being tight enough to hang loose. Think about being big enough to play small. Think," he said, staring out into the air, "think of the golf swing as a maximum of minimum. A maximum of minimum." He smiled. "Man, that's deep. How does that sound?"

"I don't think I understand."

"That's alright. You don't have to. It's the whole ball of wax, buddy, and it looks like somebody dripped it all over your swing."

I felt my cheeks warm. Behind us, I could hear my father folding his paper to be noticed, calling for a little action, a little results.

"So go ahead. One foot for the rest of the bag," Foster said. "Then switch feet. And then the other bag."

Foster Pearse kneeled in the grass, keeping himself busy by trying to stack golf balls on top of each other and laughing when I toppled over. He squeezed blades of grass between his thumbs and lips, and he made them squeak like tiny trumpets when I whiffed at the ball again and again.

"Golf's ninety percent mental, twenty percent physical, ten percent addition," he said as if he was reminding himself. He got up and pulled my three-iron from my bag and stood over a ball, clipping it out into the range, then another, and another, the perfect summer sound of snapping blades of grass. Each ball started low and climbed upward against the air, peaking, then falling and nearly landing on the ball before. Watching Foster swing was hypnotic, pass after pass after pass, slow and steady, his body simply waving at the ball. He didn't look up to see where the shots landed, as if the feel of the swing was more interesting than the outcome.

"Mind, no mind," he said, dropping his club down behind another ball and pushing it out into the field.

I could feel my father's strides in the grass, deliberate on their way toward us.

"Excuse me, Mr. Pearse?" my father said, his eyes looking down at the balls around my feet. "I was just wondering if you got a chance to see the loop at the top of his swing. I don't mean to interrupt your business, but some fellas at Fox Chase say there's a loop at the top. Maybe you could help Timmy work it out, if you know how to take care of that."

"I see. Yes, a loop. But the thing is, Mr. Price, Timmy's loop is the least of his problems here. He can hardly make contact. We'll start with contact, Mr. Price. We'll get to the loops."

"But he's standing on one foot." My father chuckled. "You don't play golf on one foot."

"Well at my range, we do. We do all sorts of silly stuff out here," Foster said. "He's not even twelve. He's got a lot to learn, Mr. Price. Loads."

I made near-solid contact ten times out of a hundred, and as I walked back to the car, my father waiting tight in the driver's seat, I could feel the heat rising off the hood. He rolled down the window, and Foster gave him a thumbs-up, patting me on the back.

"Made real progress today," he told my father. "Some good effort out there. Boy's been trained well."

"You know, Mr. Pearse, for the fee you charge, I expected you to help Timmy improve," my father said, staring straight ahead at the steering wheel.

"For the fee I charge, I will, Mr. Price."

The drive home was not as quiet as most drives. My father told me that I did not have to go back there. He apologized for his mistake and threw out a list of questions—what had I learned? Where was the improvement, the return, the value added on the balance sheet? I had no answers except to say that I wanted to go back. Foster Pearse was a good teacher, I told him, not because I was convinced that he was, but because I knew it hurt my father to love golf with everything he had and still not understand how that man could be a great teacher. It was the pain of a music lover being able to hear all the notes, to see them lying on the keys in front of him, but never being able to make the sounds with his own fingers.

I told him I wanted to go back.

During the next lesson, my father did not get out of the car, but watched through the windshield as Foster Pearse tied my feet together and made me swing the club to the click of a metronome. He didn't twist me around to tweak my stance. He didn't lay clubs at my feet or try to dismantle the loop at the top of my swing. Foster sat in the grass and watched me flail at the ball, ankle tied to ankle, and his only advice that afternoon was "See—if you swing too hard, you fall over."

I did not hit one solid ball that day, but by the end of the lesson I could feel the meter clicking in my shoulders. Later that week, I went out with my father and shot 81, and he dropped the scorecard in a trash can at the clubhouse and said Foster Pearse was a thing of the past, no matter that I felt muscles in my swing I had never used before. No matter that I hit four drives that day that were so pure I thought I might never have to swing the golf club again, as if that moment of perfection had been achieved, always to be chased and never to be repeated. And I repeated it. On one hole, then two, then three.

"I'm not paying for *that*," my father said, pointing to where the card lay on top of the garbage.

"Then I'll pay for it."

When I went back to Foster and tried to pay him with a handful of ones and fives, he smiled and said, "Keep it. That's why I charge so much for the first two lessons."

I learned balance and tempo while my father spent the forty-five minutes to and from Foster's farm talking to the air-conditioning about wasting time. I made a friend while my father convinced himself there was nothing out in that field but confusion and laziness, an eccentric lack of discipline. My father complained to Raymond Mann that Foster was a downright swindler. "A goddamned crazy," my father said with the spite of a genuinely honest man who feels he's been cheated.

People asked me if it was true that I went to Foster Pearse, that I knew where he lived. They asked if he won a pile of yen gambling on courses in Japan, if he had a kid who was half-Hawaiian, if he grew pot by the bushel up there. They asked if Foster Pearse really won the Amateur when he was nineteen years old.

I did not tell them, not even when I began to know. They liked their bigfoot how he was, so I let it all grow and fester like the mold in that stretch of ripe earth, Foster Pearse gone crazy in a field of mushrooms.

IT WAS ONE of those days the caddies said was hot as tits. Someone in the hole would say, "Steamy as a bag of dicks in here," and someone would grunt while the rest of us roasted in the quiet. The air was a heavy afternoon sort of dark, and outside, out past the doorway, the steps to the hole burned stone white in July sunlight.

By my second summer as a caddy, I was twelve years old and a regular who knew where to sit, when to be quiet, when to laugh and who to laugh at. I knew the scent of that room, all caked between my toes, the smell of something spoiled or spit from a lawn mower. It didn't matter how a caddy began the day—after a loop on a summer day like this one, every caddy came back in smelling the same. I could wipe my finger along the skin behind my knee and find it there—the scent of looping in July, the salt and the dirt, a bitter wet grime that filled the hole with the smell of a pot of boiling cabbage. My mother made the stuff once a year, on St. Patrick's Day, when she brought out her big red iron pot. It looked like toilet paper stewing in warm water, and the stench stuffed our house with sour air. She said it was the only good thing she knew that was Irish, and though I didn't believe her because it wasn't very good at all, I held my nose and swallowed it in large gulps. First you knew the scent, and then, if you waited long enough, you didn't smell it at all, not if it was boiling cabbage or the socks you scraped off your feet after caddying, not if you waited and opened your mouth and swallowed, breathing your deepest breaths.

Caddying in the damp mornings, the humidity clinging to the grass would turn your sneakers into globs of green-brown mush. It felt like walking in oatmeal. The skin on your heels and under your toes would peel away thick and white like the rind of a grapefruit, showing pinker meat underneath. Every caddy had a pair of ruined shoes for work. Some owned pairs of shoes that were not ruined at all, and some didn't, but it didn't matter who because when loopers were together it was all mildewed canvas and flaps of torn leather.

I was a member's boy upstairs, the precocious talent the other members murmured about, speculating, gloating about how I would crumble if I stayed after it like I did, all the while loving me for it. They said I was blessed and damned with ability. They said things would happen, that doors would open for a swing like that. They whispered that they would open too quickly.

Downstairs, the caddies didn't know me by golf. They called me Pricey and T-dog and T-bone. They asked me why I was so fucking skinny, or how the hell didn't I know who Dave Schultz was. They said I was a member's kid who didn't act like a member's kid. They liked me for that, and that was the thing I liked best about them—for the ways they thought I was not myself.

The day was waiting. The hole felt like the inside of a boxer's mouth, sweat and headaches and no work, and the caddies were staying away. The rabid golf addicts who would brave hundred-degree temperatures were not crazy enough to walk the course, not on one of those days when the air was paste, when the outside covered you like plastic wrap. Carts for a hot day. Caddies could wait.

I played a game of war in the corner with Jamie, just the two of us and the handful of regulars who had been braving the heat wave without a cent for their sweat. It would seem mathematically impossible to achieve dominance at the game of war, but Jamie and I played cards every day while we waited for a loop, and almost every day he beat me for a pack of Fig Newtons and a grape soda.

We were waiting for a loop that afternoon but hoping we wouldn't get one, not in that heat, but we still waited because caddying was the kind of work you had to want all the time, and then maybe you would get it some of the time. Put in your hours on your ass, especially in the lean weeks, and the caddy master might throw you a bone.

Lewis flopped down the steps, clipboard in hand, a look on his face like he had something for us that none of us deserved. He tapped his teeth with a pen while an electric fan clicked and hummed and blew the smell of X-brand cigarettes around the room.

"Alright, we've got a twosome here, one caddy. Probably the only loop that's going out today." Lewis cradled his clipboard against his chest. He was breaking out in the heat. His cheeks looked like tapioca.

"Chaumers and Johnson. You want it, Pricey?" Lewis said, and I could tell he wasn't looking for a no. It was not a bad loop on an average day, but this was the kind of day that separated caddies into two kinds: the lifers and the summer crew. The summer crew came from colleges and high schools. They had Hondas and air-conditioning and remote controls waiting at home. They had couches and excuses. The summer kids didn't do their own laundry, and they didn't buy their dinner with their tips. They needed the work to get them out of bed in July, to put money in their pockets, just so they could say they had it. They waited, but not for nothing.

The lifers had waiting, and waiting was all they had. They didn't go back to school in the fall; instead they stuck it out through August and autumn, caddying in December when golfers wore woolly caps and gloves and used orange balls to fire through the flurries. Most lifers collected unemployment on top of their caddy money, and together it was enough to keep them going through the dry spells. Some slept while they waited. Some showed up at 6 A.M. with sweaty, hungover eyes, not a bit of rest anywhere in their faces, looking for an early loop, perhaps a couple ladies during the week, maybe a pair of doctors squeezing in eighteen before their rounds. Some were sent home by Raymond when he pulled surprise inspections of the caddy hole, when he would ramble down the steps and bark that they stank like a fucking brewery. He would lean into a lifer and yell, "You want to hit the fucking road?" because he had found a few butts rubbed out on the floor. A pile of paper and ash was all it took. Raymond stored up each little piece of shit the members had dropped on his desk that day, and at the end of a bad afternoon he would come down into the hole and blow it all in our faces. And we took it, some of us more than others, because some stored their life's possessions in the rafters of the caddy hole, tucked away in brown paper bags. Some lifers spent their nights curled up in the maintenance shed. Some shaved at the drinking fountain.

I knew Chaumers and Johnson wouldn't take a lifer, and Lewis knew I knew it, and he was looking to me for a hand. I told him I was waiting for a single, and with a pissed-off shake of his waxy white head, I was assured that I wouldn't be out in the heat that day.

There were four lifers waiting that afternoon—Mick (who everyone called Tomato Face), Jeffrey, Puddy, and Position A. They did not decide how their day was going to go. They were rarely called by their real names.

Four lifers plus me, already a no, and Jamie, who Lewis couldn't put out in case Norton showed up to play. There was one more looper leaning back in the corner atop an upturned bucket, another A-caddy named Brian Seaman. Brian was two years older than me, but he talked to everyone as if they were his dim-witted little brother. He was short with swollen shoulders and thighs like tree stumps, a jaw too thick for his face, black hair clipped tighter than the fairways. He had already selected himself as future starting cornerback on the high school varsity. Brian knew about Casey Price the linebacker, so he left me alone most of the time. I suppose he liked me, on some days, but Brian Seaman didn't like anyone as much as he liked Brian Seaman. He was a gossip and a bullshitter and a stand-up act, and he would have been running the room that afternoon if it wasn't too hot to laugh.

Lewis pointed at Brian and raised a thin eyebrow. "You want it?"

He looked at his watch. "I'll pass. Thirty bucks to follow those hackers around in this heat? No way. I already got butter ass, just from sittin' here."

Butter ass was a nagging wet discomfort familiar to most loopers. Some caddies blamed it on all the walking in the humidity. Others blamed it on Schlitz.

Jamie smiled and poked a finger in Brian's shoulder. "Pussy."

"Shove it, Byrne. Just wait till Norton shows up. Then see how you like it out there sweating your nuts off."

Chaumers and Johnson were not the only members who would not take a lifer. Many of the gentlemen preferred, even demanded, A-caddies and bag-toters from the summer crew. There was something unpleasant about having a man older than you carry your bag, a man who smelled like yesterday with a nothing look in his eyes. Chaumers and Johnson would have to take a cart because those of us with a choice chose air-conditioning over Johnson's trunk of a bag and the smoke from Chaumers's skinny cigars.

I heard a voice come crackling over the intercom from the pro shop. "Who's down there?"

"Lewis here," he called. "Watcha need, Raymond?"

"Gorman and White, twosome, one caddy."

Brian and Jamie and I tried to sink into our seats while Tomato Face, Puddy and Jeffrey leaned out over theirs. Two loops was more than we expected that day, but Gorman and White was a loop for dire times. When Gorman wasn't playing the wrong hole, he was whiffing and yelling, "Practice swing! That was a practice swing!" White took apologetic half-cuts at the ball, rolling it along the fairway forty yards at a time, and he cheated with such brazenness that it embarrassed even the most disinterested caddies. Gorman and White yelled at each other from first tee to last green, and each was the only member in the club who could tolerate the other.

"Who wants it?" said Lewis, panning the room with his pen as if it were a flashlight.

Tomato Face started first. "I was here at seven." Mick came down to the hole every morning with two handfuls of coffee creamers for breakfast, popping them open and slurping down shots of half-and-half that didn't always stay down for long. Some mornings we found him sleeping in the bathroom, and some mornings we heard him in there, paying for the night before. Everyone called him Tomato Face because his skin was swollen with gin blossoms and sunspots to where he could only squint, his cheeks lumps of pink, porous meat. It was a cruel thing to call someone, yet it never seemed to bother him. Caddying didn't make you any more or less mean. Caddying just made you forget why it mattered either way.

"The shit you were here at seven," said Jeffrey. His Afro was matted and lumpy with bits of lint. Drops of sweat covered his forehead, and in the warm darkness the skin beneath his eyes looked like pools, deep and opaque. He was a bony man, his skin tight and baked by the sun. He always caddied in jeans—purple jeans, blue jeans, black jeans in the heart of the summer, the denim faded and worn soft as tissue. The ends of his pant legs were frayed, as if Jeffrey had tailored them with a steak knife. He was always Jeffrey, never Jeff, and Seaman sometimes called him shitbird and made us all laugh.

"I was here, gassin' mothafuckin' carts at seven," Jeffrey continued. "You were in there sleeping in the goddamn bathroom."

"Your ass I was," Tomato Face said, tossing an empty coffee creamer across the room.

"Yes, my sweet black ass you was. I was here at seven, Lewis," said Jeffrey, standing up to move around in his glad-handing way. There were times when Jeffrey looked like he might sink into himself as he sat there, silent, his eyes dead and plastic, and then there were mornings when he couldn't sit still, couldn't stay interested in a sentence long enough to finish it. He would pat backs and give high fives and cover everyone with compliments, especially Lewis Holmes with his clipboard full of loops and his cavalier discretion. It was Jeffrey on campaign. It was pleading with your hand open.

"You saw me," he said, his eyes wide and red and staring at mine, as if a member's son would be the best witness.

"I came up late today," I said.

"Ask Raymond then, he saw me here."

"Jeffrey, just sit your ass down," Lewis said. Lewis seemed perpetually annoyed by Jeffrey's presence, and he was not afraid to sit Jeffrey down for an entire week for skeezing loops. Skeezing meant approaching a member on your own, soliciting your own services, or working in on somebody's steady—it happened in all sorts of different ways, usually to kids from the summer crew, usually by whoever looked the hungriest. It meant screwing a coworker, which meant very little, but it also meant going over or around Lewis's head, which was as much a violation of proto-col as existed in the hole. It meant that Lewis thought you were shit.

Lewis looked around the room. "Position A." He pointed with the clipboard. "When'd you get here?"

"Seven," he said. No one would refute it. Caddying gave us all strong thighs and calves, but Position A's legs were tight and tan like a runner's. He shaved every day. He never snuck a night's sleep on the course because he kept a studio apart-ment with disability checks from the electric company. He had bright green eyes and strong lines to his face, and from the way his blond hair fell across his brown eyebrows, you might have

thought he was a model or a surfer or a face from a soap op-
era. He never had a problem getting an early loop during the
week (the only way to catch two loops in one day), because
more than one of the members' wives had a habit of request-
ing him, especially Mrs. Norton, Fox Chase's first lady. He
couldn't have been much older than thirty, though a lifer's age
was not something we discussed or wanted to know. They
were older. That was it.

His real name was Stephan, but we all called him Position A
or P.A. because of his irritating habit of cheerleading for his
players. "Oh, that's position *A,*" he would say after a shot landed
on the fairway or green, "position *A.*" What was wrong about it
was that he made himself part of their game. I sometimes paid
quiet compliments, but Position A participated, and no one was
in favor of that, golfer or caddy. The name stuck when Position A said that what he was really talking about was the way
he was bending all the members' wives up into pretzels. "Kinky
orgy stuff, Bruce Lee yoga shit," he said, "bend her over, *ahhhh,*
position *A.*" None of us doubted him. He was a handsome man
with skin that was golden in October, but he was a lifer too, for
his own quiet reasons. Caddying was a job without an application, without questions about *felonies or crimes of a violent nature,* without hours or timecards, without any chance of having
to piss into a bottle. There was quick cash and no taxes, perfect for Position A, the beautiful Stephan who not only had
aftershave and biceps, but who had another story, the ugly
everyman story he wore in spots and scars around his body.
There was a tattoo of a naked woman named *Monica* smiling
down his left forearm, a bleeding swastika stained into the back
of his left shoulder that he once told me was *a dumb thing a dumb
kid does,* and a front tooth he could pop out and rattle around

his mouth like hard candy. He was a lifer, and if asked, he would carry for Gorman and White and cheer the whole way.

"Puddy? What time?" asked Lewis, continuing around the room.

Puddy looked up from a library book he was reading about steam engines.

"I was running carts with Jeffrey," he said. His full name was George Pudlinski. He spoke little, and when he did, you couldn't see his lips moving deep inside his beard. I liked Puddy. He did not offer insults. He did not skeez loops. Puddy read library books with crinkly plastic covers that were usually about trains or ships or trolley cars. He once talked about working for SEPTA, driving the suburban trolley along tracks that ran through the towns outside Philadelphia, straight down the center of Main Street. *It was eazy, peezie, Japanezzee,* he said. *Go and stop, that's all there was to it. Sort of like caddying. Just go, and stop.*

"Hey Jeffrey, d'you use deodorant this morning?" Lewis asked, sniffing in Jeffrey's direction.

"Aww, screw you man, I'm fresh as fucking roses," Jeffrey said, running his fingers across his chest.

Lewis was only half joking about the deodorant. As a caddy, I was responsible for three things in the hole—my hat, my towel, and my bib, the green pinny a caddy wore over a white shirt. After showing up consistently for a season, I won a bib with my number on it, #36. The bibs were thick like burlap, itchy on your shoulders. They did not breathe on a hot day, but they increased a looper's earnings because they distinguished real caddies from rookie bag-toters. The bib was silk-screened with the Fox Chase logo, two golf clubs crossed in an X, a simple *Est. 1924* between them. A pouch was stitched along the bottom of the pinny for scorecards, pin sheets, headcovers. We hung our bibs from a pipe in the back of the caddy hole, and on opening day that season, each of us found a trial-size bar of deodorant in his bib pocket. Lewis said we deserved it. He said the members didn't want any more shit-stinking caddies.

The summer crew slipped their bars into the bibs of the lifers, and the lifers said it was fucking bullshit. I dropped mine in the trash bucket, but some stomped the white stuff into the floor. Some crumbled Sure Extra-Dry into members' bags. Someone even coated Lewis's car windows with the musk-scented goo. And some quietly put their bars in their pockets and took them home.

"Okay, hold on, here we go. Lewis has got himself an idea," Lewis said. "Alright—Tomato Face, Jeffrey, you both stand over here." He pointed to the front of the room.

"What do you want, Lewis? You want us to kiss your ass? It's too hot for any bullshit today. Just give me the fucking loop. Gorman loves my shit," Tomato Face said.

"Mick, you are the worst fucking caddy in the whole fucking history of caddies. You're an embarrassment to the profession," Position A said, laughing. "Get this shit. I was out with Tomato Face last week, and he was carrying for Collins and his spoiled little shit, and the little shit asks Tomato to read his putt on the eighth—"

Tomato Face interrupted, "Oh, shut your ass up about that."

"—and the kid asks him which way it breaks, and Tomato Face looks at it, like all confused and shit, and he picks up some grass and throws it in the air, like he's checking the fucking breeze!"

"That's good, all right, very funny," Tomato Face said, waving his arms. There was sweat beading up on his forehead and coffee creamer spinning in his eyes.

"Then he says, 'I think it's a little in our face.' Kid looks at him like he's from fucking outer space!"

"Alright, alright," Tomato Face said. "I didn't hear what the little prick was saying. The kid whispered, for Christ's sake. Whisperin' all day."

"Oh, that is absolutely priceless. Fucking *priceless,*" said Lewis. "I should give you the loop just for that, Tomato."

"Fine, shit, I'll take it," he said, standing up. "I haven't been out all week."

"None of us been out, man, 'cept this pussy-getting motherfucker over here," Jeffrey said, nodding in Position A's direction.

"Oh, I hear you, Jeffrey. Loud and clear," Lewis said. "Now this might be your only chance for a loop today, fellas. And so as not to *deprive* anyone, we're going to have a little contest. We're going to have us a little spelling bee."

Jamie shook his head and Brian Seaman slapped his knees like bongos.

"Get the hell out of here," said Tomato Face.

"No, it'll be great. That's what you fellas need, a little competitive spirit. You guys ready? Contestants?" He pointed to George and Tomato Face. "Puddy," he said, "you want in on this?"

Puddy shook his head slowly from behind his book.

"Didn't think so. Position A? We've got a spot for you."

"Thanks, but no fucking thanks." Position A grabbed Brian Seaman's *Daily Times* and kicked open the door to the caddy bathroom. "Gotta go drop the kids off at the pool."

"Okay, so here we go, boys and girls. The first word is," Lewis thought, grinning, his fingers stroking the nicks in his chin, "*drunk.* As in to be a *drunk.*"

"Fuck this," Jeffrey said as the rest of the room laughed, even Puddy, the steamship on the cover of his book bouncing on the waves of his belly.

"D, R, U," said Tomato Face as he stood up, taking a quick step forward to catch his balance. He coughed from the bottom of his stomach and swallowed, squeezing something sour down his throat. "I can spell it," he said, "just give me the damn loop."

"You're not there yet, come on, that's the spirit," Lewis said, rushing over to encourage him.

"D, R, U, N," he continued.

"Stupid-ass white boy," Jeffrey said.

"Do you want to give it a try, Jeffrey?" Lewis asked.

"Man, fuck all that. Just give me the damn loop."

"U, N . . ."

"Almost there, Tomato, come on," Lewis said, clapping his hands, his lips parted with excitement. "Help him out, Jeffrey. Here, here's one for you. How about spelling your name."

"K."

Jeffrey looked up from his bench, and in a voice cold and straight he said, "Lewis, do not even fuck with me." I heard him mumble under his breath, ". . . pimply-ass pillow-biting motherfucker."

"Sweet Jesus." Brian Seaman applauded. "This is classic. This is caddy history!"

"We have a winner," Lewis said, slapping Tomato Face hard on the back, and I could see as the white rushed to Tomato's face what a bad idea that was. When Lewis went to lift his hand in victory, Tomato Face's head slung forward. He doubled over, a sticky orange soup falling from his mouth to the concrete.

"Caddy fucking history!" Brian said, raising both arms over his head.

"Brian, you are such a dildo," Jamie said, and Brian stuck a fist in Jamie's shoulder.

Tomato Face ran to the bathroom door, his shoulder slamming up against it, a pink line of spit dangling from his lip to his shirt. I gagged twice on the smell, covered my nose and mouth. I stood up off the bench.

"Now *that* is how I spell drunk," said Lewis, backing away from the puddle at his feet. "Clean that up *now,* Tomato Face. Not soon. Now."

Position A had locked himself in the head. Tomato Face pounded on the door as he dry-heaved. "Let me in, you sonofabitch!" He turned from the door, his T-shirt splashed with vomit. "Lewis, I got to use the bathroom. Upstairs, I got to use it," he said, his fingers clutching his stomach. We watched him retch, nothing leaving his open mouth but the throaty sound of choking.

"Are you nuts? There is one bathroom for caddies. One. You fuck it up, you fix it."

"But I'm fucking sick . . ."

"No caddies in the clubhouse, you know better than that."

I walked out of the hole for air and stood on the first step, the sun hot on my skin, the smell still bitter in my nose.

"Where are you going? Get in here," Jamie said, and I pretended not to hear him. As hard as he played it, Lewis Holmes wouldn't tell a member's son to get off the steps and get in there with the rest of the caddies. But Jamie Byrne definitely would.

The intercom crackled. "Who's down there?" came Raymond's voice.

"Right here, Ray. Whatcha need?"

"Gorman's gonna ride. Load 'em on a cart. Too hot to walk."

"No problem," Lewis said. "Sorry fellas." His shoulders were like pins inside his shirt as he shrugged and smiled. "Hot as hell out there. You all should be home in the air-conditioning."

Lewis walked outside, passing me on the steps with a smile on one side of his face, poking my gut with his clipboard. "You should be at home watching cartoons, Timmy." His feet made quick shuffling sounds up the steps.

Tomato Face lay on a bench and closed his eyes and took shaky breaths. I watched from the steps where, in the noon sunlight, the hole was pitch dark. The men sitting there were shadows on the cinder blocks.

Brian Seaman left to go lift weights in his basement.

"What the fuck's wrong with the members, man?" Jeffrey said, looking straight at me. "Too hot for 'em? We're here. I'll tell you that much. I'm right the fuck here."

And he would still be there, even after I left to change my shirt and slip on spiked shoes and go from A-caddy to A-player, Jeffrey from North Philly would still be waiting for work. He did not care about the sun and the way the insides of your thighs would rash up from the friction and the sweat, the way the dirt and salt would cake behind your ears, the way you could scoop out flakes of it with your finger. He did not even notice, because noticing such things, wrapping them in words and calling them bad—that was a privilege not all of us shared.

I walked up the steps and slid through the front door of the clubhouse, and ten minutes later I came out with my yellow hat balled up in my hand, my spikes crinkling clean across the pavement toward the practice tee. I stayed clear of the hole when I looked like that, dressed like a fresh breath, the collar on my shirt folded neatly over my shoulders.

My eyes tightened in the sun, and as I walked out past the carts, a soggy chin stepped in front of me.

"Well Mr. Price, looks like you're itching for a game. We need a fourth here."

Judge Farthing invited me to golf with him a few times a month, playing up his boyhood Texas drawl that I couldn't refuse. His body was wide and his wrists were choked with fat, and shaking his hand was like sliding your palm into a manila envelope.

"Yeah, that'd be great," I answered, checking my collar.

He patted my shoulder and flashed me a mouthful of yellow. "Well all right then. Great to have you," he said. "Now I got a couple guests here. I hope you don't mind playing with some stuffy lawyers."

Judge Farthing played almost exclusively with guests, because even among adults, retirees, community leaders and millionaires—even among the gentlemen, there were cliques. There was popularity. There was *in* and *out,* and a member who always played with guests and asked a twelve-year-old to fill out his foursome was drowning in the bad blood of the latter. The reason why was such juicy gossip that it dripped its way all the way down to the caddy hole. The story was that the Judge sponsored his son for membership a few years before—not a big event, considering almost every member sponsored his son when he reached bond-holding age. But Farthing Junior, the young ad executive, showed up for his final interview with a wife he had met in Fiji. The problem was she wasn't a tourist, and when the Board saw the dark-skinned girl and heard her English, all tangled up around her island tongue, their eyes nearly fell out onto the table. The members were boiling. Farthing's bid for membership was already past the snowballing point of *sorry we*

aren't accepting applications at this time, and when the Board went
to the Judge to tell him to call off his boy, Judge Farthing bucked.
He threatened to pursue the matter through the proper channels,
and it wasn't five minutes before he was blackballed from every
Saturday-morning foursome in the club. Proper channels were
not welcome at Fox Chase, not at a club that thought it was being
modern when it acquiesced to opening its doors to Irish blood. My
father had been admitted in the first wave of non-WASP membership, sponsored through one of his friends from the Rotary
Club, but by that summer when I was twelve, there were still less
than a dozen Irish members. There were five or six Italians, con-
tractors and lawyers, a Greek restaurateur, and a Polish doctor
who the whispers said was half-Jewish. So Farthing's son would
wait for a bond buried beneath a pile of nothing, and the Judge
would fight his quiet fight, playing golf with whoever would play
with him.

I told the Judge that I didn't mind playing with lawyers,
not at all. I knew the routine. Judge Farthing paid for everything—cart fees, lunch, and all the bets I would have to make as
an addition to this afternoon's game where the stakes were, ac-
cording to Farthing's Texas lilt, *just a little something extra.* We
played dollar skins, birdies paid double, no strokes given or taken,
and it was nowhere near fair. Playing even up, I would be in their
pockets without hardly trying, but gentlemen never seemed to
mind handing over a few dollars to a kid who gave them something to brag about at happy hour—*got a shot at Fox Chase yesterday, helluva track, got sandbagged by the next Jack fucking Nicklaus.*

"We're going to ride, if you don't mind," Farthing said, stepping into a golf cart, the small tires wincing beneath him. "Too
hot for me. Now my guests said they might like to walk. Any
good boys left down there?"

I thought about it for a second. "There's just some of the older guys."

"S'what I figured. Got to be in a desperate way to be out here in this kinda warm," he said, waving his hand at the air. "But these fellas, they're a good bunch a boys, and they've been waiting to get out here for months. Hell, they been riding me 'bout bringing 'em out here since the day."

We rolled down to the first tee. The course was empty, and in the haze on the tee I met two lawyers from Washington, D.C. One was tall and lanky with a boyish face, and he cracked my knuckles when he shook my hand. The other was squat with a head like a nut and legs that were all ankles. He was the kind of guy who kept club pros in business, the little moneyed duffer who would buy anything that might give him a few extra yards. Elsewhere, small men pumped iron and got in fights. At golf clubs, they spent fortunes on equipment and dreamt of Ian Woosnam.

Both guests had bag tags from California and Florida and Arizona, and they both wore golf shirts with TPC logos. They were resort players, guys without home clubs whose expense accounts were filled with greens fees. They probably practiced a lot and waited for that bond to come through at Congressional, but there was no way either of them was going to muscle Fox Chase, no matter what they shot down at Myrtle Beach this winter. Resort courses were built for quick play and grandstands. Fox Chase was built to punish, to humiliate, to slap you with both hands for even stepping up to that first tee. It made worm's meat out of egos. I should have given them strokes.

I stretched for half a minute before ripping a one-iron off the tee, the ball boring through the humidity and splitting the fairway.

"This heat reminds me of a day last week when we were out here. I'll tell you, it was almost intolerable," the Judge said as

he steered our cart down the fairway. "And there was this fu-
neral procession passing down Dogwood Road. You know, right
off number four."

"Yes, sure. I know it."

"So we finish three, and we're trying to hit up on four, and
the foursome in front of us, well they're just stopped, hats off
their heads, like they're holding Sunday services or something
out there, watching this procession go by.

"So I drive out to the fairway and I yell, 'Hey, buddy, what
the hell are y'all doin' out there?' And one of the old fellas says,
'We're having a moment of silence, if you don't mind.' So I
yell right back, 'Hell, this is a golf course, not a cemetery. Move
your butts on outta here!' He looks over at me and says, 'It's
the least I can do, for Christ's sake. I was married to her for
forty-six years!'"

I'd heard it a dozen times, but I laughed good and long
anyway.

"I hope you brought your wallets, gentlemen," Judge Farthing said. "This young one is packed to the gills with talent.
His father runs a nice accounting outfit in town. Good practice,
good honest man."

The lawyers smiled and said it sounded very nice, and I nodded along. My part, as the kid player, was to be polite, to display a precocious knowledge of the etiquette, but also to show
them something raw and brash and immodest, to take large
swings and risky shots, nothing held back. Eat the course and
thrill the gentlemen who, in turn, would play their part by offer-
ing wide-eyed compliments and nostalgic musings of *oh, to be
twelve again,* as if being good was simply a matter of being young.
They would tell me how they wished they had started playing
golf when I did, and they believed that was the difference be-

tween my game and theirs, a little luck and a few extra years. And that was why I would always take their money.

On the fifteenth tee, the shorter one asked me what I wanted to be.

"Pro golfer would be nice," I said.

"Well, that's a tough row to hoe," he said. "Ever think about the law?"

"No, not really."

"Smart kid. Be an accountant. It's much safer," he said. "You working with your father this summer?"

"No, I'm looping, I mean, I'm a caddy here."

"Is that right? Well at least you're not inside. Beats an office job, I suppose."

"I can get more practice in too," I said as we watched the Judge snap-hook a drive onto the previous fairway. He cursed in three languages—English, Italian and something that sounded made up.

"Well you have quite a golf swing there, young man. I'll be looking for you on TV," he said. "But I'd keep something in mind to fall back on. A lot of guys want to be touring pros. And you can't be a caddy forever," he said, elbowing me in the shoulder.

"That's right," I said. "I guess you can't."

The short guest had not won a single skin, not until the seventeenth hole when he pumped his fist and jiggled his chin after I lipped out my putt for par. It was a five-dollar hole, and from the time he spent explaining it to himself, re-narrating the moment for us, calculating the precise worth of the skin—it made you wonder if they were paying the lawyers down in D.C. at all.

At the end of the round—and after two side bets, four presses, four birdies and an eagle on the seventh—I took twenty-seven dollars from each lawyer, and fourteen dollars from the Judge.

Since a twelve-year-old can't go into the grill and widdle his winnings away on drinks for the losers, the cash went straight into my pocket, more money than I would have made on a great day of looping. And I didn't feel bad about it, because there wasn't a moment out there when one of them didn't feel like they were better than the son of a New Water accountant.

I took my money and shook their hands. We smiled. We paid our compliments.

The sun was low, just hanging around lazy like it does at six o'clock on a summer evening. The shade and the first night breezes cooled the grass, and I could have played eighteen more. I went down into the hole to rack my bag, and there was Jeffrey, sitting in the middle of an empty bench, looking down at his hands like they were somebody else's. He lifted his eyes and looked at me, tilting his head.

"Hey, it's Mr. Price. You been out there playin', Mr. Price?"

"Actually, I was gonna practice, but I ended up getting a game," I said.

"I hear ya," he said. "And you didn't take no caddy?"

"Jeffrey, it was like a hundred degrees. You wouldn't want to be out there caddying," I said as if I had done him a favor, but he looked through me, his face half asleep, swollen and tired from doing nothing. "I would have taken a caddy, definitely, but the guys I was playing with, they wanted to ride."

"Uh-huh," he said. "I hear ya. Crystal fucking clear."

"Jeffrey . . ."

"Caddy taking a motherfucking cart," he interrupted. "But you ain't really a caddy now, are ya, Mr. Price?"

I took my bag off my shoulder and propped it up on the rack.

"Do you want a ride down to the trolley stop?" I asked. "My dad'll give you a ride."

"Nope. I'm waitin'."

"Jeffrey, it's six o'clock. No one's taking caddies this late. The course is empty."

"Ya never know," he said. "I'm stickin' it out. Day's coolin' down, ya never know. Need the duckets, man. I need that money."

I reached into my pocket, pulled out the pile of tens and fives I'd just won. "Here," I said, holding out the cash, "you can have this. You can pay me back tomorrow, when you get out."

Jeffrey looked at the money, then looked at me like I was twelve years old.

"Go home, Mr. Price. Us caddies, we're waiting for a loop."

Beneath his eyes, the skin was still wet and deep, but now there was worry there. Just a twitch, a sweaty tremble. I walked to the doorway, the steel spikes in my shoes crackling across the cement floor. That night, when my father asked me if I had gotten a loop, I told him I played with Judge Farthing and two big-shot D.C. lawyers with TPC shirts and TPC tags. I told him I shot 73, and that it could have been 70. He nodded a heavy end-of-the-day nod that was not a sign of approval. It was a reminder of how hard he worked for what we had, how not every boy got to play golf in the afternoons, how the cost of a college education was rising much faster then four percent.

Lying awake that night, I listened to our house creak and pop, the night cooling the swollen joints and beams, and I dreamed without sleeping, thinking about Jeffrey. I saw him sitting in the hole, no sound or motion around him, only a faint sense of breathing. I could not make out a face, just two shoulders hunched over himself. It was dark but still steaming at midnight, and I watched him sitting on the bench, inflating, deflating, waiting and ready and unable to budge.

Maybe he was really there, numb but awake, trying to think of one other place to be. Maybe he had to be the first on the clipboard tomorrow, no excuses, no problems, no protest.

He was the last thing I remembered, my last thought as I slipped into sleep. I was wondering about a man and how long he could wait.

EVERYWHERE IN THE bleachers were mittens and hot chocolate and pink earmuffs on little sisters. It was Friday night and the grass on the field below was bright and stiff with the cold. I watched the high school kids goofing off at the concession stand, freshmen walking back and forth in front of the bleachers looking for cooler kids to laugh with. On the opposite sideline, I saw Brian Seaman wearing his JV jacket and letting a cheerleader feel his bicep through the leather.

Down on the field, my brother's chin strap was red with blood. The final game of the season, they needed one more victory for eight wins and a trip to the state playoffs. The cheerleaders shook signs and handed out kazoos. Everyone clapped and beat the cold out of their mittens as we watched my brother run lost on the field, his feet moving like cinder blocks as he bumped his way through the plays. The crashes were coming to Casey, running backs sticking their helmets in his chest, banging him up under his face mask. He ran standing straight. Casey wasn't hitting, he was walking through plays that the coach hadn't called. He was watching the kids goofing off at the concession stand. Then he was picking himself up off the ground.

The night before I had listened to Casey and my father arguing in the kitchen. I sat in bed on top of my covers, pushing together the back page of one of Casey's old *MAD* magazines, a cartoon of a miniature golf course that transformed into an alien spaceship if you folded it right. I listened to Casey tell my father he was quitting the football team. He'd had enough of the coach, the fat guy with shades and sweaty gray T-shirts who drove him twice as hard as the other players. He was tired of getting kicked out of practice early, or having to stay late to run wind sprints. He didn't want to hear that he dogged it in practice, the coach calling him Lacey Price, spitting words in his face like *stubborn* and *disrespect* and *half-assed*.

"But did the coach make you a better player, Casey?" my father said. "Did you ask yourself that?"

I heard Casey explain how that afternoon the team had voted for next year's captains. When one of the other linebackers nominated my brother for the vote, the coach wouldn't put his name on the board. "In front of the whole team, Coach tells everyone that I don't show up ready to play," Casey said, more calm about it than I would have expected, as if the facts of his case were solid enough without the ranting. "He tells them I'm not a leader, and only leaders can run for captain. I didn't expect to win, I didn't even want to be captain. The kid that won's just a kiss-ass. But I'm the best player on the whole damn defense. Coach can think about that when I'm not there tomorrow night."

The kitchen was quiet for a moment. I heard my mother walk into the room, fill a glass at the sink, then walk back out, her plastic-bottomed slippers scratching across the linoleum. I folded together the caption beneath the *MAD* cartoon, and the letters read, "TALKE MSE THO YOUUR LEASTDER."

When my father finally answered, his voice was matter-of-fact, disinterested almost, as if the solution to the problem was that there wasn't a problem. "I didn't make you start football," he said. "I didn't. But you've started it, and you're going to finish it. I will not let you quit before the final game. And I will not let you quit before your senior season."

That, and the threat of a senior year in private school if Casey quit the team, and my father put his foot down in the kitchen that night. And, amazingly, all four of us seemed to hear it.

After the game, I sat in the backseat next to my brother. He'd showered but I could still smell the funk of mud and armpits. Our car was stuck in the jam headed for the exit of the high school parking lot, girls giggling in Volkswagens, calling over to boys frozen in jeeps with the tops down in November.

My father clicked off his news radio and spoke at the steering wheel in front of him. "Casey, if you dog it around the field like that with your head down, you're going to get yourself killed."

We pulled out of the parking lot and into the long line of cars trying to get back to the highway, a school bus pumping out chunks of exhaust up ahead of us, horns honking and kids waving hands out their sunroofs. My brother stared out the window, the reflection of his tired red face sticking on the glass.

"Who won?" Casey asked.

"What do you mean who won?" my father said. "The other team won. Twenty-eight to nine."

My father turned on the radio. We listened to news radio all the way home. Three times the weatherman called it a perfect autumn evening.

Off-season caddying was the best work of the year. We wore long underwear and woolly caps. There was no humidity, no sunburns, no rashes from the sweat, and before the snow came there was more work than the caddies knew what to do with. Lifers would lug four bags, two on each shoulder, because in the bitter November wind no golfer wanted to sit in a golf cart, freezing their behinds numb on the plastic seats. With all the summer crew gone back to school, demand for caddies beat down the supply, and even Jamie Byrne had to carry doubles.

The Saturday morning after my brother's game, the air was clear and tight and almost winter, but if you just kept moving down the fairway, the cold in your chest would turn to a better sort of warm than you ever felt while caddying in the summertime. Jamie and I took the two halves of the Norton loop, Jamie with Norton and Goodloe, me with Baker and Hall. Fifty dollars later, we headed down to the banks of the Delaware River, a lump of cash in my pocket that I was anxious to waste before I had to turn it over to my father that evening. I once asked my father what would happen if I won a scholarship to school, what would I do with all that college money growing in the bank, and all he said was "You'd be a very lucky boy."

We stocked up at 7-Eleven and carried our booty down to the water's edge, a six-pack of Mountain Dew and a Ziploc bag full of sugar, beef jerky and a chunk of string cheese because Jamie said he could make a bomb out of them. We spent an hour on the bank there, dangling our legs off a discarded slab of side-walk, our toes just touching the green-black film on the water's surface. I drank the soda while Jamie packed the empty cans with sugar and caffeine and little balls of cheese he'd rolled up in his palm. The green belches burned my nose and eyes and they made Jamie laugh as he tossed can after can into the water, each bomb fizzing dead there in front of us, then slowly floating south, tiny aluminum wrecks ready to sink.

The Delaware River was the west edge of town. It gave our town its name, but it was not something people looked at or swam in or discussed as a part of New Water. The water was not the moving kind, and it wasn't new—it slid past like a rotten soup. There were no heroic crossings here, not at this spot on the Delaware where New Jersey coughed at us from the other side. This was where buildings and barges slept beneath the flaming tips of smokestacks, metal towers like graying bones sticking up out of the earth.

"Did I ever tell you my real name?" Jamie asked, tossing the last can into the water.

"Isn't it James?"

"Nope. That's what everyone thinks, but it isn't."

I burped a low rumbler that smelled like lemon and beef.

"My real name's Jameson. Jameson Byrne. I don't think anyone knows that except my folks."

"That's a good name. *Jameson,*" I said, like it was some warrior knight.

"You know what it is? Jameson?"

"Nope."

"It's whiskey. It's a green bottle of Irish whiskey." He tugged at the long strand of blond hair hanging down over his eyes.

"Jameson. It's not a bad name."

"I don't know," he said. "Maybe not. I think I would like it better if it was someone else's. My mom, she wanted to name me Brian. Brian Byrne," he said, shrugging his shoulders.

It was the first and only time Jamie brought up his mother.

"Where is your mom?" I asked.

Jamie held his hand to his face and peered at New Jersey through the spaces between his fingers.

"Los Angeles. She's an actress. She's a stewardess on planes, and she's an actress."

"In movies?"

"Commercials mostly. I've only seen the commercials."

"Is she famous? Did I ever see her?"

"Probably not. There's only two commercials I've seen her in. There's this one where there's a mom talking to her daughter, about, like, cleaning around on her insides. My mom's the mom. She's got blond hair. They're on the beach, and she's like, 'Honey, do you deuce,' and the girl's like, 'Yeah, I deuce every day.'"

"I never saw that. You're making that up."

"No, I swear to God."

"Then why did I never see it?"

"'Cause it's for girls, jackass," he said. "And then, then there's this other commercial where she cooks dinner with low-fat oil. She makes chicken, and the whole family's at the table and they all go, 'Ooooh, chicken,' and they smile and eat it. There's this girl with real big teeth, and this goofy-looking kid with freckles that's supposed to be her son. And the dad looks sort of like Mr. Wade from Fox Chase. My mom's the mom, with the blond hair."

Our eyes adjusted to the dark. Steel shapes on the opposite bank were black blocks drifting on the water.

"She's a stewardess too?" I asked, standing up and brushing the gravel off the back of my jeans.

"That's what my dad says."

A split telephone pole lay dumped at the water's edge. It connected the riverbank to the road. As we tightroped our way back up the pole, I asked Jamie, "Do you have a picture of her?"

"She's blond," he said. I followed as we stepped our way up to the street, one foot in back of the other.

SOME OF THE caddies called Brian Seaman Spooge Boy or Spermy. He would lift a bag off the ground and pause to watch his bicep squeeze into a ball. He was a storyteller in the superlative. I listened through all the biggest and the bests and the craziest things he had ever seen. During that spring when I turned thirteen, Brian's favorite story was how he had touched pussy on the eighteenth green one starry April night.

"Swear to God. I was all over her. Her ass left two dents in the green, right there, *bang,*" he said, standing at the center of the hole and grunting with his hips.

"Sit your virgin ass down," said Jeffrey. "Only man in here gettin' tang is this nigga, and it's with all a your mommas." He reclined on the bench, hands behind his head, wet circles beneath his arms in the same spot and on the same shirt as yesterday.

"Screw that, man," Brian said, fanning out the muscles in his back, "I ain't no virgin."

"Spooge Boy, let me tell you something," Jeffrey said, lighting his next cigarette with his last. "If it was raining pussies, you'd get hit in the head with a dick."

Jamie and I both laughed good and hard, but Brian decided to slap only me in the ear with a cupped hand. "Shut your hole, Price," Brian said. "You've never even seen a pussy in your life."

He was right. I hadn't seen, at least not the genuine article in real, breathing life. If pressed, I could have fudged the details, substituting what I had gleaned from Cinemax for what, at twelve years old, was all too good to ever dream of touching. What a breast might feel like, perfect and impossible, like a hand brushing the water's surface without breaking it. Or that shadow beneath the panties in a Penney's catalogue—it was all a warm dark mystery to me.

There was Brian Seaman, with stories of how he had actually marked the earth with a female's buttocks, and then there was me, just two years younger and I had not even masturbated properly yet. I tried once after spending most of an afternoon looking at the cover of *Cosmo,* a woman with a lime dress spread open across her breastbone. She tugged at the scoop of her dress with red fingernails, her eyes peering off the page with an open mouth that wasn't smiling at all. I was doing fine until it burned—it felt like a Slinky was trying to twist its way out of me. Out dribbled a drop of what looked like Elmer's glue, and I felt so guilty I took a shower, crying and scrubbing my hands clean. And then I tried again. The soap seemed to help, yet nothing actually happened, except for me getting very clean. I already knew—no dents in the green—not for me, and as Brian told his story I couldn't help thinking about what I would do if those ass prints on the green were in my line. Would I get a drop? Was it a man-made obstruction? There was puberty in my blood, but there was also golf.

Lewis Holmes's voice whined over the intercom. "Hey cock-knockers, settle down, I can hear you up here. You down there, Jamie?"

Jamie laid his cards down on the bucket we were using for a table. "Yeah," he said, getting up and walking for Norton's bag without waiting for Lewis to tell him, "Well get Norton's bag and get going."

Jeffrey shook his head as we watched Jamie climb the steps sideways, hauling Norton's bag upstairs by the handle. The rest of us carried two bags, but we all knew Jamie outearned us looping with just that one.

"How the hell's he always get that loop?" Jeffrey said. "When's Lewis gonna throw that bag my way? Haven't been out in three days, man. Shit, I'd take a single today, no problem."

Brian Seaman picked up Jamie's cards and turned over a nine. "War," he said. We each laid down three while he turned to Jeffrey. "Like you're going to caddy for the club president. Give me a break."

"What, black man not good enough to caddy for the president but a little cripple kid is?"

"Yo, Jeffrey," Tomato Face coughed from the corner. Puddy even looked up from where he was reading the W volume of an encyclopedia.

Brian scooped up my cards and pointed the aces at Jeffrey. "Watch it, shitbird. That's out of line."

"Hey, I like the kid as much as the rest of y'all. I'm just sayin' he's no better than anybody down here. He's always turnin' the big loops, and he's not the one thumbing it back to Philly tonight if he don't get out."

"Right. Tough guy here, raggin' on a little kid. Dude's half your size," Brian said.

"I ain't raggin' on him," Jeffrey said, leaning out from the bench, elbows digging into his knees. "I'd just like to see the guys that really need that money, get that damn money once in a while."

"And that's you?" Tomato Face said.

"You're damn right it is."

Brian Seaman lit a menthol cigarette from the same pack he was showing off around the hole three weeks ago. He spewed the smoke out in one big cloud. "I don't know, man. Jamie earns it. He's a tough little fucker."

"Dude ain't bigger than five minutes," Jeffrey said.

"Yeah, but still, if he was a little bigger, that is one kid I wouldn't mess with. I've never seen balls on anyone like he's got. Did I tell you the shit he pulled at school this year with the librarian?" Brian said, and he slid the bucket out of his way, turning so the whole room could see him. He hacked up a bubble of phlegm, dripping it from his mouth and onto the burning end of his Kool, then mashing the butt out on the bottom of his sneaker. Brian wasn't very good at smoking cigarettes, but he excelled in finding dramatic ways to put them out.

"This Mrs. Gasperec is the librarian, right, and she's old as dirt. Older than dirt. She's been in that library since the fifties, man, and she's skittish as hell, just totally out to lunch. So we have to take this placement test for freshmen, some fill-in-the-dots bullshit for the school or the county, you know what I'm talking about." Brian looked at me and I nodded. "So there's like a hundred of us packed into the library, and she's the proctor, and she reads all the rules, no talking, no whatever, and nothing on your table in front of you except two fucking number-two pencils." Brian's strong brown eyes panned the room to see that we were with him. "So Jamie's not really paying attention. I mean we're all half asleep, and he's got that little plastic strappy thing he slaps to his hand so he can write."

"What thing?" Tomato Face said.

"It's like a little fake thumb, he straps it to his hand like this," he showed us in the air, tucking his thumb into his palm, "and he sticks a pen in there. It doesn't really look like a thumb, but he writes like a mother with it. So this little strap is sitting on the table, right there under Gasperec's nose, and when she walks around handing out pencils, she grabs the fucking thing and starts saying some shit about *no objects except a number-two pencil!*"

"Are you serious?" I said.

"Swear to Christ. He gets all red and shit, and I'm in the back of the room barking about how he needs that shit to write. Can't take the test without fucking writing, right? And she gets all nervous and flustered, brings me to the front of the room, in front of all these fucking kids, and sits me down at a desk right next to her. And Jamie's back there saying, 'Mrs. Gasperec, Mrs. Gasperec, I really need that, Mrs. Gasperec,' but he won't show her his hands, and I'm saying, you crazy old bitch, give him his fucking thumbs back! But she just grabs the things and chucks them in her desk and yells, 'No more talking! Begin! Begin!' So I'm just pissed off, you know? The bitch didn't have a *clue* what was goin' on."

"Crotchety old whore," said Tomato Face, wiping half-and-half from his mouth with his shirtsleeve.

"So there's Jamie, and I'm sittin' up there next to Gasperec and I'm watching him. She smells like cat piss, and I can't even start my test because I'm watching Jamie stick a pencil between his fingers,"— he showed us again, making a V with his first two fingers where Jamie tried to balance it, "and he starts writing. With his *knuckles.* Puts his head down and tears through that fucker, and the pencil keeps falling out onto the floor, the tip's breaking and shit, and he has to go to the sharpener like twelve times. So Jamie's a real smart fucker. He's like the genius in our class. So I'm watching him and drawing pictures on my answer sheet, connecting the dots and all. We've got two hours to take this thing, right? And Jamie finishes in, like, fifty minutes."

Tomato Face waved an open hand at Brian. "Get the fuck outta here."

"Maybe a little longer, but he's done before any of us. Other kids are still on the first page and Jamie is there finishing up. He closes his test book, and I'm just watching him, thinking that was the craziest shit I ever saw. Dude did it with his *knuckles*. Then he closes the book, puts the pencil down next to it," Brian's voice got quiet, "and he folds his hands on top of the book, and sits there, silent, and just stares *right at that bitch*."

"Cold," said Jeffrey.

"Cold as *hell*, man. After like a minute she comes up and tries to take the test away from him. She's all, 'When you have completed the exam, you are permitted to leave,' like she's reading it straight from the book. You know what JB tells her? He tells her he's not done yet."

"No *shit*."

"Swear to God. He's like, 'Thank you ma'am, but I'm not finished yet.'"

"Thank you *ma'am*," Tomato Face echoed.

"He just sits there, man, just staring straight at her, his hands folded on top of the desk, and I'm doing all I can not to jump up in my seat and start dancing. She gets all fidgety, her face gets all red, the veins in her head look like they're gonna pop, man, and Jamie is not even fucking blinking. He sat there like that until the end of the test, and after everyone's gone, he stands up, hands her the papers, picks up his strappy thing off the desk, and he stands right there in front of her and puts them on. That's when she sees his hands. He says, 'Thank you very much, Mrs. Gasperec,' then walks right out the door. And she's sitting at that desk, and she goes white as a ghost, and I swear she just about dropped dead right there."

"Now that, boys and girls," said Jeffrey, "is pretty fucking solid."

Jeffrey hopped up onto the bag rack, squeezing himself into an empty slot between golf bags. "What the hell happened to the kid's thumbs anyway?" he said. "I heard someone sayin' he got attacked by a dog, a pit bull or some shit."

"Nah, he blew them off. This big-ass rocket on the Fourth of July, blew both of them to bits," Brian said.

"Bullshit," said Jeffrey. "Fireworks woulda blown his whole hand apart."

"He could have been born that way," Tomato Face said.

"Nah, it was fireworks," Brian said. "Jamie was like, six. It was Fourth of July and his dad brings home a shitload of fireworks and he lets Jamie start messing around with them."

"What kind of asshole gives a six-year-old fireworks?"

"I don't know. But that's the story I heard. And I heard it from a buddy at school who said he heard it from one of the teachers."

"Maybe it was a war injury," Jeffrey said. "Maybe he lost those thumbs in Nam."

"Very funny, asshole," Tomato Face said. "You're talkin' to a Vietnam vet here."

"No wonder we lost."

Jeffrey hopped down from the bag rack and slapped our hands while we laughed, and Tomato Face leaned back, rolling his neck muscles in his fingers and sighing a warm breath. "You know something, Jeffrey? Why don't you just save me the headache of having to listen to all your bullshit. You should just stay at home and collect welfare with all the rest of your, your *people,*" he said.

The reality was that Tomato Face, Puddy, Jeffrey were all collecting. All the caddies knew, even me, but entitlements were one of the hole's few taboos. We didn't talk about welfare, not seriously, not when some of our coworkers had to abuse the system so they could eat in February.

"Maybe I will, you drunk-ass Irish motherfucker. Better watch yourself, people gonna forget you white you keep drinkin' that bathtub hooch—they might start thinkin' you an Indian redskin or somethin'."

"Fuck you," Tomato Face said with a lazy chuckle, no offense taken because between the loopers, it was a room without egos.

"See, thing of it is," Jeffrey continued, tucking his thumbs into his armpits, "you know if I wasn't here, y'all's little club would fall the fuck apart."

"Is that right?"

"God*damn* right. Just waiting for my bond," he said, flapping his elbows. "Should be coming through any damn day, then y'all be carrying my motherfuckin' sticks around, and I'll be out there whackin' the ball with Mr. Price here." He nodded at me, taking a baseball swing in the air. "Knock that little white ball into next fucking week."

"Sit the fuck down," came a voice from where the light spilled down the stairway, where silhouetted against the concrete was the six feet, six inches of Walter Kane, a handsome and heavy-shouldered black man with a chest that looked like it was fashioned from bronze shields.

He was the assistant greenskeeper, and while he was a country-club careerist, he was well above the lifers on the Fox Chase food chain. What Walter did required a degree in a specific field of agricultural science offered by only a few schools, one of them Penn State, where I had heard that years before he played power forward. He married a girl in State College who became a paralegal, and they lived in a brownstone in Philly and had a son that went to Episcopal Academy. It was his boy who everyone asked about. His name was Jimmy Kane, but the newspapers called the All-State point guard Candy Kane. Walter would bring news down to the hole about the latest letters, the way a big-time college coach would kiss ass for pages, a big famous signature scrawled across the bottom like a promise.

"Lookin' like it might be Notre Dame," Walter would say with a child's smile, a young face talking about his hero. I loved how Walter was not just a father but a fan, and I tried to imagine my father talking about me that way, bragging with blunt, unmasked admiration, but the thought of him looking up to me like that was too embarrassing to picture. It wasn't who we were, and that was as deep and as shallow of an explanation as my family ever got.

Walter had a plain, proper manner of speaking around the membership, but down below in the hole, he broke into a quick, sliding tongue that sounded as tough as we all thought he was. "Now if we can just get the boy thinking about the SAT instead of the NBA, we'll be alright. Get him out there with some of that rich Catholic pussy," he would say.

That afternoon, Walter strutted into the shade of the hole, his arms swinging at his sides. "Day they let you in this club," Walter said to Jeffrey, "y'all better be looking busy because Jesus is on the *way*."

Everybody at Fox Chase loved Walter, not just in the hole but in the clubhouse and on the fairways. Jeffrey might have been the only exception. Walter had clean staff shirts, arms with long muscles, light skin that was always clean shaven. Next to Walter, Jeffrey looked like a mistake of a man. He was shorter, sweatier, a darker shade of brown. His white shirts were yellow and his English was crumbled. To the membership at Fox Chase, Walter was the model, Jeffrey was the sin.

Walter came down to caddy in the afternoons after he finished his morning work on the grounds—trimming collars, raking traps, syringing the greens. It was Walter's job to drive the chemical sprayer down the fairways, wearing his white mask and bodysuit like some astronaut roving the hills of Fox Chase. White globs of foam fell in a trail behind the sprayer, a cart with hoses that showered down chemical juice from a clear plastic tank. In the sunlight, the foam would burn neon-yellow patches in the grass. We never asked if it was safe, and we never wondered about Walter's white suit. It was not the kind of place for that because things were never not fine.

Some days when we sat in the hole, sleepy and too bored for conversation, Walter would look at his hands, back and front, the fingertips a touch orange. Sometimes there were odd white spots trailing down each digit, and Walter would shake his head, spit on his hands and rub them together, close and fast. He would look at them again, and the orange would still be there, and he would fold his hands closed and quiet.

"No loops today," Jeffrey said. "Sorry 'bout that, better go back out to the bushes."

"Already got my loop. You think I'd come down here to sit with you fools if I wasn't set up already?" Walter said, walking around the room and slapping each of our hands hello. Walter was in high demand as a caddy because he knew every grain and cut, every subtle break on the course. He rolled each green every morning. He could read them like words on a page.

"That's bullshit. Been here since seven o'clock, and I ain't had a good payday all week," said Jeffrey.

"Hey, sorry, man. Lewis said he had a loop for me, so I'm here."

"Who?" I asked, knowing I was next in line for an A-loop.

"Don't know. Something good," Walter said. We knew that Lewis prearranged loops with him because he would hit Lewis with ten bucks afterward. But big Walter didn't skeez, he bumped, and Jeffrey was the only one who seemed to mind.

"I'm tired a this shit, where the fuck is Lewis?" said Jeffrey, brushing past Walter and heading up the stairs two steps at a time.

"Aw, shit Jeffrey, get back here," Brian called. "You're gonna get roaded!"

"Boy must be out of groceries," Walter said.

"If you can get crack at the grocery store," said Brian.

"Shit, that fool ain't doing crack. Fucking H, man. He's all about it."

"Heroin?" I asked.

"Hell yeah," Walter said, slapping at his forearm with two fingers.

"Then where's the tracks?" Brian said. "Jeffrey's got pipes for arms. I've never seen any marks."

"Have you ever seen him wear shorts? Ever?"

"So?"

"So middle of August and he's wearing those purple fucking jeans, doesn't even cut them into shorts, 'cause he's shooting it in his leg. In his calf and foot and shit. There's big fat-ass veins down there."

"No shit?"

"No shit."

Position A came rattling down the stairs, a pink and green bag beneath each arm, the sweat on his face from a six-hour loop. He dropped the bags against the sink, exhaled like it was his last breath.

"Out there chasin' that tail 'round," said Walter, opening his large palm to Position A, who slapped it. "That's my boy."

"How's my favorite point guard, Walter?" Position A asked.

"Mailbox is jammed tight."

"That's what I like to hear," Position A said. He dug into the pocket of his cutoff jeans and pulled out a piece of torn newspaper. "I've got a little something here for everyone. Get this shit," he said, unfolding the paper and reading, "'Police Beat, Philadelphia—George Pudlinski of the 400 block of Hall Street in New Water was arrested Friday morning at 2:35 A.M. after soliciting sexual services from a vice agent of the Philadelphia Police Department.' Can you believe that shit? Puddy, fucking Puddy, got caught trawling for tuna!"

"Aww, man, that library-book-reading motherfucker in the corner? I didn't think that dude had a prick to piss with," said Walter. "He got a record?"

"Yeah," Tomato Face said, "we've done a couple nights together, just some D and D bullshit. But he might have something else on there. Puddy loved those broads down on Bainbridge."

"Puddy?" Brian said. "Puddy doesn't fuck, man, no way. Porkers like that, man, they mate."

I didn't laugh with the rest of them. Puddy was one of the good ones, quiet, showed up every day, took any work. He never talked about a wife or a girlfriend, never told gap-toothed stories about his old lady like the other lifers did. I could tell he was the one in the crowd who wasn't supposed to be there. He was fat everywhere—in his ankles, in his wrists, his chin hanging on his chest like a curtain—not sweat and bones like most of the loopers his age. He didn't tell large stories, didn't reminisce, didn't complain or say he was waiting for things to get better. He just waited, a simple face behind a few simple books. I tried to imagine him out on the street early in the morning, handing over a week's worth of work to a woman with red lips and red heels and red leather. I wondered if he was thinking of the way he smelled, if it mattered to him, if he was embarrassed when he asked her what she would be willing to do.

"Pin that stuff up," Walter said, and Position A stuck the clipping up on the Wall of Shame, a patch of corkboard that held a DUI clipping for Tomato Face, a letter from a disgruntled member complaining that Fox Chase caddies were lazy and inept (reminding us all to hack up something sticky in his bag whenever his number was called), and a glossy photo of a stripper with overripe breasts signed, "To Wilson the golf pro— Looking for a hole to drive? Luv, Cheri." Cheri was the benevolent goddess of the caddy hole, and it was protocol for a looper to honor her after a big loop by kissing his fingers and touching them to the crack of her behind.

"How's the ladies?" Walter asked Position A. "Treatin' ya right?"

Position A peeled apart a damp pile of bills. "Right as rain. It's easy money, fellas."

"Shit, but we *know* you putting in that overtime. I saw you over at Norton's last week, man. What you doing over there, diggin' tunnels?"

"Layin' pipe is what he's doin," Brian said.

"What do you do at the Nortons'?" I asked.

"Oh shit, Pricey, I think you're a little young for this story," Position A said, smiling. "So cover your eyes."

Position A was Mrs. Norton's favorite caddy. She had hair that was thick with rings of all sorts of reds—apple, cherry, a little orange. She was tan in February. Her legs were thin and leathery and covered with small brown spots, and she was one of the few members who made a point to smile a hello to the caddies. She wore tight shorts and no socks. Her neck was thin with soft muscles, and hers were the only two breasts at Fox Chase to have ignored gravity. The caddies scurried like mice out of the hole to watch her pass.

Mrs. Norton spoke quietly when she asked for something. She tiptoed around her husband's club. Amanda was their only child, and the three of them lived in a cathedral of a stone mansion just off the fourteenth tee. Some days you could hear splashing from the pool as you played by. You could smell the chlorine when it rained.

"So I'm out carrying for Mrs. Norton, and after the loop, she asks me if I want to come over and help her do a little spring cleaning to the pool," Position A began, "and you know what that means. They have a guy come every week to clean that thing. She's never cleaned the pool in her life."

We all rocked back into the benches. Brian Seaman's face hung slack with anticipation, and I sat there squeezing my hands white as we listened.

"So, I go over there, and she answers the door in a freaking bikini. No shit, man, the thing is all strings and curves and *bam,* her body's looking like she's nineteen."

"How 'bout her horns?" Tomato Face said.

"Man, I've got two words for them things—*niiice,*" Position A said. "So I'm at the door, and she tells me sorry, the pool guy showed up after all, but since I walked all the way over I might as well stay for some lunch . . ."

"God*damn*."

"Swear to God. So we go back to the pool and she opens a bottle of wine, and she brings out some shrimps, and we have some wine, and some shrimps, and some more wine, and next thing you know she starts talking to me about her husband. Mr. fucking Norton, the president of the damn club, and she's sitting there telling me what a total stroke he is. She says all he wants to do is play golf and drink and play cards and how he's never home and how the prick probably has to stop and ask for directions on his way home from the club. And then she starts telling me, get this, she starts telling me that they don't even fuck anymore."

"You have got to be shitting me," Brian said.

"I swear, she starts telling me he's soft, he can't get it up. All this shit. Mrs. fucking Norton, that quiet little lady, man!"

"She's telling this to *you*?"

"What'd you do?"

"What do you think I did?"

"I think you nailed her six ways from Sunday," Tomato Face said.

"It was like chimps, man. Like monkeys at the zoo," Position A said. "Christ, you should see that body. You have not made the love until you have made the love to an older woman. And it doesn't hurt if they're sexually frustrated with a big-ass Jacuzzi in the backyard."

"You fucked in the Jacuzzi?" Brian asked.

"Oh, man, for like an hour. And the shit of it is, get this, this was nuts—she keeps looking at her watch telling me when her husband teed off, saying shit like 'He should be making the turn about now, he should be coming down the eleventh now, he's getting close, he'll be by here soon,' like she couldn't wait for it. And then, just like she said, Norton comes over the hill with his group, strolling right up to the fourteenth tee, and you *know* you can see the pool and shit from there."

"Oh, hell yeah."

"So, get this shit. She pushes me down, so I like, scooch down in the Jacuzzi. My back's to the course, so my head's just below the edge and I'm just barely out of view, right?" Position A held out his elbows and lifted his shoulders up around his ears. "Like this, all tucked up and shit. And you know what she does?"

"Oh, please tell me," Brian said.

"She puts her bikini top back on, and I think we're gonna just sit there and lie low. But get this—she fucking straddles me, slips me inside, and starts riding while she's waving to her husband!"

Tomato Face's face went crooked. "While you're *fucking?*"

"While we're screwing, swear to God! She's going up and down on me and waving, 'Hi honey, how's your round?,' gigglin' and shit, and I can hear him calling back, 'Oh just fine, see you for dinner around eight,' and man, I'm there and my heart's pounding and the bubbles are going and I'm not worried about losing my job—I'm worried about getting shot! But she just keeps grinding on me. She starts coming before he even finishes the fucking hole, all moaning and peeling off her top and touching herself, and I swear he could have seen her if he just turned around."

"Did he?"

"She said he didn't. He was golfing, man. She said he doesn't see anything else in the world when he's standing over a putt."

"Not even his wife gettin' screwed silly by a goddamn caddy,"

Walter said, laughing hard and giving Position A a loud high five.

"Not even."

"Jesus Christ," Brian said, "I think I've got to go burp the twins."

We laughed together, and then nobody said anything for a while. The day was all waiting, but it was good, and we sat there in an untroubled quiet that we all wanted to soak in for just a moment longer.

Just a moment before we heard Lewis upstairs. He was roading Jeffrey, calling him a dumb-shit waste of breath, telling him that he couldn't come back until he took a shower and used deodorant because he smelled like the fucking trash.

WHEN I WAS thirteen, I showed my best friend how I played golf.

Jamie carried my bag in the Fox Chase Junior Championship as a favor. A favor, plus half of my next loop. Myles Dane was defending champion two years in a row, but that afternoon on number eighteen, a quiet semicircle of faces surrounded the green to watch me drop my five-footer for par to seal 72. When it went in, I pumped my fists and yelled through clenched teeth, *yes,* and Jamie blushed and shook his head. Stuck to second place, Myles knocked his three-footer for 74 past the hole. He quickly raked the next putt back, missing again, then tapping the next, then the next, the ball rolling back and forth like the hole was covered with glass. For the first time, Myles Dane looked his age. He was suddenly a kid, fear soft in his face like all those children at the clinic who had to turn around to their fathers and say they couldn't do it.

136

As Myles pushed the ball around the hole, racking up strokes, a voice boomed from the far edge of the gallery, "PUT THE BALL IN THE GODDAMN HOLE!"

Jamie and I took a step back, leaving Myles in the center of our circle with a ball that would not fall, a father nearby with a swollen voice and lines in his face, a man full of blood and muscles who would not accept a son who was sixteen and already ex-champion.

Myles bent and picked up the ball and walked off to the pro shop, his lips trembling at the corners. He took a DNC on the official score sheet, no number for the eighteenth, and he finished the day tied for last place with a ten-year-old beginner who quit after four holes, the day's only other *DID NOT CARD*.

Jamie slapped me five and the members from the gallery each took their turn congratulating the Price boy, all except Mr. Dane, who I saw in the distance, standing large on the empty driving range, waiting and steaming and rearranging his ideas, his plans, his dreams of Augusta Sundays. It wasn't long before Myles shot from the pro shop with five bags of range balls swinging heavy from his fingers. His eyes were red circles. They looked like they were gasping for air.

Jamie sat by my clubs on the rail, taking it all in the way Jamie did, and he said, "Man, that was wild. I didn't expect such a big deal."

"It's a big deal 'cause he lost," I said, motioning toward the range.

"Man, my dad would never do something like that, that guy yelling at his kid and all in front of everybody. I mean, my dad doesn't know where I am half the time, so I guess that's different," he said, wiping his hands on his towel.

My father was watching golf on TV that afternoon when I came home with a gold trophy in my hands. He looked up from the television for a second, and I tried not to smile, but I did. He turned his eyes back to the green pictures in front of him and said, "Good for you, Timothy." He did not say why he wasn't there while men without sons were crowding the eighteenth to applaud me and smile. Instead he turned up the volume so he could hear the golf a little better.

My trophy was the centerpiece of the dining room table that evening. My father eyed the golden cup as if it might be stolen, shaking his head and chewing up his Salisbury steak. I wondered if Jamie meant what he had said. If it came up again, I thought, I would tell him that Myles Dane was not as unlucky as we all thought he was, that it was better to feel a father's hands pushing than to see them dug quietly in his pockets.

Casey came down from the attic to eat dinner with us that evening, and he pretended to drink his milk from my trophy. "This is plastic," he said.

"It's not plastic," I said. "It's brass."

"This is *not* brass. It's cheap, listen," he said, flicking his finger against the side, sounding a dull clunk of a *ting*.

"It's metal," I said.

"It's aluminum."

"It's wonderful," said my mother as she scooped another slab of vegetable lasagna onto Casey's plate that he didn't ask for, hoping it might keep his mouth busy.

"D'you beat a girl to get this?" he said, holding it upside down and trying to loosen the bolt at the bottom.

"No, I didn't beat a *girl*."

"Beat a bunch of girls. A bunch of golfin' girls."

"Casey," my father said. "Put that down." He grabbed the trophy to pull it from Casey's hands. Casey wouldn't let go.

"Get off, I'm looking at it."

"I told you to put it down."

"I'm looking at it."

Their fingers tightened around the cup. "Put it down!" my father said, and as he yanked the trophy, my brother let go. The cup tumbled to the floor, bouncing metal across the linoleum. One of the fake brass arms snapped off like it was made of candy.

We watched the trophy lay broken on the floor, silent, as if we sat there long enough the cup might get up and put itself together and come back to sit on our table.

My brother dropped his napkin on his plate and went back up to the attic, and my father picked up the pieces of the trophy. He held the base, the cup, the broken arm in his lap, saying something about not having the right tools. I wasn't listening. I was thinking of the next tournament, the next trophy, a wall of trophies, a room full of trophies that I could fill and refill faster than my brother could tear apart. Trophies I could pile upon my brother. Trophies I could bury him with.

Later that evening, after the kitchen was cleaned and my parents had gone up to bed, I sneaked out the back door and rode my bike to meet Jamie at the riverbank. We didn't go down to the water, but sat along the road beneath the canopy of an old pine tree. We collected pinecones in a pile as the rain began to fall, bits of rain you couldn't see in the night, the sound of thousands of pins falling.

"Come on, we're gonna get soaked," Jamie said.

"Where are we going?"

"Just come on."

I followed the trail of Jamie's tires on the wet streets. The rain subsided to a slippery feeling, like the air was sweating around us, and we rode across New Water to the north side of town, closer to the state border and Pennsylvania and the tangled gray refineries. I didn't know my way around the narrow streets with few houses and many potholes, gravel everywhere and trash cans slumped on the curbs. There was no construction in this part of New Water that some called Bone Hill, where FOR SALE signs rusted in long grass, the doors of dented mailboxes hanging open like thirsty tongues.

Jamie Byrne's driveway was two strips of mud reaching back into thin blue woods. His house was gray and white, one story and no garage, a paint-flaked *Daily News* van in the driveway sitting tilted on its wheels. The windows were dark when we arrived, and I followed him through a front door that was cracked open. Warm dust and the brown vegetable smell of kitchen trash filled my nose.

"Wait here," he said, and he tiptoed around a corner. I stood in a room where there were no pictures or paintings or vases or curtains. An unspecific yellow stain dripped down the wall in front of me, and through a doorway to the right I saw the back corner of a couch.

I stepped lightly. In front of the couch, the Phillies game was on a blurry TV with the sound off. A man lay in a leather recliner next to the sofa, a small mess of empty brown bottles fallen about the floor like sticks set for a campfire. The man had curly black hair, his face long and his cheeks rough with a peppery stubble. He was dressed in denim pants and shirt, a dark stain on the breast pocket, his body sunk deep in the chair. I could tell he was tall, his hands large and thick and black with ink. Mr. Byrne. He snored from deep in his throat.

"Jesus, did you wake him?"

I flinched and turned to see Jamie in the doorway. His face was pale with fear.

"No, I don't think so," I said.

"Good. He gets up at three in the morning and delivers the paper," Jamie said. He peeked around the corner to see his father's chest still rising and falling with sleep.

"Come on, we don't usually have visitors."

I followed Jamie back outside to where an orange light hung over the doorway, mosquitoes humming and clicking against the windows. He lifted his shirt and pulled out a silver revolver. It was long and heavy in a very real way.

"Where did you get that?" I said, taking a step back.

"It's his. He shoots stuff in the backyard with it. Targets and bottles and crap. Sometimes he pops birds with it. Or he'll get a squirrel once in a while."

"To eat?" I asked.

"No, that's disgusting. He just shoots them for targets and stuff. He doesn't do it a lot." Jamie held the gun across his open palm like a string of pearls. "Have you ever shot a gun?"

"No."

"Then come on," he said, tucking the pistol into his shorts. Jamie grabbed his bike and rode fast away from his house and I followed, pedaling through the darkness, chasing the sound of tires turning through the water.

A bank of thick woods lined the edge of Fox Chase's fifteenth fairway. If you stepped through the trees you would come to a path of wood chips that led back into a clearing where the grounds crew burned leaves and fallen branches. The head greenskeeper hired a dozen migrant workers in the winter, farmhands from the mushroom fields in Foster Pearse's part of the world, and the Mexicans would come and comb the course for a week, picking up every twig and acorn shell, every nut, every seed. They swept the course with their fingers, dumping their buckets in the clearing at the end of the day, brown bits of shells and sticks piling up into a heap that, at week's end, they lit with a splash of gasoline and a pack of matches. I saw the fire once, playing winter golf with gloves and a wool band around my ears, when I stopped to see why smoke was pouring thick and fast from the center of the trees. The burning was all cracks and squeaks and flame-ups, each scrap flashing and smoking out, but as I stood there watching, the fire began to grow. The flames grew higher and grabbed sideways, the surrounding trees leaning over the smoke like they wanted to burn, to settle there in the black hot cinders. The tired men stood close around the pile, watching in silence like it was a log crackling in a fireplace, orange and black and red flashing across their faces. They were short with meaty shoulders, heavy plaid shirts and wet brown boots, and they didn't flinch as the fire grew so large that I thought it would swallow the course green by green. But it didn't, and they watched it burn down to hot gray dust, a look in their eyes like they were already elsewhere. They left New Water later that same day, gone for another year, an immaculate golf course behind them. The members called them the best idea a greenskeeper ever had.

Jamie mentioned a fire once, a bonfire in his backyard, but a fire isn't always a good story for telling—it moves in its own directions, too many colors and a thousand different sounds. There was too much to tell, so Jamie didn't tell us all his stories.

Who knows what would have happened if he did. Who knows what kind of story that might have been.

When Jamie turned his bike up the driveway to Fox Chase, I knew exactly where we were headed. What members had inside their clubhouse, the caddies had in the clearing. Amid acres and acres of rolling open space, that spot in the woods was the course's only privacy, and on Sunday evenings it would be full of loopers, lifers mostly, with 40's and fortified wine and cigarettes. The bars were closed on Sunday, and the course shut down on Mondays for maintenance, so the caddies brought the party to Fox Chase, building a campfire and leaning against tree stumps, tipping their heads back until they were full and settled, passed out with the stars above them.

Jamie and I had once checked out the Sunday party and found some untroubled faces along the edge of the clearing, a few card games and some conversation between men with wilted smiles. But when Jamie talked me into sneaking a beer from one of the torn-open cases, Tomato Face caught me by the neck and made me drop the can there in front of him.

"That's all you fucking kids need," he said. He let me go, then picked up the beer and cracked it open and walked back into the shadows along the edges.

The rain had stopped by the time we reached the course, the gray dripping out of the sky. We ran by moonlight to the clearing, down the path, branches smacking at our faces and arms. When we came out into the open, I grabbed my knees and breathed in deep. Jamie dropped the pistol in the pine needles at our feet.

"Careful," I told him.

"It's okay. It's pointed the other way."

The caddies' Sunday had been rained out, and the clearing was empty except for a pile of beer cans, a soggy pizza box and a couple of plastic cigar tubes. Jamie and I caught our breath on the tree stumps.

"You get first shot since you're the champ," Jamie said, picking up the pistol. It took him both hands to hold it properly.

"I don't know. Someone's going to hear us out here," I said, looking at the air all around us. "Don't you think Norton could hear a gunshot from his house?"

"Oh, he wouldn't care."

"Yeah, right. He wouldn't care that we're trespassing on his course, running around with a loaded gun."

"I thought you were a member, Mr. Price. Isn't this your course too?"

"You know what I'm talking about."

Jamie lifted the pistol and aimed it at the moon. "What's Norton going to do? Even if he caught us, he wouldn't bust me."

"Well he'd bust me," I said.

"Nah, he's a good guy." Jamie rocked the gun backward, pretending to fire rounds up at the only target bright enough to see. "You know what he told me? He told me we can come over and use his pool whenever we want."

"He did?"

"Yeah. He said I can bring anyone I want. He said it's a waste that nobody ever uses it." Jamie handed me the butt of the gun. "Well, are we going to shoot this thing or not?"

I wrapped my fingers around the handle and as I thought about its weight, dense enough to put holes in all sorts of things, I accidentally pointed the barrel in Jamie's face.

"Christ, watch it," he said, whipping his head back.

"Sorry. It's heavy."

"It's real."

"What's there to shoot at?"

"Just fire one off at the trees over there. That big oak over there, try and hit that."

I stretched two hands out in front of me, pushing the pistol as far away from me as I could get it. I turned my eyes.

"Watch the kick."

I aimed for a tree I couldn't see. My finger felt the cold trigger, and I slowly pulled until I heard the sound of twigs snapping under feet.

"What was that?"

"I don't know," Jamie said, turning in circles and looking everywhere. "I think someone's on the path."

We slid into the woods and hid behind a rotten pile of wet leaves, watching from a distance as Tomato Face and Puddy and a twelve-pack of bottled beer emerged into the clearing. They dropped themselves onto their tree stumps, and Puddy opened two bottles of beer with his keys. They were arguing about something that neither seemed to care much about.

Jamie and I helped each other sneak out of the woods, pushing away branches, feeling our way through the trees and back to the fairway. We agreed to bury the gun deep in a bunker beside the fifteenth green. The moist sand turned in our hands like dough. Jamie pushed the gun down into the dirt and smoothed the sand over the top of it, then we ran from the bunker as if we had wired it to explode.

"I'm not going to be the one who digs it up," I called to Jamie. "And I'm not telling anybody either."

"Well neither am I," he said, and we stopped and shook hands and swore to each other that the gun and our secret would stay there buried. It was for us alone, a little piece of power to keep to ourselves.

We ran the fairways that night, howling across the course like animals, slipping through the trees, hiding from the dark and the shadows and the stars. In the moonlight, the greens on a golf course are all bumps. When the sun is not out to bleach everything flat, the least accidental light colors the grass sideways, the footprints and the wrinkles and the grain showing up like gashes and potholes. The fifteenth green looked like lunar terrain as we sprinted across it. We ran zigzag down the fairways, long shadows leading us up and down the slopes. We stopped to catch our breath at the bathroom off the twelfth tee, a forgotten green shack in the woods that only caddies or the greens crew used. It was sometimes a halfway house for lifers on the skids, and that night we could hear Jeffrey moaning in his sleep.

I followed Jamie around the corner to the bathroom's open doorway, and there was Jeffrey, his sleeping body half in the bathroom, half out, his head resting on the slate walkway. He hummed in his sleep, his lips chewing as he mumbled.

"Should we do something?" I whispered, but Jamie was already taking off his T-shirt. He balled his shirt up into a pile and leaned down and pushed it beneath Jeffrey's head.

Standing there bare-chested, under the moonlight, Jamie looked like he was all ribs, thin and hollow, skin poured over his bones. Maybe it was just the light, the night shadows sideways, the way late evening fairways looked like dunes and foxholes.

MY MOTHER CALLED Casey a moothogue. *Moo*-thogue. It isn't in the dictionary. When I asked her what it meant, she gave me a quiet look, like it would be better for me to guess, and I knew she wouldn't explain it in full because in our house, foggy and broken and mumbled explanations reigned. When words were necessary, we trusted brevity.

"It's Irish," she told me. Things Irish in my home were things that refused reason, things that were too simple and plain, things that didn't move. "Stop being so *Irish*," my mother would sneer at my father. "You're such an Irishman sometimes."

On her good days, her talking, smiling, laughing for hours into the phone days, my mother might spend the morning yelling at Casey. On one of those good days, a morning in early July, the rain rattled across the roof in waves, the air outside going black and cold. It was a good dark day when she railed at Casey for not having a summer job until her voice went thin and airless.

"Timmy's younger than you. He's *smaller* than you," she said. I stepped back into the kitchen doorway, digging my chin into my chest as I listened, wishing she would leave me out of all of it.

I would not usually have been home on a Thursday in the summertime, but the course was closed for the weather. Thunderstorms were kryptonite for a golfer. No one, except the most desperate or drunk, ventured out into a storm with metal rods swinging from their fingertips and metal spikes planted in the soles of their shoes. During lightning, the men's grill would be packed with disappointed players, rounds washed out, afternoons away from the office wasted for three holes and a tableful of Manhattans. Yet they rarely complained about it. They never claimed they could fix it when nature screwed every man in a room full of men who were not accustomed to being screwed, a room where golfers sat with white towels draped over their rain-spotted golf shirts, sipping from frosted glasses and telling stories about a friend of a friend who was struck from scalp to toe down in Boca Raton. They said how lucky they were to get back in when they did, safe, while they watched the outside through plate-glass windows. Patio umbrellas and chairs and branches would skid across the grass, sometimes tumbling toward the glass, sometimes knocking up against it before sliding away like salt brushed from a table. But those who watched from inside didn't flinch when the windows shook. They whistled and they smiled, and they massaged the wetness out of their heavy shoulders.

The storm above our house sounded like cars being dropped from the sky.

"And Timmy works every single day," my mother continued, speaking each word as if it were a distinct revelation, "*every single day,* Casey Patrick Price."

Casey stood across the kitchen table from her. His palms were open flat on the tabletop, his arms pillars holding his shoulders up above her. He didn't blink, I swear to Christ, but his skin boiled, his nose and ears twitching. When her words were all out, there was a loud silence, and as I watched him, I thought the screaming sound of the wind was coming from those eyes. He lifted a hand and slammed it down flat on the table, my mother's pills scattering and falling and clicking across the floor. She said nothing. Her words were over, and this was Casey's turn, and each one of us knew it. He leaned over my mother as if he were trying to smell something, and he paused. One second. His nose almost touching one of her hard dark curls. Two seconds. I watched my mother's hands go white as she clenched the bottom of her seat, and when he turned away from her, I felt a wind, swear to Christ.

Outside, the sky was like night. The air was spinning and the leaves on the trees went from green to white to green, wind howling and waving on the branches. Our small house made its own sounds in the weather. It would groan and yawn, and that would make the walls feel bigger somehow, as if the rooms above us stretched higher and wider than we knew. Yet on a plain day, our home was quiet and small—shrunken almost, without ever feeling crowded.

I had spent most of that morning sitting at the table with my mother, surrounded by candles and flashlights stood up on end, ready, waiting for the electricity to blow out. I read one of my old *Choose Your Own Adventure* books about a trip through the rain forest with a dog named Spink while my mother flipped through one of her *New Yorker*s. Casey was somewhere above us, pacing perhaps, and I imagined his footsteps in each creak, each breeze that bent back the shingles. The candle flames flickered and twisted while I sat there still. When the big bolts hit, my mother's face shook. She rattled her vitamins in her hand like dice and turned page after thin page of a magazine she had probably flipped through a hundred times before. She never read the pages in the middle of *The New Yorker,* the articles thick and crowded with bulky words. She stuck to the reviews of shows, ballets, openings—musicals were her favorite—and she read the critical blurbs, studied the theater addresses all year long for the one Saturday in October when my father would take her on the train, from 30th Street in Philadelphia to Penn Station in New York. Lunch and the show of her choice, and she would come home, walk through the door in her mink wrap, a *Playbill* in her hand and a dead-tired look in her eyes, and she would mumble something about New York being a nice place to visit, New Water being a nicer place to live. I would listen and imagine myself interrupting to tell them the things I had watched Casey do that afternoon—pissing in the corner of the basement, mixing Irish Mist with RC Cola—and what about that green-smelling smoke that poured down from the attic, how it smelled like he was burning shrubs?

"Hold down the fort?" my father would ask, slipping the belt from his pants and flopping down into his chair with a large breath. It was like watching a tire deflate.

And I always said yes, no problems, not a one.

The storm went on all morning, and when Casey came back down the stairs and walked into the kitchen, my mother spoke as if she had forgotten the things that had already been said, and I wanted to hold her head and wrap my hands around her mouth as she started in on *Casey Patrick Price, no summer job for a boy seventeen years old, a simple moothogue on his way to get a bowl of cereal.*

Moothogue. *Mooooothoawg*. It was Irish and lazy and stubborn, and my mother said it was all over my brother.

Her fingers touched her lips as she repeated it. "A *real* moothogue, that Casey Price," she said as he stood directly in front of her. I watched the windows, the water beading up on the glass, and out past the blue droplets, trees blowing and waving like they were calling for help.

I turned to watch Casey take one swift step toward my mother. It was almost invisible. No sound, just a drowning in the roar of water all around us. It was like he was swatting a fly. A snap, *snap,* hard to her cheek, and drawn back in a flash that would have been so easy to forget, a small, small moment, barely even there until it blossomed on her cheek, filled in from pink to a red shine. Casey stood there, looking at her as if she had done it, as if she was the one that made his jaw shake, made his muscles go stiff with hate, made his hand swing at her again as she tried to calm herself with a handful of vitamins.

Before they reached her lips, the pills flew sideways from her hand, rattling across the wood floor, and over the washing water came the sound of a clean, skin-to-skin slap.

I paused for a second, stuck on the clarity of the moment, realizing only as he walked out of the room that I should have strangled him purple until blood poured from his ears.

Instead I took short breaths, and I watched the wind.

On a golf course, when you are stranded in a storm, far from the clubhouse without a shelter in sight, you are in danger—dead, flashes-of-regret danger, the kind that cinches up your throat when you feel how close, how real it is. From a casual three-wood rolling down the fairway to that one crack of thunder, to your bowels going flat as you stand there thinking of the two men who have died on that very course, doing what you are doing at that very moment.

My father and I were trapped one evening in August, a hail and rain and lightning storm rolling in without warning, the heat of the week all pouring out in five minutes, wet and electric and loud enough to split wood. There is a procedure for dealing with a storm, a simple step-by-step to safety when you are stranded too far from shelter and you hear that storm horn from the pro shop echoing in the trees.

All metal must go. Keep your distance from trees. Stay low and stay flat.

We left our cart, tore off our shoes and hurled them as far from us as we could. We ran heads down, out into the middle of the fairway where we lay with our noses to the grass, our arms and legs spread while pebbles of ice bounced off our backs. My father was yelling, "Jesus Mary and Joseph Jesus Mary and Joseph Jesus Mary and Joseph," and I looked to see him next to me, the ice ricocheting off his shoulders and his back and his bare, scalp. He reached out and grabbed my hand and squeezed it like he was trying to wring it dry. He kept his eyes shut. There was a tapping on my back, soft water pinches all over, but on my father there was pounding, a drilling I saw and a deep pain in *jesusmaryandjoseph*. From somewhere on the course came the crack of hot wood, the sound of a tree tearing, branches crashing down, and my father let go of my hand and dug his fingers into the turf. He looked like he might wash away. The rain puddled under us, his words bubbling at his mouth. He dug his hands in deeper until it all stopped as quickly as it had started, and we were safe and dripping from the ears, and he stood and wiped his mouth and grabbed me by the shoulders. His yellow sweater was wet paper on his back, and his fingers were dirty up to the knuckle.

My father looked like he wanted to say something, but his mouth didn't move. He stared at me with copper-colored eyes, his cheeks slick with rain, his hair clumped and tangled. We looked down at our feet, and I smiled at our dirty, soggy socks, wiggling a wet toe, and my father turned without a word to say it was time to go hunt for our shoes.

My mother sat at the table that morning and tried to compose herself, fixing things like my mother did by rubbing her cheeks until they were both red all over. She looked at me standing in the doorway, my toes barely touching the edge of the room.

"Timothy," she started, her voice an awful sort of calm. "Do not tell your father. About this," she said, circling her fingers about, pointing to everything. "This just kills him. It all just *kills* him."

I ran out into the rainstorm, water cold all around me, white flashes clawing sideways across the sky. There was no process, no step-by-step to safety. I looked back at a small house that was dark from the outside, like the lights had finally gone out.

IN

THE NIGHT BEFORE a tournament came with nerves that turned my sheets into cold fingers, kneading my stomach until I got up from no sleep and went downstairs with heavy red eyes and a stomach full of glass. My mother would give me a shirt crisp from the drying line, and I would sit sideways at the breakfast table, a plate of eggs steaming in front of me that I knew I couldn't eat. My mother's eyes would follow mine as I glanced at the bathroom door, the sink, the trash pail beneath the cupboard. As soon as I reached the outside, her morning plate of tenderness would spill out of me, the fresh air jumping down my throat and squeezing me inside out. And she would be watching from the window, and I would hear her voice muffled from the other side of the glass, mumbling gathering up into a yell, then answered by my father's voice with his own *this is my morning off* edge.

He would tell her that she was wrong. He would tell her that it was not his fault his thirteen-year-old son was so nervous he could not keep down her breakfast. It was not his fault, he said, while she beat the kitchen counter with a plastic spoon and said that whatever this game of his was, it wasn't a game for children.

"I never forced him, Meredith. Don't ever say I did, because it is up to that boy, what he wants to do, and what he doesn't want to do, and if he wants to play golf, I will not be the one standing in his way" was what he would say. Sometimes he might add, "And if I got in the way of his opportunity, Lord forgive me. Lord forgive anyone for trying to stop Timothy from doing what he can do out there." He always followed by telling her she did not understand, that she did not play the game, that she was not there to see how people watched, to hear how men talked in the grill and asked my father what he fed me to make me hit a golf ball like that. And then there were times, times when I hoped he thought I wasn't listening, when he might tell her, "That boy is better at that game than I've been at anything in my life," and that might be when his voice bulged in his chest, when my father hit a key that was not right or reasonable but final, when he dropped a fist in his open palm and said, "And I'll be damned if I'm going to let you or me or Casey or a god-damned bad stomach keep him from doing it."

That was when he walked outside and started the Buick, roaring the cold engine until sour clouds spilled black out the tailpipe, and I slid into the passenger seat and looked away from that bitterness swirling in his temples.

And that was when my mother came to the door in her pink robe and yelled to the smoke and tires that my father was as goddamned Irish as a goddamned grudge.

But the morning of the Father-Son Championship was different. The night before I had stayed late at the driving range, hitting nine-irons with Charlie Logan propped up against a bench behind me. His hand pushed his empty Styrofoam cup around in circles, telling me, "Youngest Junior Champion ever, Timmy. Thirteen years old, that's the youngest ever."

The next morning I woke early to a blue iron sky, my parents' morning voices floating up the stairs. I could tell from the soft way they were speaking that they were drinking coffee together, and I hustled down to the kitchen and ate two plates of my mother's eggs and her scrapple, extra crispy.

Casey wasn't at the breakfast table. It had been a week since I'd seen my brother. I had heard him walking, heels knocking across the ceiling above my bed. He had been holed up in the attic since the day of the storm, the day my father never heard about.

I told my mother how Foster Pearse said I only had to be as good as I was, and how that was the easiest thing in the world to do.

She smiled and touched my hand. "That sounds like good advice."

My father shook his head. "I told you that."

"You did?"

"Sure," my father said, nibbling the blackest meat off the edge of his bacon. "I've always said that."

But what my father always said was *Is that good enough for you? As long as you are satisfied with that, I guess that must be good enough.*

On our ride to Fox Chase, my father and I spoke about our team strategy, how one of us had to zig while the other zagged. He talked about the possibilities and our chances, and he sounded impatient about this tournament, upset almost, as if he realized that this might finally be a day for the Prices, and that there should have been one long ago.

When I went to change my shoes at the trunk of the car, my father stopped me.

"This isn't a public course," he said. "A partner of mine uses the locker room."

He led me down a bright hallway filled with steam and the moan of an old vacuum cleaner. The smell was shaving cream and pine, and the lockers were tall wooden cabinets with brass nameplates, clean padded benches between them. In the corner of the room, a man with strands of black hair pasted across his scalp sat at a counter. Colored bottles, piles of unlaced shoes and a loud-looking buffing machine lined the wall behind him.

"Morning, Mr. Price," the man said. He was on the fat side of stout with a wide Italian face, and his fingers were black with polish. When his mouth moved, his chin rolled and unrolled on the top of his chest.

"Morning, Bobby," my father said, slipping off his street shoes and placing them on the counter. They shared a laugh about a George Tanner, who had been waiting by the clubhouse door at six o'clock that morning.

"I'll tell ya," said Bobby, speaking from the side of his mouth, "that guy's gotta be freaking homeless, Mr. Price. He's here when we're closed, for cripe's sake."

My father pinched up his face and laughed. I chuckled along.

"I'll tell you what, Bobby, you'd know why if you met his wife."

"Is that right? So it's the old lady. I knew something wasn't right there. So he's got himself a real tiger lady, huh?"

My father smiled, then looked down at me and shushed me off toward a row of lockers. As I started to walk away, I heard Bobby say, "Enjoy your round, Mr. Price. And Mr. Price, congratulations there on the big win."

My father tugged me by the shoulder to turn around, "Timmy, Bobby's speaking to you."

"Hey, congratulations," Bobby said, holding his large hand over the counter. I turned back to shake it, his skin worn smooth like the pocket of a catcher's mitt. "Name looks perfect on the plaque in there. Someone needed to shake that Dane kid up a little, ya know what I mean?"

I smiled and said thank you and wondered why, to Bobby behind the counter, my father and I were both Mr. Price. It was either pity or guilt that I felt, because there was something very sad about that big man tucked back in his corner, the wall behind him holding too much shine for too many shoes, but no polish for a shoe-shine guy.

My father put on his spikes and told me he had to sign us in at the pro shop, so I could go putt or loosen up and meet him on the first tee. He went one way, so I headed in the other, this big house of empty hallways whispering to me to come explore, to come push on these petrified doorways. There was a room somewhere where *my* name was hanging, where Bobby said the letters looked perfect.

I headed down a musty dark hall to a door with a bronze sign lettered in polite script, GENTLEMEN ONLY PLEASE. I pushed it open, peeked around the corner like a burglar and stepped in toe first, testing the water.

The grill room was empty of people and morning cold. There were red wood tables, tall leather chairs, a silver stone fireplace. A long window covered one whole side of the room and looked out over the eighteenth green. The smell was licorice and cigars. With the lights off and the sun just beginning to color the clouds, shadows spread across the room, shadows that did not begin or end with the furniture or the walls or the black marble bar, as if they were somehow part of the decor. White faces dotted the walls, men with long foreheads and waxy eyes behind the glass, golden placards beneath their pictures telling what it was they began or continued. It was like a museum, quiet and cold, and in some ways airless.

I froze when I saw them—two dark eyes shining at me from above the bar. I thought a fox from the course had sneaked into the room, a trespasser like me, but then I saw that it was mounted dead on dark wood. The orange fur was dusty and splotches of hair had turned the color of smoke. Its skinny legs were painted white, its mouth pried open to show a thin row of teeth—they made it look like something that would snatch a child from your yard. There was nothing left of the twitching ears and fast paws I had seen two years before. The trophy was plastic and carpet and stuffed bigger than the animal I remembered.

I walked over to where antique clubs hung in the corner, ancient golf balls packed with goose feathers displayed beneath protective glass. I could hear the green carpet crunching beneath my feet as I stepped over to the longest wall, the one without windows where the championship plaques all hung in a row, *Club Champion, Team Champions, Senior Champion, Match Play Champion, Member-Guest Champion,* all the success there to be touched, hanging side by side by side.

I walked over to a plaque that read *Fox Chase Country Club— Junior Champion.* The letters of my name were dug into a strip of black metal, *Timothy Price* etched with a thin tin gleam. The metal was screwed to a plaque of red wood, the edges caked with a cottony layer of dust. Above my name came sixty-two prior junior champions, and below it came more blank black strips screwed tightly in line.

I put my fingers to my name, and the corners of the letters were still sharp. My name was right below *Myles Dane,* which was right below *Myles Dane.* Junior champion on a wall of champions, in a room I had never seen before, that I sneaked in and out of while the morning was still orange and wet. As I left the room, I had the feeling that I would not be back in there again for many years, not until I was a *Gentleman Only Please,* and until then it was all theirs, the smell, the view, the names engraved up and down their walls. I wondered if mine would still be there when I came back, if they would really leave it alone, untouched, *Timothy Price* just the same.

I went outside to the scoreboard and read *Myles and Norman Dane, Jimmy and James Sr. Shaw, James and Timothy Price* written in pairs on a large score sheet.

"Well, we've got our work cut out for us, partner," my father said, squinting up at the names written in red marker, the thick letters curly and smudged. Eighteen empty boxes followed each name. *James Price* and *Timothy Price* and then blanks, and I stood there envisioning the numbers that would fill those spaces, fixing the sum, plus or minus, weighing it for what it might be worth at the end of the day. And the idea came to me that plaques with black plates and golden letters were for decoration, that white sheets with red numbers were what everyday people looked to every day.

In our foursome, two Prices, two Danes. We loosened up on the first tee, the fairway ahead of us a hazy green runway. Mr. Dane looked fresh from the weight room, tan arms cut with muscles and bowling balls for shoulders. The cords in his back popped when he twisted and stretched.

Next to Norman Dane, my father was a humorous aside. His yellow sweater dangled at his hips as he took small, unassuming practice swings. He offered a genuine smile. He wished everyone good luck.

Myles Dane looked straight ahead when his father congratulated me.

"You've been playing well, Timmy. You're having a helluva season," Mr. Dane said. "You sure taught this kid a lesson, I'll tell you that much. I'd say Myles owes you a thanks."

Myles smiled at his feet, and he didn't say thank you even though his father had a voice that sounded like he had found a gym machine where he could do reps with his throat. Norman Dane had a big, check-this-out swing, an arc that went ten degrees past parallel and whipped back with an elastic snap, the ball swept away like a magic trick, now you see it, now you don't.

The tournament format was selective drive, alternate shot, medal play. Father and son both teed off, the better drive would be chosen, and the partners would alternate shots until the ball was holed. Two players, one ball, one number on the wall at the end of the day. It was a format built for dissension and blame and apologies.

In the group in front of us, Mr. Norton had taken a cart because he was playing with his daughter, Amanda. I watched him call Jamie up from the caddy hole that morning to apologize.

"Had to take a cart today, captain. Amanda's mother would kill me if she saw her little girl walking the course with all us *men*," he said, knocking the bill of Jamie's hat to the side. He put his hand to his mouth and mumbled, "I do this once a year. Whole thing's sort of a joke. She's not a bad little player, but if I had a young man in the house like yourself, well, this Father-Son thing would make a little more sense."

Norton laughed, and Jamie smiled and nodded politely, and Norton handed his caddy a five-dollar bill.

"Five?" I asked as the cart pulled away, Amanda sitting next to her father with her brown hair pulled back into a short ponytail.

"Yeah," Jamie said. "He always hits me with five bucks when I bring up his bag."

"Must be nice," I said.

Jamie tucked the money into his back pocket. "It is."

Out on the first fairway, I grabbed my eight-iron and stepped to where my father's drive had rolled to a stop. My father stood to my far right, anxiously digging a heel into the grass. His drive had been the shorter, but it was in play. Better to have me approach with an eight-iron than my father hit from where my drive had landed, eighty yards out, a tough in-betweener, closer than any approach shot he was used to. Mr. Dane's drive was long and wrong, deep in the left trees, but Myles's ball was a wedge away.

Turn, and return, and I pured the ball, a thin divot of turf cut from the fairway and turning end over end toward the pin. We watched the ball drop and check next to the hole, jumping back like it was a yo-yo I'd snapped with my finger.

"Golf shot," said Mr. Dane. It was what they said out there after a quality shot—*golf shot*—another expressionless golf expression, as if there were other kinds of shots on a golf course.

Dried and double cut, the first green was like putting on glass. Both teams lagged and made pars, and the Prices and Danes stayed even with each other through the first seven holes. My father kept his drives in play, I swung for the fences. We zigged and zagged pretty well, each taking care of the other and steering away from the *ker-plunk*-in-a-pond type mistakes. Myles dumped an approach shot into a Hail Mary bunker on the eighth hole, and he and his father took turns cursing and failing to scoop it out—junior calling father worthless, then father calling son a spoiled little shit, then son kicking sand at dad until they walked off the green with an eight, the dreaded snowman. Our team made the turn leading by two.

On the fifteenth hole, my father stuck our approach shot dead in the center of that bunker, and I felt myself look around for Jamie, watching down the tree line and seeing no one. I took a hard slap at the ball, floating it up to the tip of the bunker's edge, where it hit and stopped and rolled back down the bank and into my footprint. We walked off that hole with a double bogey, and we did not argue or discuss, afraid to admit out loud that we were up by only one shot.

We went par, birdie, bogey, par. They went bogey, par, birdie, par. Still up by one, one to go, and the match went a wonderful sort of quiet, pure competition, two runners stretching their necks at the tape.

The eighteenth hole was a par five that first rolled down and then climbed up, bending left around the woods on the way back up to the green. My drive was 270 off the screws, and we decided that my father would hit the second shot. But when he stepped over the ball, he looked resolved to be unresolved about what he was going to do, and he dribbled an ugly worm-burner, his three-wood chunking up a brick of dirt. The ball skipped along the grass and died in the rough.

"Sorry. Sorry, sorry, sorry sorry sorry," he said, almost singing it as his head swung back and forth. He apologized, not as if the shot was a mistake but that he simply couldn't help it.

I laid our next shot up in front of the green, but my father, a look on his face like this four hours of effort was hardly worth a breath, went ahead and chili-dipped his pitch shot into a bunker.

It was not failure. It was worse. It was success at losing, defeat the safe idea that he sold himself on and went out and

accomplished. Practicing out on the putting green one morning, Charlie Logan had told me three successive times that *losing is just the fear of winning,* and I watched that fear in brown
golf shoes walk off the eighteenth that day, a snowman in the
last box on our scorecard. The Danes made bogey, and they were
braver by one.

We shook hands, and Myles smiled as if it were bound to
happen.

My father said it was a tough one. One of the toughest.

"What can you do?" he said, dropping his shoes on the locker-
room floor, slowly folding his socks. "We were having a lot of
luck out there, Timmy. It just caught up with us. Sometimes
the other team is just better. That's nothing to be embarrassed
about. We gave it a shot."

The sun was still high when we pulled up to the house. My
father parked the Buick in the driveway, the black car soaking up the light, bright but not shining. I waited for him to go
up the steps and walk through the front door before I dropped
my bag on the driveway, reaching into the front pocket for a
ball. I teed it up, there in the front yard, and I saw my father
standing bored and Irish in front of me, arms crossed, leaning
back against a car still glowing from the Simoniz. I lifted my
driver from my bag and ripped at that white ball like I might
crush it into dust. And this time, the ball made it to the car,
smashing the passenger-side window into a puzzle of a thousand opaque pieces.

Casey came down from the attic that night for the first time in
days. He burst into my room and punched me in the ear and
held me by a fistful of throat.

"What the hell was that all about? What the shit did you think you were doing? You busted the fucking car, fuck-face."

He twisted my nipple until I cried, then punched me twice in the shoulder. He asked me if our father had gotten ahold of me. He wanted to know if I was a dead man.

I should have told him what our father looked like when he quit. I should have explained that fathers were not supposed to be that way, not to their sons. Fathers did not shrink, not when you were thirteen. They did not fold.

I told Casey I was settling a bet, a gentleman's bet, and this dead man in his hands was a winner.

THE MINI-STATE of Delaware is a microcosm of the entire East Coast. From the beaches down in Bethany on up through the farms and the single-lane thruways and the lazy drawl of a south Delaware tongue, through the capital in Dover to the city of Wilmington and on up into Philadelphia, Delaware is Georgia and Carolina and the beaches, up through to D.C., up into the big cities and the faster-moving money. The people south and north in Delaware understood each other as Southerner and Northerner did everywhere—as the same, but then a little bit different, and each a little suspicious of how big those differences might be on the things that really mattered.

Delaware is a small state, but the tournament field for the Boys' State Championship that year was large and unpleasant. Players from downstate, from chicken farm and NASCAR country, came north with ability and attitude, jaws set firmly on the idea of whipping the city boys, the private-schoolers who played the best courses up where it rained money, where cash was stuffed into suburban Wilmington by tax-dodging corporations and a Du Pont family that seemed to include everyone.

I knew that my chances at states were solid. My swing felt tighter with every week, while Myles Dane, my main competition, had given up on practice after the Father-Son. He started to let his hair grow long and began smoking cigarettes in front of the members, and soon I was the one all the whispers were guessing about. Myles and I shook hands that morning of the state tournament, a quiet relief between us in both of us knowing that he probably would not beat me. We said good luck like boys, laughing and not believing each other, shaking our heads to show that all the proving had been done.

I shot 70 and beat the field by four strokes. Mr. Dane looked on as Myles finished his round, parring eighteen to shoot 76, fourth place. The man said nothing this time, crossing his arms in front of him, his heavy shoulders unbalanced, crooked in a begrudging surrender.

The paper said that I was the youngest ever to win the state championship. The article was headlined THE PRICE IS RIGHT, and the lead read: *There's something new in New Water. It's tall and lanky with a swing as pure as gold bullion, as fine as French wine. But this vintage is only thirteen years old. . . .* My mother taped the clipping to the refrigerator, where it would stay for years, curling and unsticking and turning yellow.

An envelope came in the mail addressed to THE PARENTS OF TIMOTHY PRICE and stamped in red block letters URGENT. My instinct was to hide it at the bottom of the trash, but I handed it over to my mother like it was a shard of one of her china plates. That night, my father spilled the envelope's contents out in front of me.

"Everybody gets an opportunity, Timothy," he told me, a glossy golf-camp brochure open on the coffee table between us. There were pictures of happy junior golfers set in perfect backswings, effort strong on their faces, and a picture of a pine clubhouse that looked like a church, glass and wood, a pool that turned in four different sections. "Not everybody takes advantage of their opportunities," he said. There was a letter with the brochure, congratulating me on winning the Delaware Boys' Championship and inviting me to *ten days of the finest youth golf instruction in the country, for players who have distinguished themselves as the premier talent in their region.* I stared at the brochure and wondered what premier really meant, better than good, imagining who decided, who knew me, and not sure why I could not find anything in those bright slippery pictures that looked anything like myself.

The price of the camp was more than my father had planned to spend on our entire family vacation. When I pointed that out, he spoke about investment and commitment, and how he was willing to pay for work and effort because that was where the good things came from.

"We'll save a family trip for next year. Your mother wanted to stay around here this summer anyway. She thought it would be best. And your brother, well . . ." he said, scratching the back of his hand. "We'll wait, if this is what you want to do. It sounds like a great thing, a chance to measure yourself against the *real* talent. Those kids down there," he said, spreading the brochure out like a fan, "these boys play all year-round. There are good players around here, don't get me wrong, but if you want to see what you've got in that bag of yours. . . ." He snapped his newspaper open and talked at me through the business section. "It's up to you, Timmy. It's just an idea."

It was his way of not pushing me, but the plane ticket was already in the mail. I would go to North Carolina, to prove how good I wasn't.

Foster Pearse and I stood side by side, hitting balls out into his scorched field. When the balls landed you could almost hear the grass breaking, the turf coughing up bursts of dust. Foster wore cut-off madras slacks hemmed with masking tape, and his hair was pulled back into a frazzled knot at the bottom of his neck. I would hit a slice and Foster would hit a hook, and we tried to time our swings so that the balls would knock into each other in midair. I hit first and let Foster chase after it, a fade shot hanging longer in the air than a draw.

We hit away without success or much conversation until I asked Foster if it was true that he had won the U.S. Amateur when he was nineteen.

"Nope," he said. "I shot eighty-four in the qualifier. Just missed the cut . . . by thirteen strokes."

I punched a cut into the air, and to my right Foster wrist-snapped a hook, a jet just zipping by the nose of my ball.

"Though I did set a record I don't think anyone in that tournament's broken."

"Highest score?" I laughed.

"You're hilarious," he said. "I had two holes-in-one in that round."

I turned and looked at Foster, his eyes watching a ball arc across the sky. "Pretty cool, huh?" he said. "You ever had one?"

"No. I've been close though."

"Horseshoes and hand grenades, Timmy." He chuckled. "There's nothing like slam-dunking a golf ball from two hundred yards away. It's so sort of . . . perfect. When the ball goes in, there's this moment when you just feel totally in tune to something. I swear it's spiritual. It's like kissing God. With an open month."

I sorted through Foster's range balls for one that didn't have a smile cut into its cover.

"You had two holes-in-one, and you shot eighty-four?"

Foster looked back over his shoulder and smiled. "Let's just say that at that point in my life, I was a very different person. The funny thing about that tournament is that nobody asks me about the holes-in-one—*that* actually happened, but nobody knows about it. They all come up here asking me shit like, did I ever get run off a golf course in Vegas? Or how's the golf in Fiji? Or did I really win the Japanese Masters? I don't even think there *is* a Japanese Masters. It's amazing the stories people will come up with if you just don't talk about yourself. That's the best self-promotion going, keeping your mouth shut."

We switched sides. I hit the draw shot and Foster the fade, but still no collision. We switched sides again, back and forth for most of the hour.

"Do you still enjoy it?" I asked him.

"What's that?"

"Golf. Is it still fun for you?"

Foster stopped and thought for a moment, then looked at me like I was the only person who knew he wasn't crazy.

"Worst fun I ever had."

Toward the end of the hour, before my father could lean on the horn to tell me to get in the car, I told Foster I wouldn't be coming by for the next few weeks. I told him I was taking a trip, and I asked him if he'd ever heard of a place called Pine Acres golf camp.

When I launched my fade up into the air, I didn't see a draw shot there to match it. I looked over and saw Foster turned around, leaning on his eight-iron and staring at me.

"*Pine Acres golf camp?* What is that, one of those golf factories where they stamp out studs for the college teams?"

"I think it's just a place to take lessons—"

"That's very impressive, Timmy," he interrupted, flipping his club to the ground. "I think that's a real smart move. I think you're just too damn good a player to be a real individual, you should sign up with the pack. Then you can play their game and be just like them."

"I don't understand," I said, looking back to where my father was watching from the front seat of the Buick, where I'm sure he could see Foster shaking his head at me.

"Exactly," Foster said, "you don't understand. You don't understand a thing I've tried to teach you up here. You want to learn from them, you go learn from them. Go learn how to be a champ, go and collect your trophies. Then maybe they'll turn you into one."

Foster gazed out at the field and caught his breath, then bent down and gathered up the remaining balls into a bag. "Time's up Timmy," he said. "When you get back from your little trip, don't bother coming back here."

He wasn't looking at me as he turned and headed for the house, and the lesson was over before my father even had a chance to honk the horn.

* * *

Telling Jamie about Pine Acres went only slightly better.

"What the hell is a golf camp?" he said when I told him about my trip. It was early on a Tuesday morning and we were down in the hole, hoping to catch a loop before the August sun came out and dried up the afternoon.

"What do you do, roast marshmallows with your putters?" Jamie said.

"I think you just practice and get lessons, and then you all play a tournament at the end. It's only for ten days."

Jamie picked up a broken tee off the floor and tossed it at my head. "Well, what am I gonna do for ten days? It's supposed to be a hundred degrees all week. It's going to be dead around here."

I told Jamie I would bring him back a souvenir. He told me, "Just bring back some good stories."

And I would. I would come back with a forward press in my swing that I didn't need, a new pause at the top of my backswing, all my bolts tightened a quarter turn. I would come back with orange leather skin and a loud boneache in my fingers. I would come back and the heat would be punishing, and they would be talking about Jamie Byrne taking some sort of vacation, a little time off, a few days gone.

I would come back and find myself on the wrong side of thirteen. For all I would see in those ten days, something would blow through Fox Chase that no one saw at all.

NORTH CAROLINA STARTED with pine trees back in the shadows along the road, straight and bare and the color of oil. The trunks poked through a forest floor of long needles, woven into a carpet that sizzled orange-red.

I sat quietly as the van from the airport wound its way through the woods. The driver introduced himself as Jimmy Niles, a short college-aged boy with purple skin on the tips of his ears and nose. The strips of sunburn beneath his eyes looked like bacon. Jimmy said he was fourth man on the East Carolina Pirates, and when I said I had never heard of East Carolina, he blew breath from his mouth like I was the most ignorant kid he'd ever met.

"Wheww, not from around here, are you? East Caralina Pirates, fourth-best golf team in the You-nited States last year. That's the north *and* the southern parts."

The ride could have been silent, but there was golf to talk about. There was always golf, only golf. Weather, clothes, cars, family—everything measured and discussed in relation to the game. For others it might be an Indian summer, but for us it was bonus golf, another hole and another round before the snow. It was not a new Suburban that fit the family or a Porsche 944, it was room for a foursome's clubs, or not damn near enough space for your sticks. It was not a family of five or a baby on the way, it was a sorry bastard who had better get his wife a beach house, or a poor guy who didn't yet understand that his best golf was behind him.

Jimmy and I talked without looking at each other. I stared outside at the trees whipping past, the pine branches blurring into a web of black and light. We talked of favorite courses and our best shots. When I asked him what his handicap was, he wrinkled his face and thought for a while. "I haven't actually used one in a while. Probably plus a couple."

That was when I knew that this was where golf was. I watched closely, noted every golf condo, read every word of every billboard for courses and clubs and shops and discount golf warehouses. Here I was next to a Jimmy Niles from a part of Carolina I had not known existed, a kid who was giving shots back to par, a player better then the golf course who was *fourth* man, driving a van for the premier talents with a look on his face like he was just so happy to be fourth. I knew North Carolina wasn't just a step up. It was a first step too.

We wound our way through the trees, moving around the swamps, the road wrapping itself through the woods like a vein, pulsing toward the heart of golf. There was wet heat all around us, stillness everywhere except for the breeze of stale vent air blowing on my face. We were the only thing moving at that moment in that part of the world.

The van rolled up a brick drive, passing beneath an entryway carved from an unbroken slab of pine tree that read PINE ACRES.

The place had the tight, careful look of a home for golf, and I stepped from the van and watched the young players with clubs jingling from their shoulders, so serious as they bounced from building to building, all rushing to play, all in a giant hurry to get better, to find out what came after *premier*.

This was golf, and golf smelled like sap and flowers and a little bit of swamp, and golf was full of long buzzing bugs that stung and zipped by in a haze of yellow.

I was showed to a room in villa #9, a small khaki-colored cottage where one of my roommates called me a Yankee. His name was Frankie Pepper, *everybody calls me Pepp*. Our suite had long cedar closets, two beds and two cots tucked into the corners. It was summer camp with carved soaps and a triangle fold at the end of the toilet paper. I dropped my bags on a cot and watched my other roommates laugh and punch one another, giggling secretly about what they had gotten away with the summer before.

I recognized the tallest of the three boys, Whitman Carlsby. The brochure opened to show his face next to a tall crystal trophy, the caption *Two-Time Camp Champion* beneath his smile. His shoulders were wide and square, and he was handsome like a man, a slight brown shadow of stubble already on his cheeks. Frankie Pepper call me Pepp paid most of his attention to Whitman, while the other boy, Deck Williams, lay on his bed laughing at the other two. Pepp spoke with a heavy drawl, his tongue sloshing around in his mouth. Whitman's accent was subtle and refined, and Deck Williams spoke with an exaggerated California disbelief. It was all *oh my God,* everything *unreal, outrageous* and *bogus.* He had the perfectly placed patch of bright blond hair hanging over his eyes, and his father had finished in the top ten that year on the PGA money list. My roommates looked older than thirteen, aside from Frankie Pepper, who was short and soft and bouncing around the room, groping for attention with all the unrest of a child trapped in a backseat on a long trip.

His stomach flopped up and down as he hopped on the bed, saying, "So where you from, Yankee?"

"New Water. It's a town in Delaware. It's near Philadelphia, sort of a suburb."

"Delaware? Ain't nothin' in Delaware I ever heard of. Y'all ever heard of anything in Delaware?"

The other two snickered as if they knew where this was going.

"Delaware? Is that a state?" Pepp said.

"Yeah. Actually, it was the first state."

"*Actually?* Listen to the Yankee—*actually.*" He drew the word out in a bad British accent. "What kind of kid talks like that?"

"Don't pay attention to him," Whitman said to me, smiling. "He gets a little too excited 'bout being a Southerner. Thinks the war's still on sometimes."

"Goddamn, war still is on. Hell, spooks runnin' the country 'cause a them Yanks like Mr. Delaware over there. Not our fault this country's turnin' to a pile of shit. South had nothin' to do with that."

Deck laughed and clutched a pillow. "Dude, Pepp, you are totally fucking whacked."

"Kiss my ass, Declan. I'm telling ya, Frankie Pepper don't cross words, tell you that for certain," he said. You could almost see someone else's lips moving on his face, someone older and more swollen than Frankie who might be called Pepp too, someone who convinced young Pepper that it was best to act twice your size.

He bounced higher and higher, spinning as he turned, the bed wincing and tossing him back up with a metal squeak.

"What war?" I asked. I honestly didn't know. Wars were over. We were born at the end of Vietnam, but even that war was never entirely real, just a vague sense of mistreatment that lingered in movies with tired-looking helicopters and angry Green Berets, a true fiction about soldiers left behind, bad blood, black and white flags.

Pepp stopped the bouncing. "What war? What *war*? What they teach you boys up there in Delaware City? The fucking war of all wars, man. The war of Northern fucking aggression."

"He's talking 'bout the Civil War," Whitman said. "And Pepper, you can shut your damn hole about all that. Making us Southerners sound like a bunch of rubes, ya jackass."

"Hey, I'm just having some fun with the boy, Whitman," he said, changing his tone. "Just giving the new guy a little heat, no problems here."

Pepper extended his tan hand. It was fleshy and felt like a palm full of pudding.

"Welcome to North Carolina, my great home state. Whitman there's from Georgia, but it's not his fault. Kid hits the ball like a fucking animal. That sonofabitch there was born to play golf."

"First thing out a your mouth made sense all day," Whitman said, his eyes on me. "So where'd you say you play at?"

"It's called Fox Chase, in New Water."

"Uh-huh," he said, unimpressed. "And where's that? D'you say you play in Delaware, or Philadelphia, or, what'd you say?"

"New Water, that's the town, in Delaware, but the closest city is Philadelphia, or Wilmington, but it's really a Philadelphia suburb."

"Philadelphia's connected to Delaware?" Pepper said.

"Well, sort of, I guess."

"So do you tell folks you're from Philadelphia, or Delaware?" Whitman said.

I thought for a second.

"Ya see, where you're from, now that's one thing I would not want to be unsure about. That's a pretty big thing." Whitman laughed. "I didn't mean to confuse you."

"It depends," I said. "I guess it depends who's asking. Some people don't know where Delaware is. Some people think it's a city," I said, looking at Pepp, who wasn't paying attention but flexing his flabby white biceps in the mirror.

"Well the real question is, how do you play?" Whitman said, looking at me sideways. Pepper looked over from the mirror where he was flexing the meat on his chest, his chin wiggling with the effort. Deck propped himself up on a pillow and set his eyes on mine.

"Well?"

"I guess that's what I'm here to find out," I said.

Frankie Pepper let out one hard *Ha!*

"You will," he said. "You sure as shit will."

The putting green at Pine Acres was the size of a pond. The driving range was perfection, flat and long and wide, with nameplates and bright white boards sectioning off each camper's hitting space. There were acres of tight green grass to hit from, and when it rained we could back up beneath sheds, keep the work on, keep the gears cranking and the shoulders turning. There were heaters in the shed for winter lessons. There was an outdoor studio for film work, for pictures and fifty freeze-frames of each position in your swing, every moment from address to follow-through, and there were dozens of staff in white shirts, shuttling balls back and forth, tan instructors in green shirts flipping through piles of photographs, fast-forwarding through films, tweaking turns, discussing planes and angles and V's and the elusive *first move*. There was effort everywhere, shiny foreheads damp from the heat and hard with the work of the game.

Southern heat was different. It was like walking into a sponge, tougher to breathe. The ground had a hot sandy crunch to it. The sun hissed white, and white arms went pink.

I saw Jimmy Niles in a group of the other counselors at the end of the range. They leaned on their clubs and watched each other swing, laughing and whistling and clapping and laughing some more. They were real college players, their bags embroidered with STATE this, UNIVERSITY OF that, headcovers from the U.S. Amateur. They played the type of golf that made careers, and they watched as someone in the group would take his backswing, pause at the top, then wait for someone to call out a shot—*low fade, high hook, knock it down, dead straight,* then execute that shot on demand from the top of their backswing. And when some of them did, it looked just like magic.

I watched Jimmy Niles shank a prescribed high cut, then dig into his pocket for a few bills, handing them over to a tall blond counselor who rubbed Jimmy's hair like he was one of the precocious talents spread down the edge of the driving range.

"Let's beat some balls," Whitman said as he passed behind me with a tall bucket in each hand, his bag strapped across his back like a quiver.

I settled in at my slot, spilled over a bucket of freshly washed balls and breathed in deeply, looking out at the range, the distances marked with white marble stones. There were none of the sagging white flags they had at the range at Fox Chase, but there was grass and there were balls, and the grips of my clubs felt soft in the warmth, my fingers melting into the rubber.

I did what I was supposed to do. From first to last ball, it was just play. My ears were full of the clicking and ripping of steel through soil, the pure and premier all around me, better or worse or whatever they were. I stood with shoulders full of balance and, with swing after swing after swing, it all slipped away, leaving me alone and content, not even watching where the shots were going because they were right in my hands. The sweat was good, oil bleeding beneath my arms and dripping down my sides, more sweat than there was up in New Water.

I stopped to dry my grips between my legs, wiping my forehead on my collar. Deck Williams was standing behind me, his eyes wide.

"Dude, where'd you say you played?"

"Delaware. The town's called New Water. The course is called Fox Chase," I said.

And soon after there was Pepp with Deck, now quiet with a dumb twinkie smile. Then a few more campers, then a group of counselors. It was Fox Chase again, Timothy Price the driving-range freak show. No one said I was pure, no one whistled. The silence was steam, some bitter perhaps at what they had found. No one said anything, not until Jimmy Niles's voice came in the middle of my backswing. "High cut."

And I saw a high cut behind my eyes, just before I dropped my body into the ball and saw the shot taking off, a ball climbing up the face of the humidity and sliding gently off to the right.

"Low hook."

And then there was a ball cruising low, hardly hanging above the grass, ducking left as if it were taking cover.

I stood on my left foot, swing, clicked a five-iron out at the 150 marker.

I stood on my right foot, swing, clicked one that hit the 175 marker, bouncing high into the air.

"How good is *that*," said Jimmy Niles.

I turned around to see some of the younger players gaping, the older ones behind them with doubt and competition and sweat rolling down their foreheads. The counselors at the edges laughed and slapped each other's shoulders as if they had just found a new toy. And there was one face there that was surrounded by brown hair bunched in soft curls. Hair just past her shoulders, cinnamon-colored shoulders slick with suntan lotion. Green eyes and peach-colored cheeks, and she smiled to say she knew I saw her. She was the first to walk away, shaking her hair off to the side, legs swimming past each other that looked like they were poured from her short round skirt.

I hardly noticed the next feet to go stomping off, Whitman Carlsby with a look like he had just watched nothing, the first of them back to work all the harder.

Premier, I was learning, was a small, crowded word.

There was breakfast, putting, instruction, lunch, putting, eighteen holes, rules seminar, course-management session, dinner, and then night sessions at the driving range, fluorescent lights in the muggy evening that brought out the long yellow mosquitoes. Before bed there was film work, a review of our swings, marking improvements, highlighting regression, putting the pieces together day by day by day. The staff gave me a few pointers, angle your foot this way, dip a shoulder here, move a finger there, but most of them just watched and nodded. When Jimmy Niles watched me swing, he always said, "How good is *that*," and one of the teaching pros with aviator sunglasses introduced himself as an assistant coach at the University of South Carolina. When the man smiled, I saw small brown teeth that were rounded like candies he'd sucked for hours.

"*Gamecocks.* Helluva program we got down there. Now I want you to hold on to this, Timmy," he said, handing me his card, "and I want you to give me a call from time to time and let me know how you're doing. You need to use my name to get into any tournaments, I want you to feel free. And when you start thinking about college, you remember us down here. Friendly place to play, not a bad place to go to school either. You look to me like the kinda player who's gonna deserve a full-tuition scholarship, with a good word from a friend from Pine Acres."

He showed me into the clubhouse and walked me down a hallway covered with pictures of past camp champions, players who had gone on to Division I programs, guys who made a nice living on the tour. "Take a look around, Timmy. You're in some fine company here."

The black-and-white photos showed boys in crew cuts swinging old wooden-faced drivers, their bodies bowed in long fluid follow-throughs. Some of the pictures were of kids with high curly hair, butterfly collars and bell-bottoms above their saddle shoes, and one of those faces I recognized, a boy who went on to win the United States Open.

I looked down the plaque of past champions, and the names burned into the dark wood read like a PGA leader board. But there was a name there that stuck out from the others, a name the man from South Carolina might have known nothing about, a name that was written there more times than any of the others—next to *1970, 1971, 1972,* I read *Foster Pearse, Foster Pearse, Foster Pearse.*

The ten days flew by the way summer days do, but they were more than golf because there was Angela. Angela Ray, the girl from the driving range. She was sixteen and she talked to me when there were breaks for lunch or snacks or an early evening swim.

"You look older than thirteen," she told me. "You're taller than me. And you talk like a regular gentleman, Timmy Price."

She was a vegetarian, and she said that made her something of an individual. Her father was a plastic surgeon in Savannah. "Now I don't have the slightest interest in being much of a golfer myself. Every summer Daddy makes them try to turn me into a superstar, and it just kills him that they can't. But you," she said, "now you are really something. Northern boy, coming down here and showing these fellas up. Don't you think it's exciting?"

I felt my breath move with the waves in her drawl, up and down and settling on her lips. I did not say much at first. I told her she was the nicest person at the camp, the nicest person in the entire South. I gave her a flower I snapped from the top of a reed at the edge of the water. She laughed when I told her she was beautiful.

We ate our meals together. She held my hand and talked and it was a nice voice to listen to.

"Timmy, you *are* different," she told me. "Do you see the way some of these boys look at you? I swear, it's like they love you, and they hate you. It is the most fascinating thing. And I do not believe that you even care one eyelash about what they think. Boys in Delaware, they must all be so mature."

I never did try to explain to her how I was not mature but afraid, not an adult but a kid whose idea of adult was a plodding numbness to the things that might hurt you. I did not tell her that I was afraid of everything but golf, not as we walked together after lights-out. Instead we talked about our hometowns. We told a few stories about our families. She said she felt sorry for my brother, and I thought that made her the kindest person in the world.

When Whitman Carlsby saw us together, he looked straight at her, his eyes small, shaking his head like we were a grave mistake.

"Don't mind Whitman," she said. "We used to be a bit of an item. Last summer—you know how things happen and go on, Timothy, specially in the summertime. Now, if he gives you trouble, you just remember." She brought her face closer, her skin like soap against mine, "You just remember me."

I felt her hair fall down around my cheeks, the scent of strawberry and suntan lotion. Her lips were water against my face, a small space of soft heat.

It's the breathing I remember, the sound of it close in my ear, how warm it was that first time, when her breath was all mixed up with mine.

Whitman Carlsby turned me into a void, an empty space in the cot in the corner. Pepper would joke with me, punching me in the arm when he made cracks about Whitman's girl, and Deck laughed too much. We were scarfing down hot dogs between practice sessions when Deck asked me how I'd found out about Pine Acres.

"A brochure came in the mail," I said. "They said it was an invitation or something."

"Right. You must have won something big this year."

"Well, I won the Delaware Boys'."

"That was probably it. That's how they got your name."

"States' a big-time win." Pepper spoke, a pink chunk of pork mushed up in his mouth. "How old are you? Fifteen?"

"Thirteen."

"Dude, you're thirteen years old? Jesus, man. Thirteen?"

"Why," I said. "How old are you guys?"

"I'm sixteen," Deck said. "Porky here is fifteen. I figured you were sixteen, at least."

I looked away and said, "Well the boys in Delaware are especially mature."

Pepper laughed. "My ass they are. Thirteen and you won *States*?"

"It's a small state."

"Still, dude, that's a monster win," Deck said. "Looks sweet on your résumé, I know that."

"You have a résumé?"

"Of course. You have to to get into national tournaments. Christ, mine's half made up, but it doesn't matter."

"So's mine. Mine's a sinful bunch a bullshit," Pepp laughed.

"They let me in most of the tournaments because of my dad. It's good PR or something, for the tour."

"There's a tour? For you?" I said.

"For *us*. Dude, where have you been? What do you think we do with the rest of the summer? We fly around the country playing AJGA, bro. It's kind of sweet, I'm not gonna lie to you. Hotels, sweet-ass courses, planes, sponsors giving you all sorts of free shit."

"You fly around all summer, and the tour pays for it?"

Pepp licked ketchup from his fingertips. "Hell no. Our folks pay for it, but it'll pay off for them. Or at least that's what they're thinking. Deal is, you build up the résumé, no matter if you end up being great or not, get enough AJGA play, and you get yourself a scholarship. That's how it's done. See Whitman there? S'got three wins so far this summer. Surprised you haven't heard of him."

"Actually," Deck said, strapping his glove on his hand, "I'm surprised we haven't heard of you."

The next time I spoke to Whitman was the final day of ten, on the first tee at the Camp Championship. Deck, Whitman, Pepp and I were grouped in the day's final foursome. Eighteen holes, medal play for the tall Waterford crystal cup that I had envisioned at the center of my kitchen table—silver glass atop a green tablecloth, my mother and father on both sides of it, smiling at each other through thick sides of cut crystal.

Whitman shook my hand and said, "Titleist one. Good luck."

"Titleist four," I said, and we each identified our balls and wished each other the best. It was the etiquette and we all understood, but people who talked about the majesty of golf in the idea that you cheered and wished well for your opponent, no ill sentiment anywhere on the links—they were people like my father, people who did not know what it felt like to play big tournaments, to win, to blow it, to hear applause go up for someone else. They were the ones who watched from the ropes, safe to believe what they believed about the last great game on God's green earth.

We set off that first tee, four balls in the fairway, bags rattling across our backs, four troops moving out into the silence
with stares that were too old for teenagers, like time had crept
into our pores and showed up angry on our faces. There were
no more wishes of good luck. After nine holes out, I was down
three shots to Whitman, down one shot to Deck, and nine up
on Frankie Pepper, whose golf game had descended into a state
of hit and giggle.

On the holes coming in, Whitman made six pars and I made
two birdies. We came to the sixteenth hole, Deck's honor, then
me, then Whitman. I was behind by one shot. Whitman's face
was swelling. I could see his breath moving up and down fast
beneath his damp yellow shirt.

The sixteenth was a 180-yard par three with swamp stretching from tee to green. Muck guarded the entire left side of the
hole, hookers beware, where dragonflies buzzed around the
weeds, tickling our ears. The smell was heavy and rotten, and
the black soup pulled down the few reeds of rebel swamp grass
growing there.

Deck turned a ball over from right to left, a flaming plane
falling sideways, out of control. The swamp swallowed the ball
with a *schloomp* vacuum sound. Deck re-teed and hit another
ball, this time swinging out of his socks, ripping a hook that
sailed twenty yards deeper into the muck.

"Hit a turtle!" Frankie Pepper called, laughter bubbling at
the corner of his mouth as we watched the ball float out into a
lake of black water, more of a gulp than a splash.

"You got that shot down," Pepper said, delighted to be joined
at the back of the pack. Deck Williams was now playing for third.

I took the tee and looked over at Whitman and saw sweat
dripping from his eyes. I turned, and I returned. One hundred

eighty yards, six-iron, and I saw it bounce once before we heard a thin pin-smack, then a hard rattle from across the swamp. It was so perfectly lucky that it didn't feel lucky at all, just hit the ball straight and it goes in the hole. Yet I still fell to my knees in shock and slapped the ground like I was trying to beat the dust from the dirt.

"DUDE! DUDE! DUDE!" Deck yelled as he picked me up. We jumped around the tee in circles while Pepper could not stop laughing, chin rippling, his body rolling in all its soft parts.

There was no congratulation from Whitman. Instead he asked us if we would please act like we were on a golf course. There was a fear in his face that I had seen in Myles Dane at the club championship—dead fear from the moments when you had to show those watching you what it was that made the voices say you were *a real player*. It was the worry of being shown you were not something you had to be.

Whitman made his par and dropped back one shot as we headed to the seventeenth hole, a dogleg par four tucked into an alley cut through the forest. My approach shot dropped short of the green and into a pebbly bunker, while Whitman juiced his ball over the green and into the trees and pine needles.

My ball was buried, a fried egg in the sand, and I played as safe a shot as possible, settling for bogey with my opponent still looking for his ball in the forest. We helped Whitman search without success, then putted out and waited while Whitman paced back in the trees, a hunched shadow, spit and curses and searching all over.

"He's gonna have to go back, dude. He's gonna have to go back and hit another. We can't look all day," Deck said, placing the pin back in the hole. "What'd you make?" he asked me.

"Five," I said.

"Game over," said Pepper. "Ain't no way he's making better'n double."

"Got it!" yelled Whitman, and we all whipped around to see him standing over a ball to the far left of the green, several yards deep in the shade but with a clear opening to the pin.

"Must have hit a tree," he said.

He carefully addressed his ball, holding a wedge above the needles, careful of what the staff had warned during a rules session, how grounding your club on a bed of pine needles was dangerous because touching just one needle could touch another and another connected to that, a webbing of twigs until one moved beneath the ball, rolling it that smallest turn that would cost you a stroke. But Whitman played it careful, picking the ball clean off the needles with his blade and dropping it next to the pin, the ball curling toward the hole.

"Holy shit," Pepp said as we watched the ball turn for the cup like it was being reeled in on a string, turning, turning, then ramming into the base of the pin, hopping straight up and banging straight down.

"Sweet mother a' God!" yelled Whitman as he leaped in the air and came running for the green, pumping his fist in my direction. "Thought you were gonna have all the luck today, didn't ya!"

I waited for my voice to say something back, but nothing happened. I was down one with one hole to go. I had a chance to lose with a one on my scorecard.

I reached into the hole to grab Whitman's ball and toss it back to him. I could not even think to say nice shot. I looked down at his ball still warm with luck. Titleist. Two.

Whitman Carlsby was a picture of guilt buried beneath elation. Talk fast, hurry off to the next hole, maybe no one notices the shame turning black behind your eyes.

He held out his hand to collect his ball. "Thank you very much, boy."

"What are you playing?" I said, holding the ball in my palm.

"What am I playing? Hell, I don't know. It's a Titleist."

"Titleist what, Whitman?"

"Oh hell, I forget. It's a red Titleist. And I forget the number so give me my goddamn ball, you rude son of a bitch."

He grabbed the ball from my fingers.

"I'm playing a Titleist two, all right? Right here, red Titleist two."

"You said you were playing a one. On the first tee, you said Titleist one."

"Bull fucking shit. I'm playing a two, this goddamn two right here."

I looked over at our partners. They were trying to look away.

"Pepp? Deck? What did he say he was playing?"

"Whitman, dude, I swear to God I don't remember," Deck said. "I wasn't even listening. I heard Titleist. Geez, I mean I'm playing Maxfli."

"Pepp," I said, "come on—didn't you hear him? We all said what we were playing."

Frankie Pepper looked down at his fingers, tan and plump and a little wrinkly. Cold little sausages.

"Frankie?"

He shook his head from side to side without looking at anyone.

"You got a lot of balls to come down here, come down to this course and call *me* a liar, ya rude bag a shit," Whitman said, safety settling back into his voice. "Someone ought to teach you some *goddamned manners.*"

He walked to the eighteenth tee, but the real match was over and we both knew it. I played the last hole politely. I watched

Whitman Carlsby become three-time Pine Acres Camp Champion because I was Timmy Price, no résumé, from a town no one heard of, a Yankee who didn't fit anywhere but between.

People talked about golf being a great game because a player called penalties on himself—a game of honor, a game where your conscience was your referee. Rules that never changed. Rules with dust on them. Rules, rulings, ruled. It was more bullshit from men who had nothing but a game of sticks and balls to cling to, men who found faith in two-stroke penalties and golf as the great metaphor for life. *The cheater is the only one who gets cheated, your honor is all you have in golf and in life*—it was the shit they would say, the lines they would peddle, those same smiling men who patted Whitman on his back like they were trying to burp their prodigal baby, the same faces who passed down the idea of success to us like it was the only thing worth breathing for, then sandwiched it between sugary talk about fair play. We were all Whitman Carlsby with an extra Titleist in his bag. There was no honor. There was just a trophy, crystal and heavy and bigger than my head.

A wide man with a green jacket stood at the edge of the eighteenth green, clapping and whistling with the rest of the gallery as Whitman wrapped his fingers around the trophy. His face was Whitman's with a few more rolls around the edges.

I held my hands to my face and felt my skin warm with embarrassment. Losing was the taste crawling up the back of my throat. Losing was not open for debate or discussion. It was stasis and it was safe. Combined with acceptance, it was really rather peaceful, an un-revolution that my father bought into years before. I stood there watching Whitman Carlsby cradle that cool blue base of Waterford crystal, and I thought about the trophy being from

Ireland. I don't know why. It was a strange feeling, losing that way, part loss, part surrender. It was like I was going to burst into numbness, go mad with patience.

"Check it out," Deck said. "Mr. Carlsby wore his fucking Augusta jacket, man. That is so sweet."

"He won the Masters?" I said.

"Shit, naw," Pepp said. "He's a member at Augusta."

We watched as Mr. Carlsby took off his green jacket and slid it over his boy's shoulders, the crowd applauding behind them.

"My li'l master!" he yelled to the gallery, holding his son's hand up like a boxer. They posed for pictures and Deck went off to sign his card. Pepper stood next to me, shaking his head.

"Timmy, I don't know, man. Back on that first tee it sounded a helluva lot like a Titleist one."

I turned and saw Frankie's throat tightening.

"Deck and me, we know. We know you're the best damn player here, man. Trophies aside, that was some serious golf you left out there."

"You fat fuck," I said, looking him straight in the face. "You fat fucking pussy. You knew that, and you said *nothing*. What, are you afraid of your buddy over there? Mr. Augusta fucking National?"

He looked at me and shook his head. "You don't understand."

"What don't I understand? Why didn't you say something, Pepper? Why?"

Frankie Pepper shrugged his shoulders and looked over at the father and son holding a tall crystal cup between them, smiling for a camera.

"Because."

And that was all there was to say.

* * *

That last night, I packed and put my bags by my cot and left the cottage to find Angela, and we sneaked out behind the practice shed and kissed, holding our lips together for minutes at a time. She told me that night that she had a boyfriend at home, a friend of the family she could take or leave. I was special, she said, and she would write. Every day was what she promised.

The night was clear. We went to the pool and Angela held my hand, leading me through the gate and around the lounge chairs. Light from the parking lot reflected off the waves lapping on the water. Our eyes adjusted to the night, and the darkness faded into a deep blue.

Angela pulled me to the edge of the pool, and she asked me if I had ever seen a woman naked before. She took off all her clothes, untying her top and slipping out of her shorts, and I looked down at my shoes, a chill shooting from my feet to my forehead. She stepped closer and said it was all right, and she lifted my hand to her breast. Cold, her skin like white icing, and my whole body going tight. She said I could keep my clothes on, that it was all right, and I could only think to tell her I would be fourteen soon.

She went to swim and said I could only watch. She giggled and moved through the water, her pale body shimmering and slipping past as I squeezed my elbows against me. I felt bigger than myself, happy with a thousand feelings trying to push their way out of me, and all I could think was to remind myself to remember, remember, remember. She swam, and I watched, and next to my feet on the concrete lay her underwear, white silk bunched small and quiet. In the blue night, I listened to her giggle, imagining Angela's skin sliding past as I looked down at her underwear and thought how beautiful it was, how in the July night it lay there like a cool bit of snow.

* * *

North Carolina to New Water. I told my father how six shots were three down there, and he told me it was a lesson. He did not explain where the lesson was, just chalked it up to something I would learn from. And I would. And he would learn that I was just a few years too old for that kind of hollow advice, and I decided that he was not going to hear about the hole-in-one. The idea of not telling him—if he could only know I wasn't telling him—it would have been one more thing for my mother to see when she looked around our house and said it all just *killed* him. I dropped the scorecard in the trash can in the kitchen, and I let the big 1 with a circle around it die there.

I rushed back to Fox Chase with a head full of stories, ready to tell Jamie about the tournament and the stomachaches from Southern food and the bugs the size of birds. I wanted to tell him how a man talked about a scholarship, how another man said *how good is that,* how my hole-in-one felt more lucky than perfect because the only perfect thing was the way Angela Ray's underwear looked balled up next to my feet. I wanted to tell him how she talked to me, the way her breast fell from her shirt and made the most amazing shadow. And soon I would want to ask him why he thought she didn't write, not soon, not every day.

The sun and the steam followed me from North Carolina like a mood. We were in a full-fledged heat wave, no golf, no work. I found the caddies sizzling away in the hole, talking as little as possible, wondering where Jamie Byrne was and why he was missing his loops.

AT THE END of August the Member-Guest tournament came like manna.

My hair was still streaked gold from my ten days in a grassy pocket of a pine forest. Brian Seaman said it made me look like one of those private-school pricks that spent their summers body-surfing at the Jersey shore. There had been no work, just heat and retold stories and the sound of footsteps shuffling above us, Raymond Mann's weight squeaking in the rafters as he paced the pro shop, golf shoes crinkling across the concrete outside. You could identify people from the crunch of their spikes. The men had a heavy, inert rhythm, metal rolling across the pavement from here to there, a pace of lunches to rush, tee times to catch. Their wives' shoes clicked by, airy and undeliberate. Their feet sometimes paused or moved sideways. They excused themselves. They apologized.

The hole was filling up with emptiness. The heat wrapped everything like a hairy wool blanket, and I had the feeling as I watched us wait each morning that the peace was going to crack. When Jamie left, something left that had made the hole more hopeful than it was, and what remained was a room of men impatient and bitter, and worst of all bored. Jeffrey was back caddying, but Lewis wasn't putting him out. There was an empty heroin ache in his face, and when he began to shake one morning like his veins were full of ice, Lewis stuffed him in the bathroom and told him to stay the hell out of sight.

All the stories were stale that week. Brian told us three times about Miss Gasperec and Jamie's hands.

"Just try and think about all the things you can't do without your thumbs," Brian said. "Can't tie your shoes. Can't button your pants."

"You can't be a soldier. At least you'll never get drafted," Position A said from back in the corner where he was painting red stripes on golf balls he had found in the woods and the weeds. Raymond Mann paid a dime each for a red-striped ball he could use on the driving range. Position A used nail polish to apply the stripe and his fingers looked like a rash, covered with red blotches that didn't come off with the soap we used to clean golf clubs.

"Can't be a priest without your thumbs," Tomato Face said.

"You're full of shit."

"I swear to Christ. Priests needs two things. Priest doesn't need a prick to piss with, but he needs two thumbs for holding up the host at Communion. That's sacred. They don't make exceptions about that."

"Well, all I know is Jamie Byrne's never missed this many days caddying before," Brian said, peeling the paper off his cigarette until the cherry fell to the floor. He tucked the yellow butt in his back pocket.

"Well he sure picked a good time to go on vacation," Position A said. "This is as bad as it's been up here in ten years."

"You know where he's at?" Brian asked me.

I looked down at my hands, back and front, pretending I hadn't heard their question.

"Price, you know where Jamie's at?"

I thought for a moment, then looked up at them. "Yeah. I think he's on vacation."

The room was quiet until Brian started to ramble about a sophomore named Tina, a girl he called *the closer* in the hopes we would ask why. We didn't. We were hardly listening as Brian tried to sell himself on his own stories.

A bad sort of silence.

Upstairs they talked for the noise of it, conversing in groups, each gentleman listening only to himself. There was never quiet, always motion and mumblings as if the empty moments hurt their ears. Downstairs the quiet was an entity, something you could cup in your hands, another friend, another body lying next to you on the bench.

Jeffrey was not in good shape, drops of heat falling from his face.

"S'bullshit, man," he said one morning, swaying around the room, dragging his feet. "I hear them carts up there. Motherfuckers out there, they're out there playin', having themselves a candy-ass of a time while we're wastin' down to nothin'. Bunch a damn fools, that's what we are. Man, I'll tell you what, we should go on a goddamn strike," he said, sticking out his ribs. "We should go the hell up there and picket and show our goddamn faces, man, see how Raymond and Lewis and all the motherfuckers feel about that. Stir up some *shit,* man, get this place fired *up*!"

Tomato Face straightened himself on the bench and spoke with a headache in his voice. "Sit down, you stupid son of a bitch. There's fifty scabs ready up there. Gas-powered scabs. They've even got a little place to hold your damn beer."

Position A laughed. "Take it easy, J. Weather'll break. We'll all get out."

"Naw, naw, here's what we do. We just slit those little-ass tires tonight, no more carts, motherfuckers'll *have* to take a caddy. We'll have more work than we'll know what to do with," Jeffrey said, the walls heating up, his eyes big and brown and a little bit crazy, like he could see the money there in his fingers. "Be throwin' duckets around, man, rolling around in all that cash."

"Why don't you just quit?" Tomato Face said. "Save us the pain of having to listen to your bullshit. Take your skinny ass back to North Philly."

"Maybe I will, motherfucker. Bet you'd like that."

"You're damn right I would."

Position A cut them off. "Relax, you're making my fucking head hurt." He calmed everyone down with a story about turning Mrs. Norton upside down on a chaise lounge. His face was contorted, the expressions piling on top of themselves as he tried to describe the way her body folded, the way she twisted, the way she tied him up with a section of garden hose. It was not a pretty story, but it was a good story for making the steam settle.

I did not tell them about Angela. I didn't want to have to stretch it, to spice it with fleshy details, because to do that, to compete with Brian the bard of ninth-grade ass, would be to lose even that small, good thing it had become, peppermint breath and snow on cement. The truth was, I had only watched, and she didn't write, and that didn't make for much of a story in the hole. But Angela Ray was already a story, memory and unreal, whether I told it or not.

Walter Kane spent little time in the hole during that heat wave, but he came in every few days to entertain us with news about his boy.

"Charlie Logan's up there, kissing my ass 'cause he heard Boston College is riding Candy." It was strange to hear a father call his son by his nickname, like a fan or a reporter or a high school crush. "They're gonna put Logan's name on a building up there. He said he's guaranteeing my boy a full boat. He's talking about a little boat too, for his old man."

Walter told us about the piles of letters coming to his house, shoe boxes full, each box separated by conference. Jeffrey leaned back and cocked his head, unimpressed.

"Tough little nigga, that boy a yours. How's things down at white-boy prep? Surprised a brother make it out alive," Jeffrey said, smiling at Walter.

Without a word Walter gave him one clean slug to the tip of his jaw, a quick bone smack. Jeffrey just rocked back and forth on the bench, holding his chin in his palm and giggling like a clown, and we all felt a little bit like he looked, speechless and ridiculous and past pissed off, fools waiting there for nothing.

The time got stuck, days piling on days, but somehow a week became a weekend, and a Tuesday became a Thursday, and Thursday came with a blue breeze that slipped down into the hole like a whisper. As the tournament approached, the movement above us went from a buzz to a frenzy, Lewis screaming for carts to be washed, Wilson rumbling through the hole, calling off names and bags, Raymond barking for clean range balls and clean windows and more vacuuming vacuuming vacuuming. New faces and fair-weather caddies poured into the hole, squeezing themselves into the corners, scavengers there to nibble on the excess work. The tension was beautiful. A pause in the waiting.

Jeffrey rubbed his hands together like he could see his entrée on its way from the kitchen, and Tomato Face said, "That's right, here they come, boys, here they come."

Friday morning was our winning ticket, the first day of the three biggest paydays of the year—Friday, Saturday and Sunday of the Member-Guest tournament. It was the apogee of the club's social season, three days of golf and gambling, liquor and boasting amid flattered and influential guests. Member-Guest was a pissing contest culminating in tuxedos and lobsters the size of cats, and that year it might have saved the lives of the lifers in the hole.

Every loop would be a good loop because the real tight-pockets didn't play this tournament. The fee was four hundred a man, for golf, dinners, drinks, and a black-tie ball on Sunday night. Not to mention the gambling—it was five hundred per team to get in on the calcutta, and the tournament winners took home the whole thing, over ten grand apiece of that "unofficial" money. The winning caddy would take his chunk as well.

The summer before, Jamie was the winning looper, carrying for Norton and the guest he'd brought from his racquet club.

"Norton's up for grabs. It's open season on that loop," Jeffrey said. "Jamie can't go taking no two weeks off and think he's gonna come back and take that bag."

"Lewis wouldn't let you within ten feet of that bag, Jeffrey," Brian said.

"Well, we'll just see about that, little man."

I was afraid to go to Jamie's house, worried his father had found out about that night and us and the gun, nervous he might be coming down hard on Jamie about it. I tried to call him to tell him it was tournament week, to ask where he'd been and let him know they were fighting over his steady loop. But Jamie had never given me his phone number, and when I called the operator, the voice on the other end said the line had been disconnected. *Due to an outstanding balance,* she said, though I hadn't asked her for a reason.

Part of me was glad I couldn't find him. If I got Jamie on the other end of the phone, then there would have to be an answer, a reason why he left. I didn't want to hear that he quit. I didn't want to know why he wouldn't come around to hear my stories.

By 6 A.M. on Friday morning, the hole was packed from side to side and in between the racks. There were the new high school kids with whiteheads around their mouths, and there were college kids with tans, guys back from the shore for the most profitable time of the season. There was no respect for either of them, not even from a kid like me because I had the eight ugliest men in the room behind every step I took. We were there in the warm, and everyone else was a pink-skinned Johnny-come-lately, a worthless fucko chasing our easy money. There was some respect for the ex-loopers and the friends of lifers who showed up, guys who had at least done the work before. Some old-time caddies even used vacation days from their county jobs to come to Fox Chase for the three days when the cash fell at our feet like petals.

Lewis came down the steps with a don't-fuck-with-me-today look on his face, a cardboard box dragging behind him, his clipboard guarded against his chest.

"Where the hell were all of you last week?" he said, looking around at the new faces like a priest surveying his Christmas congregation.

"We've got fifty pairings. That means one hundred golfers up there, so for Christ's sake, stay out of the way. If I see anyone on the steps, if I see anyone walking around upstairs, if I see you when I don't want to see you, you're done for this tournament. And if I catch anyone skeezing loops, so help you God, you can forget about it. You're *out*. There's fifty guests here this weekend, so everybody better be on their best fucking behavior. That means everybody, all of you, showered and fresh as fucking roses. Got it?"

No one offered an answer. We looked at Lewis like he was a pile of skin.

"Now, when you get a loop, come pick out your shirt for the tournament. No pinnies this year. Mr. Chadwick donated real golf shirts for you, so if you see him, you better say thank you. And say it loud, because he can't hear shit if you don't yell it at him. Wash your shirt every night after looping. You hear me? *Wash* it. Here's the list," he said, pinning a piece of yellow paper to the wall of shame, "and these are the loops. No debate, no argument, no dicking around with this. If you're not on this list, the golf committee's paying for spotters this year, so stick around." Spotters would sit along blind holes and watch for balls landing where players on the tee could not see them. It was seven hours of dodging and hunting, the bottom rung of the ladder, the most boring twenty bucks on the course. "And God help you if you get a loop today and miss it on Saturday or Sunday, boys," Lewis continued. "Fucking God fucking help you."

As Lewis went to leave, he turned. "Anyone seen Jamie Byrne?"

No one answered until he was halfway up the stairs and Brian said, "Yeah, I saw him last night, givin' your mom the hammy slammy."

We rushed to the list like lions on warm meat.

"Shit, I got that cheap bastard Riley. Maybe his guest'll pay."

"How much does Elliot pay, huh? Hey, anybody know what Elliot's good for?"

"Crawford, shit, man. He stiffed me twice this month. Lewis probably thinks he's my damn steady."

"Who the fuck is Utz?"

Brian Spooge was there next to *Norman Dane.* "Money. Money money *mo-ney,*" he said, high-stepping across the concrete floor. The lifers were spread out among modest loops. *Tomato Face* next to *Mollit, Jeffrey* next to *Woolridge.* Position A found his name next to *Richard Norton.* He laughed out loud.

"D'you think Lewis knows?" he smiled. "I bet that asshole knows."

Before I could read down to the bottom of the list to see my name, Position A said, "Hey Price, I didn't know your old man played this thing."

He didn't, not any year before. The sheet read *Price* and *Price is Right* in Lewis's misfingered scribble. I went to the box and pulled out a shirt and slipped it over my head. We stood around the room, trying not to laugh at each other, draped in thin, cheap cotton, our new shirts shining white. Our fronts were all wrinkles and folds from the factory, and our backs were lettered big and green: CADDY.

"I OWED HIM," my father explained, raising his chin toward the practice range where Al D'Angelo was loosening up. "He did me a favor. Financially, he did me a favor, or believe me, I would leave this tournament to the gamblers and the sandbaggers."

D'Angelo's bulky red golf bag was strapped to a dented aluminum pull-cart. A label screwed to the handle read *Property of Rock Valley Public Golf Links.*

"What do I do with this?" I said, pointing to the pull-cart.

"I don't know," my father said, looking around to see if anyone had spotted it. "Can you hide it down in the hole?"

When I came back upstairs, I saw Brian Seaman stalking the rail, trying to look busy as he circled Mr. Chadwick. Brian bumped shoulders with the old man, who always played in knickers and high black socks and a floppy tartan cap. Chadwick owned drugstores in every mid-Atlantic state, but he was most famous to us as the member who lobbied for a caddy dress code. The pinnies were his creation, and he even pushed for fines for loopers whose appearance was not up to snuff. Our new shirts were not the product of generosity. They were a way for Chadwick to make his club a little more impressive to his guest, a way to cover up one of golf's most obvious unpleasantnesses, that somebody had to carry the bags.

"Oh, excuse me there, pardon me," said Chadwick. Brian mouthed back an *I'm sorry, excuse me,* no sound coming from his mouth.

"Pardon? What's that?" Chadwick said, leaning in with his right ear.

Brian lipped *excuse me* again, and Chadwick smiled and nodded and said, "That's a mighty fine-looking shirt you got on there, caddy."

"You think? I could go get you one. It's a nice fifty-fifty blend, good for chafing," Brian said, scratching his armpit. His free shirt was a medium and his biceps were choked by the sleeves. "I personally think you'd look phenomenal in one of these numbers, Mr. Chadwick. You're already the best-dressed member in the whole club."

"What's that, son?" said Chadwick, utterly confused.

"Now don't be modest. All the caddies say so."

"All right then," he said, nodding at Brian's smile. "Did they tell you boys where those shirts came from?"

"Yes sir. Lewis Holmes bought them for us." Brian enunciated loud and slow. "You know Lewie, the caddy master."

"Excuse me?" he said, leaning in again with his good ear.

"They were his gift to us. He's not a bad guy, that Lewis," Brian said. "See, because he really didn't have to do this, but he did it anyway."

Brian walked past me and winked, and Chadwick stared after him with a face like his hearing aids were in backwards.

* * *

Mr. D'Angelo made his way down from the practice range, a muddy cigar sticking out the side of his face, his hair a perfect black shell. He was big all over—not fat, but bruising, an Italian specimen with hands like a bunch of bananas. His shirt was a busy mix of green and blue lines, and he wore white shorts better suited for tennis or for high school football coaches than for golf at Fox Chase.

"That freakin' bag, let me tell ya, my wife gave me that load of a bag," he said, pleased that I had switched it for a canvas Sunday bag. "My first wife, Tina, I'm talking about. She was good at one thing—spending my money. Tell you what, kid." He pointed a wide brown finger in my face. "Stick to the golf, stay away from the ladies. Or better yet," he peered in at me, "stay away from any woman who eats Kobe beef. Got that?"

I nodded like it was gospel, no clue what Kobe beef might be.

"Kobe beef. Am I right, Jimmy?"

My father offered an appeasing smile.

"Woman sees that on a menu and says, *oh dear, that looks interesting,* you run, my friend. Tina, she'd eat it for breakfast. Lucky Denny's didn't serve the stuff or she'd a been grand-slammin' me to death." The colors of his shirt splashed around on his chest as he laughed. "You know how much that stuff'll run ya, Jimmy?" he said, not waiting for an answer, and I could not help but smile at this man calling my father *Jimmy* when no one called my father *Jimmy.* "'Bout a hundred fifty bucks a slab. No shit. These cows," he continued, moving his large hands like he was molding a filet right there, "they never even stand. They lay on their asses their whole entire life, and they get massages and drink beer."

My father politely interjected, "Oh, come on, Al. They don't feed beer to cows."

"Hey Timmy, does it look like I'm making this up?"

I smiled and shook my head. I believed him, if for no other reason than Al D'Angelo was a person who believed himself.

"See, Timmy knows. Massages and beer all year-round, keeps their meat tender. It's like brown butter that stuff is. So once a lady gets a taste for it," he smiled, walking off toward the tee, "better get yourself a good attorney."

Alfred D'Angelo was a walking piece of the South Philadelphia that went suburbs, a man who traded in the family business for a law degree, who dropped the keys to the row house for a four-bedroom home with a three-car garage in a development with short trees spaced at regular intervals. He was nothing like my father, but he made my father smile when he normally wouldn't have. Mr. D'Angelo was everything a membership committee at Fox Chase would see on an application and quietly lose somewhere in some unspecific pile.

"Ready to kick a little ass, Jimmy?" he said.

"Al," my father said in his best South Philly, "dat's what I do, I kick asses."

The tournament format was 54 holes, three days, one calcutta. Each team of one member and one guest would play eighteen holes a day, subtracting their handicaps from their scores. The team with the lowest score after 54 holes took home the calcutta, the unofficial money that was distributed to the winners in unofficial stacks of hundred-dollar bills.

Al D'Angelo was a golfer designed for member-guest tournaments. He was a twenty handicap without being suspicious—his shorts and his bag screamed *I play once a year in Orlando,* but his swing was a curious exercise in precision, twelve pieces and three weight shifts coming together to meet the ball square and hard at impact. Fast but functional, it was a swing stuck between dumb luck and smart luck. D'Angelo was a walking breach of taste and etiquette, but it was obvious after a few holes that this twenty handicap could throw up an 83 amid all his wisecracking about ex-wives and the size of his belly.

In our first eighteen holes, my father and Mr. D'Angelo whipped Richard Norton and his guest, a man with an English accent who traded bonds in New York and Hong Kong. The guest talked about Yale and told a story about the selection of Scotch on the Concorde. Standing next to Al D'Angelo, he made my father's partner look like a big sloppy sandwich. When he asked D'Angelo where he had studied, Al said, "The library," then turned and walked up to the green where he would chip in for par and finish the Norton team off.

My father was playing well, and Counselor D'Angelo was showing that he was a man who simply knew how to win. He did not know how to make it look good, but he had the bumpy rind of experience. He could beat you and make you smile about it.

Our team won side bets of twenty dollars apiece. Minus D'Angelo's generous handicap, we were seven strokes under par after the first round.

"Nothing better than taking money from an Ivy League guy, I'll tell ya that much," D'Angelo said, sniffing the bill. "The money smells smarter, don't ya think?"

He handed me the twenty, and I pretended to sniff it.

"Definitely."

"Keep that," he said. "I'd feel bad spending that money. S'like stealing. Guys like that, T, I'll tell ya, you'll take money from them for the rest of your life, in whatever you do, 'cause they think they're better then they are. Worst disease there is, T, is to believe your own bullshit. Fastest way to lose your money. That English guy was a seven handicap in his wet dreams, you know what I'm saying?" he said, elbowing me. "Go to the Ivy League, kid, you get yourself a degree in confidence. But it's not the good kind."

We walked toward the clubhouse, three in a team, and my father had the dizzy look of a child stepping from a roller coaster, his eyes saying *well that wasn't all that bad.* He was playing as well as I had ever seen him play, and having Al around seemed to keep him patient and loose. There was such a thing as having too much reverence for the game and the course, and my father's tried plan of attack was to surrender with his first swing. Watching Al D'Angelo walk through Fox Chase Country Club as if it were just a field with eighteen holes in the ground—it helped remind my father that that was exactly what it was.

Club President Norton had crept off the final green behind us. Position A carried his bag. Norton looked thin and tired, his eyes pink and sagging open. The man who screwed his wife in his own backyard was grinning from behind Norton's bag, and his chum from England couldn't stop questioning this American turf and why he couldn't get his ball airborne. Three days and thousands of dollars already shot after four awful hours. But it was more than the waste. Something else was weighing down Mr. Norton's footsteps. I felt bad for him, for laughing at the stories about his wife, the images we all had of her begging, naked and wet. And Jamie wasn't there to steer him straight, his caddy going away before the biggest golf of the year. Day one, and Richard Norton was already lost.

DAY TWO BEGAN early.

The sky was still damp and gray when I hopped out of the Buick and scrambled back to the hole. The parking lot was just beginning to stir, cars with headaches behind the wheel, golfers bleary-eyed from the first evening's late-night cocktail mistake, laughing and patting each other's backs, walking stiff like swollen boxers.

Everything was country-club tight, a perfect place made a little more perfect. Outside, the clubhouse walls were scrubbed hospital white, the cobwebs and wasp nests scraped from the corners. The driveway was swept, the fallen petals around the front door, violet and yellow and red, all gathered up and thrown away. Down in the hole, caddies were jammed against one another in their not-so-washed-last-night caddy shirts, each looper hopeful that the work would go well, but knowing it was too crowded down there for everyone to have their share of the day.

All caddies had to be in at seven-thirty, no matter that most of us weren't out until eleven, because Raymond and Lewis and Wilson wanted us down there, waiting to jump at the first word to come crackling over the intercom. A pocketful of caddies meant they were not the low men on the pole, not with fifty of us to anchor the basement. We kept the clubhouse balanced.

The lifers and the regular summer crew leaned back in the benches, eyeing the new mouths who showed up for the extra work.

"All you new fellas," Tomato Face said from a broken chair in the corner, his blue-green fingernails tucked into the top of his pants, "you all better think twice about coming up here every day. There's barely enough work for us fellas here," he said, pointing toward our half of the room, "so you all better go back to the beach or your mother's house. We don't need any new caddies up here, thank you very fucking much."

Only the smallest kids seemed intimidated. Most didn't look his way, not a blink, because they knew after only one day that it was not a job of seniority or deference. It was waiting to go out and walk in a circle to come back in and wait some more. With time you earned calluses, not respect.

Among the new faces, grape-jelly cheeks, sleep-crusted eyes, all the necks that needed sunblock, there was still no Jamie. And he was not the only looper missing that morning. Jeffrey was nowhere, his bags only a half hour from the tee. Missing an arranged loop was the one transcendent caddy undoable, and doing it at Member-Guest was an unforgivable fuck-up.

"If Jeffrey doesn't show up pretty damn soon, Lewis is going to turn his ass into wallets," Brian Seaman said.

"Jeffrey, this is not a smart thing, man," said Position A, genuine worry in his voice. If anyone actually liked Jeffrey or not, that didn't matter now. We knew this would set him back hard, and we all shared an uneasiness, each looper thinking *there but for the sound of my alarm clock go I.* No one wanted to see Jeffrey roaded and hungry again.

Except maybe Walter.

"You wanna know where that fool is?" Walter said, ducking through the doorway. "I'll tell you where he is. He's back up in Philly, probably sticking needles in himself. I was out with him yesterday, and get a load a this." He took the space on the bench I made for him. "He's carrying for Woolridge, and I got Charlie Logan, and yeah, he's still got his lips wrapped around it about my boy going to play up at BC. So we're going along, Jeffrey's fucking up as usual, making all sorts of noise, putting down the wrong bags, walking through lines. All the shit you could do to fuck up, man, he's doing it. Worse caddy than Tomato Face I think."

Even Tomato Face laughed at that.

"So on the back nine, he starts falling way behind. His guys are waiting on their clubs, and Jeffrey's face is all sweaty and he's stumbling all over the place. I don't know if he's DT-ing or what, but he looks sick, I mean *real* bad. He looked whiter than the members, man. He's twitching and coughing and shit. I ask him if he's gonna make it, and he just tells me to leave him alone. So we keep going along, and then about the tenth hole, something just starts stinking to high fucking heaven. I'm talking like a fresh farm stink. We go along, twelve, thirteen, fourteen, and this shit stink is following us. So then about the fifteenth hole, sure enough, Jeffrey raises his hand like a little kid in school and says, 'Uh, Mr. Woolridge, I think I might have had a little accident here.' And Woolridge's like 'Might have! Man, did you shit your pants or not?'"

"Caddy history!" Brian Seaman called from the corner where he sat atop his bucket. We all began laughing, lifers, new guys, people with no idea who Jeffrey might be.

"Poor bastard's got the runs and there's no bathrooms out there after number twelve. He was just stranded out there, sweating and shaking and dropping bombs in his fucking shorts."

Puddy sat back in his bench, laughter rolling from his chin to his belly, a picture book about castles resting closed on his belly.

"Jeffrey was done after that. Woolridge sent his ass straight back to the clubhouse, do not pass Go, do not collect two hundred dollars. They carried their own bags, and there goes Jeffrey hoofing it back through the woods. It was fucking priceless. Only Jeffrey could fuck up that big. You've gotta work hard at fucking up before you can pull something like that off. It took Lewis about two seconds to give Jeffrey the boot. Right in his shitty shorts." Walter laughed. "He was gone, roaded off the property before the rest of y'all even got back in."

"I don't know if you can ever recover from something like that. That's a career-ender," said Position A.

"You ain't lying." Walter shook his head. "It's no damn good."

I watched the rest of the caddies ship off in twos as their teams were called to the tee. My group was in first place and would tee off last, with Dane and guest just two shots behind.

I had to smile when I saw Mr. D'Angelo on the first tee, chewing his cigar like jerky. He was wearing a golf shirt emblazoned with a bold Philadelphia Eagles logo, a bird with wings spread and a football in its claws.

"You ready, T? I wore the good stuff today," he said, knocking a fist into my shoulder. "Didn't want anyone mistakin' me for one a these freakin' Quakers. So Jimbo," he said, turning to my father, "I drove my truck today to carry all the money home. I'm thinkin' we should have them bring out a backhoe at the end of the day, and they can just drop all the dough in the back of the pickup."

"Let's not count our chickens before they hatch, Al. One hole at a time," my father said.

We matched up against Norman Dane and guest for the second eighteen holes of the tournament. Brian Seaman carried their bags, and Myles followed his father around in a cart, sunglasses propped up in his long bleached hair, a tall cup of iced tea jingling in his fingers. I had not found Myles's name in the newspaper for the Mason Invitational, a local junior tournament I missed while I was in North Carolina. The papers printed only the top ten scores. Maybe it was a misprint, or maybe sixteen-year-old Myles didn't place at a tournament he had won when he was twelve.

"Dude, I didn't even ten," Myles explained when I asked him what happened. He slid his sunglasses down over his eyes. "I didn't fucking ten, man, no ink, no nothing. I played like dog shit."

"Really? What d'you shoot?"

"Fucking eighty-two. I came in with three doubles. It was weird, I made the turn at four over, and the dude I'm playing with is one under, and man, I just stopped giving a shit. I couldn't wait to get out of there. I wasn't marking my balls or taking practice swings. It was weird. I was just totally not interested."

"Well, you won it before anyway," I said.

"Yeah. Fuck, I almost don't care," he said, resting his chin on the steering wheel, looking out at the fairway stretching away from us. "I'm getting tired of all of this crap. For real. I mean for good."

"But what about school? I thought you were getting a scholarship?"

"I don't know. Maybe. Maybe I don't want to play in college," Myles said. "But listen—don't say anything in front of my dad about me shooting eighty-two. He thinks I shot seventy-seven, in case it comes up. I told him I tied for eleventh, seventy-seven."

"Yeah, of course."

And seventy-seven it was, because five strokes mattered, to some of us more than others.

As we set out down the first fairway that morning, my father was quiet. He walked out ahead of us, alone, tight with concentration and nibbling his lips white. His swing had accelerated a few notches. My father was pushing to play better. He was playing outside himself.

Norman Dane's guest was a pediatric surgeon named Dr. Seavey, a short, balding man with freckled skin and a permanent grin, as if he found everything outside the operating room to be pleasant and pretend. As we waited for the group ahead of us to clear the third green, Dr. Seavey talked about his annual summer excursion, when he would take two weeks of his vacation to go to Vietnam and do surgery for sixteen hours a day, putting children's hands and faces back together. We made our way between the sand traps to the third green, Dr. Seavey globbing on sunscreen and telling us a story about holding a child's heart in his hand just that week, massaging it until it started to beat.

"My God, what the hell does that feel like?" Al D'Angelo said, his face askew with the image.

"It's, well, it's sort of like holding a heart, I suppose. A child's heart is obviously smaller and lighter than an adult heart. They tend to be a little softer as well. They're a bit less muscular."

"*That* is the craziest shit I ever heard. That, I could not do," said D'Angelo.

"It's really just a matter of training."

"Aww, horseshit. Training—I've got training papers hanging all over my office. BA, JD, NBA, whatever, and a freaking monkey could do my job. Strike that. A greedy, mean-spirited monkey could do my job," D'Angelo said before rolling in a twelve-footer for par.

"A monkey can't do that," Dr. Seavey added.

"No Doc, he certainly cannot."

Al D'Angelo barreled on around the course that day, the essence of ugly but effective. He carried my father, pulling out par after par, getting up and down from two bunkers, chipping in from the fairway. After the front nine we were still in the lead, yet my father's game had fallen into a state of gibberish as he barked at himself under his breath, calling himself half-spoken profanities. He looked a little nuts and I almost laughed, but I couldn't. The pressure was bending him around, a self-loathing boiling up red against the inside of his face, and as I watched my father it started to make sense why he did not play these tournaments. I had been wrong—it wasn't that he feared success, or that defeat brought him his own sad security. My father wasn't about winning or losing, because all my father wanted in the world was something steady. It was all he had ever worked for, a place to stand easy. Yet that place wasn't his home, and the truth was, it wasn't his golf club either. As I watched my father flounder from fairway to green, I didn't laugh, because my dad might never know a place where he could just let out his breath.

"A Learjet, Alfred. It's not the craziest investment you could make," Dr. Seavey explained as he strolled up to a ball smack in the center of the tenth fairway.

"I don't know what you think lawyers make these days, but it ain't the kind a money you're talking about. If it weren't for you doctors fucking up all the time, Christ, we'd all be outta business."

We all laughed, except for my father, who was searching through a patch of fuzzy-leaved bushes for his ball.

"What the hell do you need a freaking jet for?"

"Surgeries. Sometimes. Actually, I use it mostly for basketball."

D'Angelo eyed the short doctor. "Let me tell you one thing. You might be able to breathe life into kids, but I guarantee you can't play basketball worth a lick."

"You're not kidding," Norman Dane laughed, giving D'Angelo a hearty slap on the back.

"No, no," Doctor Seavey smiled, "I watch the games. I did my undergrad at Duke, so I try to take in the home games when I'm not on call. I just fly in, fly out, and I'm only gone four hours. I saw fourteen games last season."

"I'm in the wrong freaking business," D'Angelo said.

The doctor smiled, small and satisfied. "It's not a bad life."

WE WERE WAITING for the group ahead of us to clear the eleventh green when Al D'Angelo pulled me aside.

"Listen Timmy, your old man, we gotta get him back on track."

"Yeah, he sort of rode you that nine."

"No shit. I've got the spur marks to prove it. Do me a favor," Al said, waving his large tan palm at my face, "how 'bout straightening him out a little. I'm not gonna go giving him tips, 'cause a lot of guys don't like hearing advice from their partners, especially when their partner's got a twenty handicap and wears a shirt like this." He tugged on his Eagles polo shirt. "But we gotta get that swing back in working order. Maybe if you just gave him a couple pointers to get him settled down."

"I don't know, Mr. D'Angelo. I'm just a caddy."

"Just a caddy? Right, and I'm just big boned. Your old man tells me you're this unbelievable player. You're a prodigy is what he tells me."

"He does?"

"Oh hell yeah. To tell you the truth, Timmy, I'm a little tired of hearing about how good you play. He's got that scorecard of yours with that hole-in-one on the wall in his office. There's nothing else up there but a dusty old diploma and that scorecard."

The thought of my father leaning over the trash can in the kitchen, picking garbage off that paper card and pinning it to his wall—it was a little too much for the son of a tight-lipped, small-shouldered Irishman. In my family, we didn't say I'm proud of you, we didn't say I love you. Some might consider that a problem or a failure, but it isn't, not if you don't expect to hear those things. The problem is finally hearing it and not knowing what to do about the warmth you feel behind your eyes as you pick up your bags and head down the fairway, hiding your red face and swallowing it all down.

My father stood alone off to the edge of the eleventh-tee box. He was shaking his head at the hole, a long par four up a hill that, at that moment, must have looked utterly hopeless.

"You know you're falling off the ball," I told my father.

He looked over at me like I was speaking Spanish.

"What?"

"Your backswing. In your backswing, you're not turning and you're falling off the ball."

His face was confused turning into incensed, as if I was trying to show the accountant how to fill out a tax return. He took a heavy breath, then looked over at his partner and Norman Dane, who were busy inspecting Dr. Seavey's 14-karat plated putter. He turned to me and said from the side of his mouth, "What do you mean, falling off?"

"I mean, you're bringing the club back so fast that all your weight," I said, showing him by making a short turn into my backswing, "it's whipping back and falling over your right foot. You slide your hips instead of turning them."

He wasn't buying it.

"You're off balance. You can't hit the ball solid because you're off balance. Look," and I showed him a simple tip from the range at Pine Acres. "Your power is in the coil, but your hips slide back instead of rotating. Think of it like baseball. You need your weight moving forward, like a batter stepping into the ball. Or like a pitcher with his foot on the rubber," I said, showing him how his right leg had to stay strong to keep him on top of the ball. "At camp, kids would hit balls with a block under the edge of their foot so they wouldn't fall off the ball. It gets you to coil and uncoil. Turn and return. It keeps it all going forward."

My father slowly made a subtle pivot, turning at his hips. "Yeah?" he said, coiling around a solid right side like a younger player. You could see him feeling the tension in his back, discovering new muscles. "Turn, and return," he whispered under his breath.

"It's about time Timmy started giving lessons," Mr. Dane called from the other side of the tee. "Your honor, gentlemen. Shall we?"

And we did, and my father played golf as if it had been si-phoned into a needle and stuck in his veins. It was not just the swing, it was the spirit, how he finally smiled when he sank a fifteen-foot slider on the thirteenth hole for birdie. When his second shot on the par-five sixteenth bounced up just short of the green, rolling to a stop in the first cut, he shrugged his shoulders and laughed as if to apologize.

"They're gonna make you piss in a bottle, Jimbo," D'Angelo said.

My father swayed up to each shot. He watched from behind the ball, envisioning the flight and trusting his swing to move the ball out into the fairway, up onto the green. Turn, return, perfect for those few holes for my father. He'd played the game his whole life believing in those Ben Hogan moments, one-irons at Merion and one click of pure contact, and though he didn't hit a single shot as well as his hero, by the end of that afternoon I think my father knew he was right to believe those shots existed.

It was him and me walking off the eighteenth that day, up four shots and running for the calcutta.

CALCUTTA DAY WAS more than cash. At Fox Chase, it was everything. It was the handshakes at the gala. It was the chance to buy champagne for every loser in the house and still have your pockets stuffed with their money. It was a chance for the South Philly wop and the middle-class mick to be toasted by the New Water establishment, a chance for the Prices and the Nortons to share a photograph, a chance to envy a New Water accountant.

It was a morning to wake up vomiting.

It had been months since my last case of tournament nerves. I wouldn't have to hit one ball that day, yet there they were, three wet heaves in the bathroom sink. Not the toilet, the sink for some reason, as if throwing up in the toilet would just be too obvious. My mother was waiting in the kitchen, her hair pulled up in a brown pile of curls. Her robe hung open as she leaned over a crackling black pan, her chest dotted pink and brown above her nightgown. I picked pulp from my orange juice while she mixed bacon and mushrooms into a special Sunday omelet. My father was already up at the club for the Member-Guest's final-day breakfast. My mother said he did not sleep well last night. She said he tossed and turned until it was light out.

I couldn't eat the food my mother put in front of me, a yellow slab of steaming eggs. She shook her head like she didn't understand.

"Do you know the last time we all sat down and had a normal breakfast? I think you were three years old. Your brother must have been seven. Your father would make pancakes every Saturday. He loved making pancakes. And he would do the dishes, and I would stroll down in my robe whenever I felt like it, and the table would be full of food. It was nice," she said, taking my plate from me, "but now I guess you have to be a golfer to be part of this family. I can't say that I understand it, but if it means so much to all of you, well then, there it is."

The omelet slid buttery from the plate and into the trash can, untouched.

The only time I could remember my family without golf, without any mention of it, was a trip to Disney World when I was eight years old. We spent five days in Florida, about three days too many, all four of us packed into one room to save money. Casey was twelve and already a screeching terror—nasty, never satisfied, and a kicker in his sleep who, on our second night in the Magic Kingdom, heeled me so squarely in the balls that I woke screaming from a dream, a pain in my gut like a testicle was headed for my windpipe. The worst part was that my mother made me go to the park infirmary and drop my pants in front of a cold-fingered nurse who told me to keep my eyes on Mickey and cough. For those five days, I behaved and said thank you, and I enjoyed myself as much as one could in Casey's shadow while he wore my mother numb. I remember seeing a lot of my father's back that week as we walked through the park. He stayed a few paces ahead of the three of us, as if the redhead whining behind him, the one screaming to passersby that Mickey Mouse was a fag, the boy there next to the sagging woman, was not his son, no, not at all.

And on our last day, while we stuffed wet bathing suits back into our suitcases and gladly zipped up our things for the trip home, Casey gave my mother a stuffed Mickey Mouse from the hotel gift shop. I don't think any of us knew how to act just then, so the four of us sat in opposite corners of our small room, watching my mother cry with a three-dollar doll in her hands.

The morning of calcutta day, I left without a word because I knew I could not explain it to her. I couldn't tell her the secret to golf, the mystery of what made the game everything, what pulled my father out of our house so early on his days off. Perhaps part of it was that he didn't like waking up to Casey anymore, or that the only thing he seemed to enjoy except golf, those pink and red rosebushes, were now bumps of spotty growing grass, nothing left to clip on a Saturday morning. But what I could not explain to my mother was how badly those gentlemen wanted to be boys, how much accountants wanted to be heroes, to prove themselves, to win and lose and play. I couldn't make her understand that there was never just one hole, but another and then more, tomorrow and next week, that it was a pursuit of worth and perfection and purity, always just one swing away for those of us with golf in our blood. Golf led you on, down the course, no promises, breaking your heart. It was simple, and it was profound, and it was the illusion that there was always another chance to play the hero, always another way to figure it all out.

I did not explain it because it would not have made sense to her, and she would have been right, my mother the golf widow.

The hole that morning had the smell of a bad idea—one free shirt to be worn over three humid days. The cheap white fabric was turning gray, tissue clinging to sweaty chests. The room was alive that morning, my friends fussing over me and patting me on the back, celebrity for the hour.

"Ten percent of a win, man," Position A said. "That's standard cut. That's what they get on tour. Ten percent of twenty-five grand, man. Not bad."

"S'no way they pay that much. You're lookin' at five hundred tops," said Brian.

"That'll buy you some fuckin' bubble gum, Timmy," Tomato Face said, pointing a cup of coffee in my direction.

"Don't count your money yet, kid," Walter said from the sink where he was wiping grass stains off his sneakers with a towel. His Afro was tight from a fresh haircut. His white shirt was crisp with detergent. "My boy Logan's only three back. Three, am I right?"

"Three shots," I said, nodding.

"Hell, that's nothing. Just wait'll I put the heat on him. He'll be playin' like it's the motherfuckin' Masters," Walter said, slapping me five. "You and me are going to have some fun out there."

"Definitely."

From the doorway came the sound of detached soles flopping down the steps. Jeffrey slipped into the hole with his head down, sliding in sideways and trying not to be noticed.

Walter stood up off the bench, chest first. "What the fuck's this fool doing down here?"

Jeffrey looked around like he might be talking to someone else. He spoke low and plain. "I'm looking for work."

"Lewis told you to hit the road, asshole. You're wearing the same fucking pants there you shit in, man, that is just fucking disgusting. You're a walking fucking embarrassment is what you are."

"I washed 'em. I washed up and I'm just looking for a few dollars." Jeffrey didn't look at Walter when he spoke, and his face looked thinner, the whites of his eyes a touch too yellow. He looked at the floor, his fingernails, and a few times he glanced up and looked straight at me.

"Just everyone mind they own fuckin' business."

Lewis came hurrying down the stairs, slapping his clipboard like a tambourine. "Hey, where's Spooge Boy?" he whined. "Dane lost a headcover yesterday. Anyone seen it? Brian?"

Brian leaned back, tilting on his bucket in the corner. "Yeah, it's right here, keeping my pole warm."

"Listen, no bullshit today, dipshit," Lewis said. "I used up all my patience days ago."

When Lewis turned and saw Jeffrey standing beside him, he coughed on a burst of laughter, then sighed and swung his head back and forth, and we all knew there was nothing we could do to stop him from pulling Jeffrey apart into pieces.

"Are you fucking kidding me? Are you fucking *kidding* me? Do you have shit in your ears too, Jeffrey? What didn't you understand about *hit the fucking road and don't ever come back*? Huh? Are you that fucking stupid?"

Jeffrey stood there taking it, back straight against the wall, eyes barely open and his mouth screwed shut. You could see the muscles working in his jaw as he chewed his bottom lip. The rest of us tried to stop hearing, tried to look in a different direction.

"I wouldn't put you out if you were the only fucking looper in the hole," said Lewis, "not if every cart was busted and the members were up there carrying their own fucking bags!"

Lewis turned to the group of us, pointing his finger. "I ask you guys one fucking thing," he said. "Don't fucking stink. Wash your shirts and don't stink. Which, I can see, none of you assholes did. And Jeffrey, who the shit do you expect to caddy for today? All the loops are out. It's Member-Guest, buddy. Even you can remember that, can't you?"

Jeffrey did not move, his eyes focused on a spot just beyond the end of his nose. "I wanted to maybe get some work spottin'."

"We've got spotters. Bobby, Fran? And Kevin. Kevin G? You here?"

Three small boys sitting on the floor in the corner raised their hands.

"See? We've got our spotters. Bobby, Fran and Kevin, three best spotters in the club."

Jeffrey looked at Lewis. "Maybe something will come up."

Lewis laughed. "Sure Jeffrey, you just wait. You just wait right here. Maybe something will come up. And maybe I'll be the fucking president. And maybe, just maybe," he said, leaning in close, his finger jabbing at Jeffrey's face, "you aren't the stinkiest, stupidest, laziest waste of skin I have ever seen. You know something, Jeffrey? It's people like you that fuck it up for everyone down here, 'cause you make caddies look like shit. If you had the brains for a real job, you wouldn't be here. You wouldn't be here pissing off the members who come and bitch—

to who? To me. Do you know, Jeffrey whatever the fuck your last name is, who has to apologize for your ass? Huh? Do you know who, asshole?"

Jeffrey stood stiff as a nail, chin up, his nose reaching for air as Lewis leaned in, splashing words and spit all over him.

"It's me, Jeffrey. It's me. And I'm done dealing with it, so you can get the fuck outta here because you know what? You make me stink, asshole. You *make—me—stink*."

It was Puddy who grabbed him first, shot straight across the room without a sound, and that might have been why the rest of us watched instead of breaking it up, too shocked to move. It was like watching a tractor-trailer speed into a tricycle. Puddy's weight swallowed Lewis, his forearms driving down into Lewis's chest, fists falling like rocks on Lewis's mouth and nose and eyes. It was a mess. When his skin split, we could hear Puddy's knuckles pounding the moist spots. Walter finally stepped in to pull Puddy away, and Puddy stood there, breathing hard, a cold no-fear look in his eyes as if he didn't like what he'd just done, but it was not the first time he had done it.

Puddy ran from the hole before Lewis could even get to his feet. Lewis's nose was purple and bent, two red lines running down past his chin. His eyes were wet and bloody and a piece of his eyelid hung open. There was too much blood for it to seem real. It looked like paint pooling up in his hands.

Lewis spit red and a line of bloody mucus stuck to his shirt. He held his hands open in front of his chin as if he were waiting for his nose to drop off. Jeffrey didn't smile, not even as Lewis stumbled up the back steps, hiding his face, no crises allowed during Member-Guest. We wouldn't hear another word from Lewis that morning, his blood black on the cement floor.

Puddy left without stopping to grab his books piled beneath the bench. We found a pictorial biography of the Wright brothers, another book about World War II submarines, and a thin paperback, *Too Fit for Fat,* all from the library and all overdue. The diet book was dog-eared and highlighted, and it ended up in the garbage with the rest of his things.

In the morning's final foursome, we were matched up against Charlie Logan and his old college roommate, Paul Tierney. Walter was on their bags, and by the time we made it to the tee it was obvious that Logan and Tierney had started the day off with a brown-liquor breakfast.

"Be glad you're not playing this kid, Paul," Charlie said, waving his Styrofoam roadie full of Scotch beneath my nose. "This kid here is pure as the driven snow. He's sure won me a couple bucks."

Paul Tierney's bushy gray eyebrows came together as he looked me up and down, not sure if he was supposed to recognize me. He finally answered, "Is that right?"

Logan and Tierney took the tee box, and Walter dropped one of the bags off his shoulder. From inside a pocket came the clank of bottle knocking bottle.

"I've never seen anyone drink like these two motherfuckers. I'm carrying half a bar in here. There's more booze in these bags than there is golf clubs," Walter said. "Logan's been talking about helping Candy out, so I just put on my big smile and keep their cups full. It's worth it for eighty grand of college."

"No kidding," I said. "So he's going to BC?"

Walter lowered the other bag from his shoulder. No matter how big and unwieldy any golf bag looked like a purse beneath Walter Kane's sturdy arms.

"Candy had a little trouble with his boards," he said, "but Logan said he could pull some strings for us. He said the people up there owe him some favors. So it might be BC. It might be Ju-Co, I don't know. All I know is we got half of the city keeping their fingers crossed."

Our round began as the day before had ended—like a train. Price and D'Angelo didn't look where they were going, they just grabbed the tracks and kept swinging and I did my best to stay up with them. While we were waiting to tee off on number ten, our team ahead by four strokes, my father came over to his bag and put out his hand.

"Thanks for the tips, coach," he said, joking, but I shook his hand anyway and said, "No charge." He was starting to turn the key that unlocked golf, you could see the discovery in his eyes, and it was wonderful to watch but a little sad too. He was beginning to believe in his game, to trust it, but I knew it would leave him just as easily as it had come. It was the only thing in golf you could count on.

On the fifteenth hole, my father banged a five-iron into a meaty patch of heather below the green. The ball hopped straight up, spinning forward out of the rough and rolling to a spot inches from the pin. You could almost see the luck on the wind, pushing the ball toward the hole.

Tierney's eyes looked like they might spill down his face, and Logan's shoulders sagged so low he could hardly lift his hands to put them in his pockets. There was no cut of the calcutta for second place. Our opponents walked up to their balls, defeated, counting the steps it would take to get back to the grill room. Logan stabbed a five-wood at his ball, yanking it left into the junk. I watched him stomp over to his bag and rip down the front zipper, a tall bottle of brown falling out. He filled his cup to the brim and took a gulp that hurt my stomach to watch.

The sixteenth hole was a par five, reachable in two with a couple big knocks and a fortuitous bounce. The seventeenth was a par four that stretched back along the sixteenth, the two fairways running side by side. Charlie Logan's drive on sixteen barely stayed above the ground, skipping off the grass like a stone off a pond, coming to rest in front of a creek that even Fox Chase's shortest hitters cleared from the tee. With a three-wood wiggling in his hands, Charlie addressed his second shot, his body waving over the ball. His eyes would focus in tight, then blink, then focus in again, peering and getting lost and shaking his head as he tried to remember what he was supposed to do with this ball beneath his nose. His feet were too wide and his knees had too much bend. His fingers held on to the butt of the club, and it looked like Charlie Logan had fallen asleep standing up. I looked over at Walter, who was shaking his head to say it had been a very long three days. But just when I thought Logan might fall over on his ear, he drew his three-wood back, barely raising it to his shoulder, whipping the club down at the ball like a wet noodle.

A crashing sound came through the trees, from the seventeenth tee, a distant voice following it, calling *fore*.

"Wait! Mr. Logan! Heads up!"

But it was too late. Walter Kane yelled, and Charlie Logan jerked his head up and spun out of the way, hacking at his ball and nearly whiffing. He topped the shot, making just enough contact to roll the ball over and into the water.

Walter saw the wild drive coming from the seventeenth, heading for Logan's head and whistling by, missing his nose by a foot. Charlie never saw the ball, but he heard Walter, loud and clear. Charlie's face shook, his pickled tongue unable to get the words out fast enough. You could see the booze bubbling purple in his neck.

"You dumb fucking jigaboo! You have to be the stupidest son of a bitch I've ever seen! You dumb, dumb, dumb son of a *bitch*!"

Tierney tried to calm his partner, holding Logan's arms to his sides.

"Charlie, relax buddy, relax."

"Did you hear that fucking nigger! Did you hear him! Well that idiot son of his can forget about BC! Forget about it! I'm protesting this match! This is all under protest for interference!"

I watched Walter stand there with a bag under each shoulder, motionless and big as a wall, his hands balled into fists and trembling with all his strength. I thought blood might juice up between his knuckles. He would not take his eyes away from Logan's, not even as he shrugged his back and slung the straps from his shoulders. Bottles crashed as the bags hit the ground.

Walter turned away and headed into the woods, striding back toward the clubhouse.

"Where the hell do you think you're going!" called Logan. "Get back here! Or you can kiss your payday good-bye! Not a penny! Pick up these goddamn bags, you big black son of a bitch!"

"Charlie, shut your goddamn mouth."

My father was looking Charlie Logan dead in the face.

"Enough. You hear me?" my father said, angry lines dug into his forehead.

Logan leaned toward my father and pointed at his chest. "Who are you? Huh? Who the hell are *you* to tell me enough?"

"Who am I?" my father said. "I'm nobody. But I'll break your jaw if you don't shut your mouth, you drunken son of a bitch."

The color ran from Logan's face. He closed his mouth and lowered his eyes, all that anger hanging embarrassed on his face. He didn't move his feet, yet he seemed to take a step backward.

D'Angelo and I watched my father turn and walk away from Logan, stepping toward a ball down the fairway far ahead of us.

I picked up my bags and hurried to catch up.

As we headed back to the clubhouse, my father told me my cut of the calcutta was going into the bank at four-percent interest.

"You'll get your fair share," he told me. "You earned it."

I dropped the bags on the rail where Position A was leaning with his ears bent, scoping all the action. He told me that Walter came back in like a box of steam and that Raymond had him in his office right now, still trying to calm him down.

"He could have killed that asshole, Timmy. They're lucky he didn't break Logan's head open."

The brown door to the pro shop banged open and Walter stepped out, brushing past Position A and me and walking toward the hole. He didn't speak, pulling in a long breath through his nose, eyes wide and watching the pavement as he moved. Al D'Angelo came running out of the shop behind him.

"Walter, wait Walter," he said, catching him at the steps. We could hear D'Angelo talking under his breath. "See, if Logan's a member, he's got a bond of ownership here. Now, with you as an employee of the club, and with that jackass as an owner, I'm telling you, we got a great case here. It's called creating a hostile work environment, buddy. It would be a slam dunk."

Walter walked halfway down the steps, feet touching the shade from downstairs. He stopped there and looked back up at D'Angelo. "You're a lawyer?" he said.

Al D'Angelo stuck a soggy unlit cigar in his mouth. "In the worst fucking way."

"Well I don't need a lawyer, 'cause this is all over," Walter said, turning his back and shuffling down the cement steps into the hole.

I picked up my bags and headed downstairs. The shadows in the hole swallowed up the afternoon sun, and there on the bench was Jeffrey, his eyes barely open, spit dried white at the corners of his mouth. Walter was gathering his keys and his gym bag when Jeffrey turned to me and said, "What's it like out there? Big bucks?" His eyes were foggy, like he was talking in his sleep. "Big bucks for all y'all. Man O man O man."

I dropped my bags against the sink, trying to stay out of the way as Walter blew past, keys jingling impatient around his fingers. As he started up the steps, Jeffrey sat up and called after him, "Did ya get rich today, nigga?"

Walter stopped. He looked back at Jeffrey, and Jeffrey smiled back. Walter pushed his keys down into his pocket, then kept moving forward, up the steps, out of the hole two steps at a time.

Jeffrey made a sleepy little laugh, then turned to me and spoke. "Uh-huh. Tell you one thing. That nigga got paid."

MY SPORT COAT had mothballs in the pockets and smelled like spearmint. It was hanging in the kitchen when I got home from the driving range, right next to a tall crystal cup cut at a hundred different angles.

"Too bad," my mother said when I told her my blazer didn't fit anymore. She said it was a special night, so I was wearing it, too bad that the navy blue had faded and that it pinched me in the armpits.

My father wore a tuxedo that I wouldn't have believed was hanging somewhere in our house. He came down the steps, tugging at his cuffs like a movie star. He looked handsome, gray hair smooth across his scalp, black silk tight around his neck. The tips of his ears were pink and he smelled like shaving cream and leather.

"You'll be the best-looking caddy at the party, Timothy," he said, trying to tighten my tie even though it was a clip-on. I did not know that the winning family was invited to the gala, not until that afternoon when I was told that my brother would be the only other guest who I didn't have to call mister.

"Jim," came my mother's voice from the top of the stairs. She held the banister and made her way down the steps, white silk draped down her back, hanging from her elbows, covering her fingers. White swept between her feet along the floor. She was careful and beautiful, watching for each step to place the next heel. Her hair was pulled up into a turning stack of curls, ivory clips on either side of her head. Her shoulders were bare and slight and her cheeks were rose-colored. Her neck was long with quiet muscles. I had never seen her like this, wrapped in a dress that looked like it had been waiting years for a summer evening and a tuxedo at the bottom of the stairs.

Her eyes smiled as my father took her hand.

"Meredith, you look incredible."

"Thank you," she said. She blushed, and they kissed.

"Are we going to be outside tonight?" she asked, looking out through the screen door.

"I think so. At least for part of the evening."

"It's such a warm night," she said.

"It'll be fine," he said.

"I know. I'll be with the handsomest gentlemen in the club," she said, leaning over to kiss me on the cheek. She smelled like strawberries and baby powder.

"Oh, look at that," my mother said, peeling a long glove off her fingers, licking her thumb and rubbing lipstick from my cheek. She rubbed until my whole cheek was pink, but I smiled anyway.

My father called up the steps, "Casey, come on, we're leaving." There was no reply except the sound of Springsteen, twangs and thumping muffled from the attic.

"He really wasn't interested in coming, Jim," my mother said.

"Of course he's coming. The winner's family is invited, and he is part of this family."

My father planted a polished wingtip on the first step, but instead of climbing the stairs and pounding on the attic door, rattling the lock and yelling for my brother—instead of doing what he always did, my father stopped on the first stair. "He really said he didn't want to come?" he said to my mother.

"He's going to the movies with his friends," she said.

"Is that right?"

My father held out his wrist, gazing down at his watch. He studied the numbers for a moment, just a moment longer than he would have needed to discern the time. He nodded to himself, then pushed open the screen door. He smiled as wide as he could and held an open hand out to my mother. "Shall we?"

I followed her out the front door, my Easter loafers clicking along our brick walkway. The Buick started on the third try, and we headed out into the evening.

The night of the gala was drinks, dinner, dancing, then a small fireworks show over the course, the final chance to impress the exhausted guests, gentlemen in black and white holding their bejeweled wives while sparks showered down, red and blue reflecting on their faces. But before the booming colors, I had to make it through the drinks, dinner, dancing.

Inside the dining room, long-stemmed glasses swung from fingertips while a silver-haired band blew their horns, brass moaning over the rattle of a top hat, dancing wives spinning around their husbands. I sipped a Shirley Temple and walked through the glass doors, out onto the balcony patio that overlooked the putting green. I saw Mrs. Logan alone, looking bored in a slim red dress, smoking a skinny cigarette. Her husband might have been tucked back in the men's grill with the rest of the gin players. There were men who never left that room, members who were separated or divorced or soon to be both—the group of them was dubbed *the homeless* one winter when the heating broke down in the clubhouse. The homeless still came to the grill that January, bundled up in winter jackets and caps and scarves, sitting in their leather chairs, drinking hot toddies and holding their cards in mittened hands. They could see their breath inside, but they stayed. Their homes couldn't have been much warmer.

My family sat at a long table at the head of the dining room. Our dinners came under silver domes. Our horseradish potatoes were scooped for us. You could slice the filet with your spoon, and when I cut mine it sweat red all over my plate. Some of the members made their way past the table to offer congratulations, and Al D'Angelo took it all more seriously than I thought he would, collecting tributes from behind his piles of food. His wife was a dark-haired, light-skinned Italian beauty. Her hair was loops of black plastic and her dress sparkled a silver and white that on any other woman in the room would have looked like a trip to Vegas. But Mrs. Al D'Angelo pulled it off, not gaudy, but gutsy, with a soft olive face that made it all look right. I don't remember her actually speaking, but she did laugh at everything we said. She even chuckled when my father said, "Horseradish makes mashed potatoes so much better," after which Al shot her a look, and the laughing stopped for a while.

After the dinner plates were whisked away, Richard Norton approached our table to offer us the president's congratulations. His face was drawn and pallid, and his tuxedo seemed to wave from his shoulders like a towel on the drying line.

"Well done. Well played out there. You are deserving champions," Norton said, shaking our hands, his palm damp and spongy. I wiped my hand on my pants afterward.

"This is a great place you have here, Dick," D'Angelo said, nodding with each syllable to the point that Norton started to nod along. "This is one serious operation. You've got your own little world back here."

"Well thank you very much. We're glad you could be our guest."

"I could get used to this I think," D'Angelo said, putting his arm around his wife. "This is a helluva way to live. If you guys are looking for any more members, I want you to keep me in mind, alright?"

"We will, Mr. D'Angelo," said Norton, smiling at a spot a few inches above D'Angelo's forehead. "We certainly will."

As I looked around the ballroom, searching for anything that might not bore me, I saw that I wasn't the only son in attendance. In a corner by the door, Myles Dane stood next to a suit of armor. The suit was an heirloom of the club, a gift willed to Fox Chase years before by an English member whose name and coat of arms were engraved into the rust-spotted breastplate. That evening, Myles's father had brought his secretary to the gala. The Danes were separated, and dating your twenty-five-your-old secretary was such a country-club cliché that when it happened—and it happened at Fox Chase as often as any other cliché—people hardly took notice. But Myles noticed, and he was drinking himself stupid on rum and Cokes. I watched as he turned to the empty metal suit, mumbling something and smiling, his head unsteady on his shoulders. When Myles tried to put his drink in the suit's gauntlet, the glass fell to the floor and shattered on the hardwood.

Norman Dane rushed over and grabbed his son by the arm, spitting whispers in his ear, every eye in the room turned to them. Whatever his father was saying, it was turning Myles's eyes wet, and he pulled away hard and rushed toward the door, knocking into a waitress and pushing between a white-haired couple. When he brushed by his father's date in her low black dress—two young breasts pushed together for everyone to see— Myles stopped and said, "Fuck you, whore," good and loud. Waiters hurrying to wipe up the spill, faces turning to look at faces, but only a moment before the band started back up, and the cliché walked themselves out of the ballroom.

Dessert came on a brass cart, ice cream on fire and brown-candy booze in fishbowl glasses. A waiter brought long cigars that were the color of tar, Cubans from the club president's private collection, he explained. The room started to heat up with after-dinner cigarettes, and when D'Angelo fired his cigar, a few sucks and a smoke storm, I knew I had put in enough time at our table.

"May I be excused?" I asked my mother. "I want to get some fresh air."

"Okay, dear. Just make sure you're back for the fireworks."

"I will be," I said, and I walked across the dance floor and out the front door. I peeled my jacket off straightaway. It was a cool night, and I enjoyed soaking up the air, away from the voices drowning voices, the fake laughter trickling from their lips, the sound of knives squeaking across china plates. I wandered out to the parking lot, where the lampposts cast a fluorescent metal shine on the cars, blacks and blues, whites and chromes and candy-red curves, all blending into an unnatural shade of orange.

A group of waiters stood in the trees at the edge of the lot, smoking, with their bow ties undone around their shoulders.

When they saw me, the four of them crushed out their cigarettes and walked away. I was alone with Logan's Alfa Romeo and Dane's Ferrari and my father's Buick, and sitting there beneath the buzzing light, it was all just a row of empty metal boxes.

Then I heard the sound of a stone skipping across the pavement.

In the corner of the parking lot I saw a man. He was standing alone, leaning against a car that could have been black or green or blue. I stepped forward, tightening my eyes to make him out of the shadows, and from the slope of the hood, the silver metal shine of the bumper, I could tell he was leaning against Norton's Bentley. I turned and looked for the waiters, anyone I could inform about this person in the lot that might be looking through windows for purses or stereos, maybe grabbing at door handles until one clicked open. But they were all inside the clubhouse. I could hear a whisper of their party, the laughter and a saxophone playing in the distance. And as I scanned the lot I saw it parked at the far opposite end, out from underneath the lampposts, a blue-black newspaper van slumped dead on the asphalt.

THE CADDIES TALKED about eight fingers and how they got that way. A garbage disposal or a birth defect, wood shop or a pit bull or cherry bombs. There was a story there, a reason, a picture or a sound or a mistake. There would always be the way it did happen, and the way it might have happened, and somewhere in between was a moment that I would piece together after those summers with Jamie, a fifth of July and a bagful of bum fireworks. A son standing over a pile of burning sticks, watching fallen marshmallows bubble black on the kindling, flames snapping at the summer bugs. A father watched his boy silhouetted there as he lay back in the hairy night grass, maybe fingering a brown bottle of beer that was not very cold. Maybe he handed the boy his Zippo, or maybe the boy used one of the cinders to light the fuse, something to make sparks fire from the hands of the seven-year-old, no colors just a cloud, a cloud with no drift to it. The smell of burnt silver in the back of your throat and an accidental sound, a hard pop, and a red and blue rocket fell to the ground and lay on its side, white smoke spilling from its charred bottom. A boy looking up into the smoke, his cheeks spotted with bits of something wet and red, something that looked black in the twilight.

Or maybe it didn't happen that way at all. Whatever happened, no one saw. The truth of that moment was Jamie's—he carried it around in his pockets every day. Jamie Byrne had stories that were not good stories for telling, and that made them more real than most.

I ran for the newspaper van parked at the far end of the parking lot, and I found Jamie sitting in a ball in the passenger seat, forehead pressed against his knees.

"Jamie, Jamie," I said, smacking the glass until the van door slid open. I followed him between the torn leather seats and into the back of the van. Two narrow blocks of light came through the rear-door windows, and I saw Jamie slide his shoulders down the wall of the van until he was sitting, legs tucked to his chest. His eyes were somehow deeper in their sockets. He wouldn't look at me.

I sat down on a stack of yesterday's *Daily News,* and in the back of his father's newspaper truck my eyes adjusted to the dim light, the dark tiring to gray as Jamie told me moments. Instead of the story, Jamie gave me the syllables, the points and edges of a rumor that the people around Fox Chase would pick at for years. Down in the hole or in a golf cart on a quiet afternoon, they would snap off a piece of what happened, sometimes gumming it up with speculation, sometimes pushing it toward what I had heard about in the back of that van, those moments I never told any of them about.

It was the Sunday I left for the airport and Pine Acres. The humidity was sitting down on New Water, the air yellow and still. The heat packed the golf course that afternoon, burnt-orange spots like sores on the fairways and the greens dried to a prickly green dust. Jamie would want to go swimming whether I was there to join him or not. In a heat like that, what else would you do?

The house must have seemed like a hotel or a showroom, all the couches no one ever sat on, ceilings high enough to play basketball inside. A television in the kitchen, a phone in the bathroom in the pool house out back. Jamie would have brought his own towel, never thinking there would be fresh ones piled at the ends of chaise longues, towels sitting there like fluffy white cakes.

He rode his bike past the entrance to Fox Chase, back through sycamore trees lining the tight old roads. He found a green steel gate that swung open to reveal a brick driveway, a place important people visit all the time, he must have thought, when he walked through the unlocked door and saw the dining room with its dozen tall lonely chairs for a family of three. But the family wasn't there that Sunday. He would have noticed that Amanda wasn't swimming in the backyard pool, turning fourteen and just getting bumps to fill out her sleeveless polos, hips for her golf skirts to hang from.

They kept their hulking stone house sterile with air-conditioning, and stepping from the den to the patio was like stepping into a sauna. Amanda would have been down the shore with her mother, windows open at the beach house, the two of them sunning themselves on the deck with an ocean breeze brushing past them, wondering how he could be playing golf back in New Water on a day like today. But a pool was near good as a beach, and Jamie swam with a lifeguard watching over him. The man watched from the edge of the water, legs crossed on a chaise longue. He watched and kept it all safe. He watched to see if anyone was passing by.

And when he offered a ride home, Jamie accepted. He took the ride and pushed his ten-speed into the trunk of the Bentley. They drove toward the north side of town, Jamie having to give him directions and warn him of every turn. And then, somewhere between the tightly paved roads of Fox Chase and the gravel spit across the streets in Jamie's neighborhood, they took a different way than Jamie knew, and the Bentley stopped. It stopped. And later, when Jamie got out of the car in front of his house, he ran. He didn't wait or turn around or think to pull his bike out of the trunk.

In the heat wave, it made sense that Jamie wouldn't go to Fox Chase. Mr. Byrne wouldn't have found it strange, he would trust Jamie to know when the weather broke and the money returned. But never leaving the house made his father wonder about the bike. Where was the bike, he would ask every day, where was the bike he had bought with his Christmas bonus? And when he had asked enough times and had enough to drink and shaken the boy enough to get an answer, Jamie told his father something that made him scream until their house shook. Jamie said he punched a hole in the bathroom door, that he pulled the refrigerator out of the wall and pushed it over sideways on the floor. They had driven past the green steel gates and come here where Mr. Byrne had been waiting, for hours Jamie said. He wouldn't go inside.

Jamie rocked back and forth on the floor of the van, squeezing his knuckles, mumbling that his father was going to do something terrible.

The van's back doors rumbled. When Mr. Byrne hit the doors again, the metal box shook as if every screw were loose. "Who the hell's in there! What's going on! Is that one of those caddies, one of those fucking caddies?"

Jamie pushed me up to the front of the truck and out the passenger-side door. I ran and didn't turn around, away from the truck and the parking lot, and I could hear Mr. Byrne yelling, "You tell that bastard I'll be here! I'm waiting for him! I'll be right fucking here!"

I couldn't feel my legs as I ran, away from the clubhouse and out into the golf course that was mine. The greens and fairways where there was always golf, only golf. Running too hard to breathe, the only sound was my feet pushing off a damp carpet of grass.

There was not a square foot of the golf course that came without a story, stories like ghosts in a giant field of memories and fictions that all seemed more real in the dark. There were the places Brian Seaman claimed he'd done it, the nooks where loopers had spent the night, the tracks of Jamie and me chasing each other under moonlight. In the air I saw the trails of impossible shots I'd made. On the greens were the arcing paths of long putts I had drained and easy putts I'd missed, replayed in my sleep until I woke with my fingers squeezing the sheets in a textbook interlocking grip.

I ran beside the empty driving range, along a plateau overlooking a sea of abandoned golf balls. They were bright like white grains sprinkled through the night grass. As I passed one of the leaning old oaks, I saw a pair of heavy wet eyes in the darkness, a man holding himself up against the tree. It was Charlie Logan alone in a tuxedo, no Styrofoam cup at his fingers, waiting there for somebody to watch.

I cut behind the range to the fourth green, scraped through a dozen yards of brush that opened up onto the fifteenth fairway. The sand bunker up ahead shone in the moonlight as if it were full of rain. When I reached the green, I stamped my foot on the short grass and fell to my knees. I sucked for breath and spit up bits of my dinner. I rubbed an open palm across the green's spiny fur. I felt dirt on the grass that could have been top-dressing, the hard gravelly bits they sprinkled across the greens in the summer. The greens crew spread it over the turf like icing to keep the grass from dying out. But as I looked around me, I saw that the dressing on this hole was not rolled smooth. It was just spots, brown shadows in a trail. I touched one, and I rolled in my fingers the sand that wasn't top-dressing at all, but footprints.

I rushed to the edge of the trap, and I saw that it was torn apart. It was clawed away. There was a dark empty hole in the center.

Three quick bursts, *boom boom boom,* and from the edge of the bunker I saw white fire whistling up over the trees. Then an explosion in the sky, and a purple shower rippling out in circles and spilling down black.

Three more pops and one hard cannon slam, and I ran back toward the clubhouse, my feet falling out in front of me as I came down the hill from fifteen, slipping beneath the branches of pines and over to the fourteenth tee where I stopped for just a moment. I saw light glowing from inside the Norton house. The back of their home was like a huge crystal box, glass and gold sparkling off the pool. And standing there next to the pool was Amanda Norton, wrapped in a pink robe and her hair wet. She was looking up at the fireworks and smiling, all the colors reflected in the water there in front of her.

From the shadows I saw through the glass to a living room, a long vanilla couch with auburn curls spilled about the cushions.

Static flickered on the television in front of her. She wore a red robe and she didn't move, asleep perhaps, too tired for a gala, tired of all her husband's occasions. But maybe, I thought, she stayed there sleeping because she knew the nightmare things about Richard Norton.

I cut sideways across the fairways and up to the putting green, to the clubhouse with its pointed roof raised like an eyebrow. I heard glasses clanking and the moan of a clarinet. Perfume and cigarettes wafted down from the patio where, at the balcony's edge, bracelets and diamonds dangled like bait from the wrists of members' wives. People moved as if they were swimming in the air. Drunken gentlemen leaned against the patio rail, and I watched from the putting green, waiting for one to come tumbling over, scanning the crowd for the club president.

And suddenly, as I stood there wiping sweat from my forehead, a sound came that grabbed them all by the throat. Three hot snaps, *pop pop pop,* then three more. There were no colors in the sky, the blasts too close to be fireworks. The echo was the sound of trees splitting all over Fox Chase.

For a moment, there was no sound, only staring. Men and women looking at each other, at the air, at themselves. One man pointed at me. Frozen along the balcony, they looked like passengers on an ocean liner who had just felt metal tearing beneath their feet. When a woman inside the clubhouse screamed, "Oh my God!" the bodies began to move, pushing accidental and sideways, and I ran around the building to where I knew the echoes had come from.

I heard engine belts burning as I rounded the corner of the building. I made it in time to see the square top of a newspaper van leaning from side to side as it screamed down the drive. They were gone, two red lights and a snaking cloud of fumes.

Bugs buzzed around the lampposts, tapping at the glass. In the orange light I could see Norton's car, smoke pouring from its grille and rising through three bullet holes punched into its hood. The windshield was blasted white and had fallen back into the front seat. The car hissed and leaked. It slumped over a tire that looked like it had been blown inside out.

Jamie's father had stood in the parking lot, chewing on all that anger but afraid to walk up the clubhouse steps and push open the door. It was something the place could do to anyone—it could make you wait. There were lines and there were lists. There was pecking order and there was precedent. Caddies went their entire lives without ever seeing the other side of that door, but Mr. Byrne must have finally tired of the waiting. There was impatience all over that Bentley.

The crowd made its way out of the clubhouse, timid at first, then some stepping closer to get a good look at the car. A woman wearing white gloves leaned over and touched one of the holes in the hood. The crowd shuffled and parted way for the club president, but when Richard Norton saw his car he would not go near it. He stood three cars away and leaned up against a Mercedes, holding his fingers to his lips as the whispers began to circle around him. He turned to look at me, and his eyes were the plainest kind of scared.

At that moment, I wished I was like my brother, that I could fill fast with blood, take pain from the bottom of my stomach and whip it into a ball of rage unstoppable. I wanted to turn Richard Norton into that smoking wreck, that whining broken shell.

Instead I just stared at him until his eyes met mine. I stood there, back straight like the little gentleman I was, and I gave Mr. Norton a look that said I knew why those holes were there.

*　*　*

As we drove home that night, we passed the police cars and the tow truck headed for Fox Chase. I watched from the backseat while my mother wiped her cheeks and forehead with a handkerchief, and I thought about Mrs. Norton. When would she figure out about the Bentley, who did it and why? There were so many questions from that night, so many secrets to the place. But Mrs. Norton only had to get one of the answers right before the pieces of the real story would start to fall, raining down on Fox Chase until we all were drowned.

I wondered if Mrs. Norton would believe it, if she would be too embarrassed to leave. Maybe she would find a room in that house that had no windows. Maybe she would sleep it off, maybe lock herself in. But my story that night was that Mrs. Norton survived things, so what she did was call her caddy. She picked a car, and she brought him into her garage, and she fucked him in the front seat until the windows dripped with steam, the leather slippery and stained.

It was as real a story as any, and I could hear Position A telling us, "Christ, fellas, there were four fucking cars to choose from."

THE DISTRICT ATTORNEY drank stingers. A circuit-court judge enjoyed Gulden's mustard for dipping his pretzels, and a superior-court judge was allergic to peanuts. He wouldn't even allow them at his table. The leader of the Republican party in Delaware would not play gin with any of them, because he only played with a group of three men with complexions like brie cheese. He was a short man, but his playing partners were shorter, and towering over all of them was the Pennsylvania congressman who was granted an honorary membership many years before, for reasons no more elaborate than patriotism, duty, and that he loved the game. His bag was packed with the most expensive space-age equipment, black metal clubs covered in long socks that the caddies joked were specially made for congressmen at NASA.

Boardrooms and committee meetings with leather chairs and long mahogany tables—these are the places people think power resides, the places that make our finances flux and policies fix, that keep the country grinding forward. But at Fox Chase, even a thirteen-year-old knew that the real power to punch things in a new direction, or to hold them right where they were, was fostered and flexed between first tees and eighteenth greens, in relaxed rooms where men licked liquor from their teeth and sat safe behind a sign that read GENTLEMEN ONLY PLEASE. Every CEO and every commissioner and every council member played the game, and they all wanted to play Fox Chase, and that kind of demand made all the difference. Other people didn't understand that an invitation to a course like that was the new kind of tribute, the modern business way of kissing you on both cheeks and tucking an envelope in your pocket. Eighteen holes could win a contract or settle a suit or kill a piece of legislation, and the people who didn't believe it were the people who didn't play.

Their club, their rules, and one thing that was not going to be spoken about in that room was a scandal involving the president of their club. No one in New Water or Wilmington or Philadelphia would touch it, a story that was quashed like heresy, that took place in a club few people knew existed, marked by two stone posts and no sign.

There would be no case and no suit, not one that anyone could win. No one saw what happened, but we all saw the problem go away dead. The whispers said Mr. Byrne was paid off well into the six figures, some said over a million. Whatever the men from Fox Chase did, it was enough to make the Byrnes leave New Water without a word.

I never told anyone what happened that night, what Jamie told me in the back of his father's van. I didn't go back to Fox Chase, and I spent the final dying days of that summer holed up in my room, trying to concentrate long enough to read *Of Mice and Men* and finish the summer reading list for new freshmen at New Water High. My mother left me alone up there, pleased that I was thinking about my schoolwork instead of golf.

I wasn't. For days I lay on my bed staring up at the ceiling, my eyes tracing the hair-thin cracks snaking across the plaster. In my head I was preparing the call I would make to the police, what I would tell them about Richard Norton and a caddy at Fox Chase Country Club named Jamie Byrne.

It was a call I never made.

The neighborhood where Jamie lived was eventually flattened and paved. The trees were pulled up like needles from a pin-cushion, and what was left was mixed up and rolled out and covered with metal rods and quick-dry cement. I think there is a parking lot there now, or the appliance warehouse, or the bulk-food megastore, or the liquor-rama where you can buy handle bottles by the pallet. The Dane Development Company scooped up homes and businesses all over the north side of New Water. They threw up billboards and stamped out a long stretch of Delaware's finest tax-free shopping. No driver from Philadelphia or Jersey could pass through the state without being funneled through this gauntlet of no-sales-tax stereo equipment, air conditioners, Jet Skis and televisions. They turned a north-side movie theater into a jewelry store.

I did not know where Jamie went, but it didn't take long for me to stop imagining him taking up half a seat in a 747, his mother, bobbed hair and a blue uniform, tightening his seat belt. I would see the commercials, these women who I knew were not his mother, and I would hope that Jamie really did believe what he had told me, at least for that time when we were kids. It was a good story, television and blond hair and airplanes going anywhere, a New Water version of our American dream.

The night of the gala did not go away easy. Questions and rumors lingered for months, and the members came to agree that Jamie Byrne was a bad caddy, a quitter and a runaway, white trash from a white-trash father who would put his son up to that, trying to milk money from the hardworking half of New Water. They would shake their heads in sad disbelief, and they would wonder to one another when people would finally learn that there was no free lunch.

On a Friday afternoon late in September, my father went into Casey's old room at the end of the hall. He unlocked the door, went inside and closed it behind him, and he didn't come out until we had all gone to bed. For the next two days, my father emerged from that room only to eat and sleep. I saw him once in his work pants, moth-eaten corduroys he used to wear when working on his roses. He had dust in his eyebrows and black dug under his nails. When I asked him what he was doing, he shrugged and smiled and locked the door.

That Sunday afternoon, I sat in the den watching golf while my mother read a self-help paperback, something with a number and the word *Path* in the title. I was in the kitchen refilling her iced tea when I heard my father's call through the ceiling.

"Tim, come on up here."

I hurried up the steps and looked down the hall to where Casey's door was pushed open and the room inside was bright like a beach. I stepped in the room and found my father sitting behind a wide cherry-brown desk. The magazines and the sewing machine were gone, and the hardwood floor was waxed and polished to where the center of the room was white with sunlight. The crusted yellow wallpaper rotting orange at the seams had been peeled away and replaced by a cream color that was fresh and wet. Above the desk hung my father's photograph of

Ben Hogan, resurrected from the garage. The black-and-white picture shone behind a clean sheet of new glass.

I walked over to where the window was pulled wide open. I smelled the outside and looked at our front yard and our driveway meeting our quiet street. It was a view we had wasted for a long time.

"Well?" my father said.

"That looks much better up here," I said, pointing at the photograph of Ben Hogan's one-iron shot at Merion.

"You know, after Hogan hit that, he said that it was the last shot he had in him," my father said. "He'd been in a terrible car accident, and the doctors said he might never walk again, but there he was on the last hole of the United States Open, completely exhausted, one shot from victory. He'd walked thirty-six holes that day, and he needed to hit one-iron to get home, maybe the toughest shot in the whole game," my father explained. I didn't tell him I already knew the story, because I wanted to hear him tell it. "He could hardly stand and he just stepped up and stroked that shot. Look at that. Perfection. See the ball there, headed to the green?" He pointed to a white speck on the grainy background. "They say he was quiet. He was all business. He outworked them—he practiced twice as much as anyone else."

I looked around and saw the nicks in the floor where Casey's toy chest had been, the chest that was always empty because he would leave die-cast cars and crumbled-up action figures sprinkled across the floor. I could still make out a rough spot in the wallpaper where he had stuck his foot through the plaster when he was nine. In the corner I saw where we would build Tinkertoy forts when we were small, plastic pipe castles you could see straight through, where some days our mother would sit inside and play Queen and we would play knights protecting her.

A bookcase stood over a dark patch on the floor where Casey's bed had been. The shelves were filled with books my father had amassed from birthdays and Father's Days. There were history and horticulture books mixed amid all the green spines—golf instructional books, golf meditation books, golf books by doctors, golf quote books, golf joke books, golf coffee-table books, even a golf cookbook called *Living on Greens*. There were thin golf novels about sage Scottish caddies and miraculous, redemptive rounds.

Next to the bookcase, a framed parchment map of Delaware hung on the wall, an antique script along the bottom proudly announcing it *The First State*. He loved his state. Smaller, but better, and my father believed it.

"What's Casey going to say?" I asked him.

My father swiveled in his chair to face me. "About what?"

"About turning his room into an office."

"Your brother lives upstairs, Timmy," he said.

He looked at the picture above his desk, eying the photograph as if the ball were still moving, inching impossible across the gray.

"You know, when he finished that day, Hogan said that it was the last swing he had in him." I stood there watching the two quiet men with their backs to me, looking deep at that white speck and willing it where to go.

My father leaned back, tilting his chair on its back legs. He put his hands behind his head and teetered there for a moment, back and forth. Then he held the edge of his desk and gently lowered his chair, and he breathed in deep.

On some afternoons when my father was at work, I would search around the room and his desk and the shelves, looking for my scorecard with the hole-in-one, never finding it there. It was still his secret, and that was fine because that was who we were. We needed to hide some things because we were still the

Prices, and the four of us were still as goddamned Irish as a goddamned grudge.

That year my brother's football team made it to the state play-offs. The Saturday night before Thanksgiving, we went down-state to watch the semifinal game against a team from Cape Henlopen.

The opponents looked irate in bright black and yellow uniforms, jerseys cut off above their stomachs. My mother joined us in the bleachers that evening, a blanket wrapped around her knees. She watched every snap, Casey flying around the field and dragging players down by the ankles. On third and five my brother blindsided the quarterback, knocking the ball free inside their five-yard line. We jumped in the bleachers and waved blue and white pom-poms at the air. The players peeled off the pile, body by body, until it was just my brother facedown in the grass, arms wrapped tight around the football.

My father yelled and squeezed my mother around the shoulders. Fans and parents slapped our backs and stomped on the metal stands. But as the cheering died down to a murmur and the heads in front of us began to turn around, we saw my brother still lying there. Casey didn't lift his head off the turf, his empty hand grabbing at the back of his leg. Both sidelines went quiet as coaches and trainers ran onto the field, the New Water players taking a knee and locking their hands. The two other linebackers finally lifted Casey up off the ground, his arms stretched across their shoulder pads. They carried him across the track and into the locker room beneath the bleachers, just as my father began pushing his way down through the crowd. My mother didn't watch. She hid her face in her mittened hands.

When my father climbed back up to our seats at halftime, he sat down next to us and didn't speak until my mother grabbed him by the sleeve. "What happened—is he okay?"

He gazed out at the field as the teams filed back onto the sidelines. "They said he's going to play the second half."

For the next twenty-four minutes, Casey hauled his left leg around and finished play after play. He was late getting to tackles, but when they ran into his hole, he wrapped his arms around the ball carrier and waited for help to come wrestle him down. When the offense was on the field, he held a blue bag to his knee and rocked back and forth on the bench, then popped back up and went back out and chased the ball around for another four downs.

Thirty-five to seven when it was said and done, and the New Water stands swelled with congratulations. Cheerleaders conducted chants and dances in the bleachers. Football parents hugged and some mothers cried as they began planning their trips and their tailgate parties for the state championship game in Dover.

We waited in the parking lot for Casey. He came out of the locker room before the rest of the players, still wearing his cleats, a sopping brown T-shirt, his football pants smeared with grass stains and mud. He limped across the lot and opened the Buick door without a word, backing himself down into his seat, his lips tight with pain.

We pulled out of the parking lot in front of the rest of the traffic.

"What happened?" my father asked him.

"I quit the team," Casey said.

My father clicked on the radio, turning through the stations. He finally found the news radio and said, "That's good."

I did not play again until the spring I turned fourteen, when after school one day I took my clubs out of the downstairs closet and went to the driving range at a public course called Rock Valley. It was a crisp May evening, my fingers stinging as I hit balls beneath the spotlights, bouncing shots off Astroturf mats that were ground down to the black rubber.

At the far end of the range, the wind began to swirl in the trees. The sky turned purple and I went inside the pro shop and waited for my father. The building was a prefab metal hangar, and I watched the rain outside, the water clinging to blades of grass that shone beneath the spotlights like little sticks of ice.

I dug a quarter out of my golf bag and walked over to a pay phone jammed between an empty water cooler and the men's room door. I had been thinking about calling Foster for months. I missed hitting shots at his range, but I wasn't calling to ask if I could come back. It was good that I was here, a new place I think he would have liked. The balls at Rock Valley were cheap and the driving range was surprisingly peaceful, just the sound of club heads whipping across the mats, each golfer quietly puzzled by his or her swing. I dialed Foster's number because a part of me wanted him to know that I was swinging the club again. I had chosen to put them in the closet, and now I had chosen to take them back out. It was my game, and I finally felt like I had earned it.

I listened as the phone rang and rang, and I decided then that Foster Pearse was away, gone until summer or maybe much longer. Maybe he was anxious to do some roaming, headed for the beaches of the youngest state he could find. The buzz of that empty phone line was the sound of Foster knocking shots across islands of clover-green, his spikes sinking into spongy fairways along Hawaii's jagged black coastline. I hung up the phone, glad I hadn't tried to explain myself to the last person in the world who needed any explanation.

When the Buick pulled into the parking lot, I dodged the puddles and ran out to the car and took the front seat next to my father. We made it almost the entire way home without saying a word, until my father told me that the Phillies game had been rained out. That was all he said, that the Phils game was canceled, and all I said was *huh* as if it was only mildly interesting. I watched the drops bubble up blue on the window, sliding sideways off the glass.

We pulled into the driveway, our house sagging beneath the rain, and I thanked my father for coming to pick me up. "Thanks for the ride" was all I said, and he looked at me a little puzzled, like it was a funny thing to hear. Maybe it was not a thing a father was supposed to be thanked for, maybe it was something a father was just supposed to do, but I said thank you because maybe fathers got it backwards, pushing their boys to hold them close.

* * *

I don't play for trophies, and I didn't let them turn me into one. But I cannot choose to forget the game because the game chose me. The choice I did make was to only play the places where Jeffrey or Tomato Face or Puddy could tee it up. Gentlemen are honest, courteous, classy and bright. My friends in the hole were all of those, and none of those, and they were better than any of those words because the only thing they really needed in the world was their next day. And when the next day came, they took it with a quiet satisfaction that was more real than anything in the world you could touch beyond the top of those stairs.

And so I play the public courses. I line up in the cold mornings and I wait in the afternoons with the T-shirt golfers we'd mocked at Fox Chase, the six beers and three balls in his bag player who plays the game because it is the most fun an athlete can have without running. The swings are sometimes ugly, sometimes dangerous. The greens are ratty and the etiquette is vaguely interpreted, but what I have learned on those courses is that this game does not belong to the country-club players who hoard it behind bonds and membership committees and long winding driveways. The ones who truly love this game line up at the first tee at four in the morning, carrying their own bag and paying thirty dollars they can't afford to pay, all to play an eight-hour round on a course that could pass for a cow pasture. When I could not think of one player at Fox Chase who would put up with that simply to play the game, I knew then that those guys in line in the T-shirts—they were the real golfers.

You can find me in the early dark mornings, waiting in line with those who will always play for that balance, for those times when the game is pared down to the clean precision of a moment, when the fireworks stop and the sparks have fallen and the light pauses for that *pop,* that click of Surlyn on steel that sounds a full emptiness, that we chase like children with dreams on our faces. I chase the good story where there are still the times—there still have to be the times—when Timmy Price is pure.